It Burns a Lovely Light

PENNY MCCANN PENNINGTON

To Jen's sister Gloria,
I'm sorry I didn't
meet you — Jen says
you are AWESOME!

Penny

Copyright

For John.
Each day, I fall in love with you all over again.

And for Alex, Daisy, John Philip and Sally,
The loveliest lights in our lives.

My candle burns at both ends.
It will not last the night.
But ah, my foes and oh, my friends,
it gives a lovely light!

First Fig, by Edna St. Vincent Millay

It Burns a Lovely Light

It Burns a Lovely Light

It frightens me, how much I have forgotten about you. But I can still feel your spirit. You were beautiful. And when we were together, I was beautiful, too.

Chapter 1

July, 1970
Williams Air Force Base, Arizona

It was rare to see fathers at the Officers' Club pool. As fighter pilots on an Air Training Command Base, they were usually too busy training or flying their jets.

But on what threatened to be the hottest day of the summer, as Farley James looked toward the fourth grade on yet another new base, her father announced that he was taking his family to the pool. Maybe he felt bad, since he was flying out tomorrow for a month. Or maybe he just knew that Farley and William hadn't made any friends yet.

William looked up from his book. "I didn't think dads were allowed to use the pool."

"Only on special occasions, professor," said Jack, reaching across the breakfast table for the catsup bottle. He put catsup on everything, even his eggs.

Farley's mother, Pauline, took her time spreading strawberry jelly on her toast. "Jack, half the boxes aren't even opened yet."

He waved his fork at the piles of pans, dishes, table linens and silverware lining the countertops. "Sheets are on the beds, Farley's movie star dolls are back on her dresser, William found his disease books, and the TV is plugged in. All the important stuff is done."

"They're not dolls." Farley had to get that in. "They're 'collectables.'"

Pauline cut William's sausage into bite-sized pieces, her knife and fork making delicate clanking noises against the plate. "You guys go ahead. I won't feel better until we're completely moved in."

"No way." Jack winked at his wife. "'Us four and no more,' remember?"

'Us four' was Pauline's favorite saying. She was a firm believer in the 'tick-tock- the-game-is-locked' approach to families. To her, it meant that the four of them really only had each other. That no matter where in the world they were stationed, as long as they were all together, they were home. Which was more than fine in Farley's book. Over the years of moving from base to base, most of her friends had had at least two or three brothers or sisters. They shared bedrooms - often with a line drawn down the center - and fought over stuff like clothes and bathroom time and second helpings at dinner.

Jack pulled Pauline's chair toward him and made a big show of getting down on one knee. "Come on, gorgeous. Let's go have some fun."

She thumped him on the head. "Oh, for crying out loud. Everyone finish your breakfast and we'll dig out our bathing suits."

Farley smirked. As if she ever said 'no' to him. As Veda Marie - her mother's friend from way back - loved to say, 'Pauline would jump straight into the sun for that man.'

With pictures and curtains yet to be hung, no one had to yell to be heard in their new house. But William couldn't help himself.

"Mom, I can't find my Speedo!" he screamed, digging a finger into his ear.

"Hold your horses," she called from down the hall. "I know where it is."

Ever the Air Force wife, Pauline had packing and unpacking down to a science. For William's sake, each new house had to be as similar as possible to the one before, from the placement of the furniture to the board games on top of the hutch.

Bath towels were always on the center shelf of the linen closet. Socks and underwear went in William's top drawer, shirts in the next, followed by shorts and long pants, with pajamas and happiness cloaks in the bottom - everything folded 'just so.'

No matter where in the world they lived, the kitchen windowsill was never without freshly planted citrus trees in terra cotta pots. Pauline would save seeds from fresh lemons, limes, and grapefruits, and push them into potting soil. Within weeks shiny green leaves would emerge. She cared for each plant until the next transfer, only to give them all away and start over in the next house.

Farley opened the cardboard box labeled in black Magic Marker:

Private Property of Farley James

Snoop At Your Own Peril

Usually she saved this box for last, after everything else had been unpacked and put away, because it contained the finishing touches that would turn four white walls into 'Farley's Room.' But she seemed to recall packing her swimsuit in there.

She took care in removing each item: a smooth, flat rock from a creek in Colorado, her diary with the broken lock, a worn copy of E.L. Konigsburgs's *From the Mixed up Files of Mrs. Basil E. Frankweiler*, her cork bulletin board – all cleaned up and ready for new memories – a rumpled *Plan 9 from Outer Space* poster, and the Chunky Bar she stole from the snack bar last year but had been too guilty to eat.

She found what she was looking for underneath her autographed picture of *The Sound of Music's* Christopher Plummer in his Austrian escaping-over-the-mountains get-up. Holding her breath, she wriggled, tugged, and squeezed into the shiny yellow one-piece. Forget happiness cloaks. All a girl really needs is her lucky bathing suit to fly.

Outfitted in a white girdled swimsuit that seemed to be made expressly for her, Pauline stuck her head in Farley's room. With her blue eyes, long white-blonde hair, longer legs, and slim waist, she was prettier than any movie star – with the possible exception of Audrey Hepburn. Not that Pauline cared; she stood firm in her belief that beauty came from one's ability to love. Of course, Farley knew this was something only an attractive person could say with a straight face.

Pauline pointed to her daughter's rear end, where the fabric had already ridden up. "Don't you think that's a little tight on you, hon?"

'Hon' was a Pittsburgh word. Pauline grew up there, until she fell in love and got married and had 'us four.' She didn't use other Pittsburgh words, like 'Stillers' instead of Steelers, or 'yins' - the Pittsburgh version of 'ya'll.' But 'hon' stuck.

"It must have shrunk over the winter," said Farley, blushing as she tugged on the back. "Or maybe I'm getting fatter."

"You're not fat; you're big-boned." Pauline opened Farley's closet. "Where's that striped two-piece we picked out in Mesa? That was adorable on you."

Her mother did have a point about the two-piece, but Farley wasn't taking any chances today. Only her lucky bathing suit would do for the first high dive of her life.

The Officers' Club had recently installed a high diving board. Farley heard about the new board from Ben Porgie, a sixth grader with a severe dandruff problem - and, as William pointed out, an inability to chew with his mouth closed. Ben and his parents stopped by the previous night for a Meet and Greet. Meeting and Greeting was a big part of military life, and Farley was all for it, particularly if they brought fried chicken or lasagna.

The Porgies had come bearing a platter of pigs-in-a-blanket and a giant canister full of Chubbie's Potato Chips. Captain Porgie carried a sweaty glass pitcher of whiskey sours. Jack put Herb Alpert and the Tijuana Brass on the reel-to-reel and Pauline loaded up a tray with ice, high-ball glasses, an alabaster ashtray and a can of mixed nuts. Then, the adults disappeared out to the patio.

Once Ben Porgie started raving about the new high dive, there was no stopping him. He leaned in and talk-ed fast and low, as if he had a dark secret to tell. Farley smelled potato chips on his breath.

"It's only been up for three weeks," he said, licking his lips. "Already, Steve Dorfman had to be rescued by a lifeguard because his dive turned into a belly flop."

Farley nudged a concerned looking William with her elbow. "No wonder, with a name like Dorfman."

"That's not funny," said Ben. "He needed mouth-to-mouth and everything." He shoved a handful of chips in his mouth and looked Farley up and down. Mostly up; Farley was a head taller than Ben. "How old are you, anyway?"

"Ten. I'm mature for my age," said Farley, modestly. She overheard her mother telling Aunt Claire this during one of their Sunday night after-the-rates-went-down phone calls, and it made her proud. She *did* do a lot of reading.

"You're big for your age, too," said Ben.

Biting into her pig-in-a-blanket, she made a point of chewing with her mouth closed before she spoke.

"Gee, nobody's ever told me that before."

William beamed up at Ben. "Farley can do a back dive and everything!"

Ben continued, as if William wasn't there. "Good thing you're ten. No one under ten is allowed off the high dive. It's too dangerous because…"

"Because," William piped in, squinting through his glasses, "the wrong dive from that high up can cause whiplash or abdominal trauma. That can lead to hemorrhaging, which often goes undetected.'" He scratched behind his ear, staring at his shoes. "And of course, there is always the spleen…."

Ben's mouth fell open. Farley saw chips.

"My brother is really smart about some things, especially medical stuff," she explained. "He's going to a private school off base."

William pumped his fists to his chest, hero style. "A school for amazing super-children!"

William had an uncanny talent for memorizing indefinite amounts of medical information. At age four, he could reel off the names of every bone and major muscle in the human body. At five, he used his mother's eyebrow pencil to write the four key tissues found in animals - Epithelium, Connective, Muscle, and Nervous - on the wall next to his bed. These days, he enjoyed reciting the primary symptoms of whatever disease Pauline could come up with while she helped him dress. Unfortunately, he couldn't fully comprehend most of what his mind so easily absorbed.

After weeks of tests at Johns Hopkins, puzzled doctors concluded that William's abilities were a 'fluke,' a 'phenomenon.' Of course it was William who defined his condition best: His mind was 'way too full of some things, and not nearly full enough of all the rest.'

That night, Farley lay in her bed, too excited to sleep. She pictured herself leaping off that high dive.

...climbing out of the pool after a casual-yet-picture-perfect back dive...kids crowded around, wanting more...what's your name...would you do that dive again... come to my sleepover party...be my friend...be my friend.

From the empty dining room of the Officers' Club, Farley and her family watched the laughing, screaming swimmers on the pool deck. A teenage boy with whitish blonde bangs hanging in his eyes pretended to pull a girl toward the water, while the girl made a big show of resisting his efforts.

"This part is always the worst," said Farley, trying to sound laid-back. "I don't know one single soul, and no one knows me."

Pauline tucked a strand of hair away from her daughter's face. "It never lasts long, hon. Just keep that beautiful smile on your face and the rest will take care of itself."

"You should do what I do," said William. "On the first day in a new school, I walk *really* fast, like I have somewhere important to go. Even though I never do!"

By the time they stepped onto the pool deck, it was Adult Swim. Other than a few women in rubber bathing caps, chatting and side-stroking along the deep end, the pool was empty. Some kids warmed themselves on the wet cement, fists clenched under their chins, shivering and talking. Others sat at the edge of the pool, legs in the water as they kept an eye on the clock over the snack bar. The air was thick with the intoxicating mixture of chlorine, cheeseburgers, and fries.

William spotted the baby pool. "I'll just be a second, Mom."

Pauline gripped his shirttail. "Oh no you don't, mister."

"Why not?"

"Because you're seven." She steered him toward the men's bathroom. "I'll wait for you outside the door."

Farley watched with pride as her father arranged their chaise lounge chairs in a straight line. Other fathers didn't make everyday things special like he did. One by one, he spread their beach towels high into the air and let them float down over the plastic chairs. In his black swim trunks and matching jet black hair, he was the most handsome man in the world.

Pauline approached, holding William's hand. Jack bowed and swept his arm toward her chair. "My darling, your chariot awaits."

"Oh, my God," Farley groaned. She covered her face to hide her delight. People were starting to watch. Then again, she couldn't remember a time when people weren't struck by the star quality of Jack and Pauline James.

Pauline untied her short terry robe and rubbed her baby oil and iodine mixture onto her legs, while Jack smeared lotion on William's pallid skin. Leaning back on her chaise, Farley smiled and tried to look friendly. Her face was starting to hurt.

She observed the high divers from her chair. One by one they jackknifed, swan dived, and cannon-balled their way off the board. She wriggled her toes and clenched her hands in excitement. So far, not a single back dive in the bunch.

"Want to give it a shot, Pauline?" Jack teased.

"Ha, ha." She reached over and poked him in the thigh. "Very funny."

As a teenager Pauline had had a bad experience with heights. She and her twin sister Claire had been sunning themselves on a high ledge overlooking the Monongahela River. Far below them, their younger brother Ryan skipped stones out into the water.

Bored and seeking attention, Ryan swam away from the shore. He began flailing his arms and screaming for help, pretending to drown. Pauline leapt off the ledge and into the water, grazing a boulder on her way down and injuring her back in the process. The result: two operations, nine months in a body brace, and an understandably extreme and lifelong fear of heights.

It was time. Farley was ready. Index fingers tugging at the bottom of her bathing suit, she did the run-walk pool scoot all swimmers learn at an early age. There were at least eight kids ahead of her, but she didn't mind. Standing in line was just another way to meet people. Maybe by lunchtime she would be eating with her new friends. Then they could all sit together and wait for their food to digest. Waiting a whole hour was always torture, but nobody wants to die of a cramp. Someone tapped Farley's shoulder. That was fast!

Turning, she smiled at a girl with thin lips barely covering a railroad track of metal braces. "Hi."

"Hi. Can I take cuts? My best friend is in front of you."

Finally, it was Farley's turn. She skipped a rung as she started the climb – a little something she picked up from watching the other divers. Once she was higher than the fence around the pool, she spotted her new school. A few rungs more…she could see the beginning of the housing area. Another step, slower now. A jet touched down on the flight line. Beyond, the desert shimmered in the heat. The slightest hint of nausea emerged. Her body began to tremble.

Farley stopped and leaned in to the ladder. Her heart beat faster and faster. To calm herself she looked down at her family. William stood next to his chair, bouncing from one foot to the other and squeezing his weenie through his Speedo. That meant he was wound up.

"Keep going," he shouted, waving with his free hand. "You're almost to the top!"

To buy time, she turned what she hoped was a calm gaze out across the pool and pretended to look for someone.

"Go, already!" said someone from the line below. Someone who would definitely not be her friend.

Farley continued to climb, but her legs seemed to be moving in slow motion. She reached the top and knelt on the rough surface. Clutching the side guardrails, she stared straight ahead. Petrified.

"Come on, any day now!" Some little monster shouted.

"Awww, man!"

"Get off the board!"

It was like one of those dreams where you try to move but your legs won't cooperate.

"Jack..." Farley heard her mother say from the safety of her pool chair.

From the corner of her eye, Farley saw her father walk toward the board.

"All right, kids," he said. "That's enough."

The yelling and complaining promptly stopped. There were even a few 'Yes, Sir's.'

"Farley," said Jack, "everything all right up there?"

There was a rushing sound in her ears. Unsteady, she tried to close her eyes, but the darkness made it worse.

"Help," she whispered.

His wedding ring making a clanking sound as he touched the ladder.

"Can you find the ladder with your feet and crawl back down?"

"No!" Her voice was shrill, as the horror of the situation began to sink in.

"I could come up and piggyback you down." He tried to say this quietly, as if she had any dignity left to save.

Farley shook her head. The thought of being carried down from this height was even scarier than jumping. She watched as a lifeguard climbed down from his stand; probably dying for a shot at a good rescue. Moaning, she wondered if she would need mouth-to-mouth like Steve Dorfman.

"You don't have to be afraid!" cried William, thrilled to see his sister frightened for a change.

Jack took his time with each word. "Farley, I want you to listen to me very carefully."

She knew that voice. It was the voice the hero in the movie used when he was talking the crazy person down off a ledge, or telling the desperado to put the gun down. *Easy now, partner. No one needs to get hurt.*

"Keep your eyes on the end of the board and crawl toward it. Then, sit, and drop into the water."

Please, God. Let this be a bad dream. Let me wake up now.

"Farley, do you understand what I just said?"

She nodded.

"She nodded!" screamed William.

Not that he had to. The pool was quiet, everyone eager to see how the chunky girl in yellow would get down off the high dive.

Farley's hands and knees dug into the prickly board as she crept forward. Every part of her body was trembling.

"Take all the time you need, hon," said Pauline.

Thanks a lot, thought Farley. I'll bet you're off your chaise lounge now.

Her pace was hideously slow. The closer she got to the end of the board, the more it bounced. Her knee slipped over the edge, scraping her thigh. Frantically, she struggled to regain her balance.

That's it, she decided. Show's over, folks. She locked her arms around the board and gripped the sides with her feet, allowing her bathing suit to return to its familiar wedge. She pressed her forehead against the rough surface and closed her eyes. They could bring in a helicopter for all she cared; she wasn't moving another inch.

I've made a complete fool of myself before I even made a single friend. Maybe Ben Porgie will be my friend. Better yet, I just won't have any. I could use a year or two to myself. The mysterious loner...Lana Turner in Madam X...chlorine sure is a lonely smell...

"I'm here, hon."

Lifting her head, Farley turned around as far as she dared. Behind her, squatting and clutching the board for dear life, was her mother.

"Let's show these folks how it's done," said Pauline, gesturing with a tilt of her head toward the crowd below. She was shivering so hard, Farley could hear her teeth clacking.

Stunned, Farley managed a twitchy, spasm-like nod.

Below, Jack cleared his throat. "Pauline?"

"We're fine, Jack!" said Pauline, loud enough for the entire pool to hear. "This poor thing...I asked her to wait for me so we could go off together. By God, she waited!"

Pauline crept forward until she was crouching directly behind Farley.

"I've got a good grip on the board," she whispered. "Use me to steady yourself and stand up."

For a moment they stood, trembling and clinging to each other, high above the rest of their lives. And then, one by one, they soared.

Hair swathed in a towel, sunglasses on, Pauline leaned back in her chair. "Wait till I tell Claire."

Farley giggled into her towel. That ought to shake up the old bat's day. Not that she didn't love her aunt, but Claire was always so...*stern*. Librarian-stern.

Pauline placed a hand on her husband's thigh. "Darling, why don't we drink a toast to our new home?"

Jack summoned a waiter, gesturing toward his family as if they owned the place.

But then, he had no reason to believe otherwise.

Chapter 2

Pittsburgh, Pennsylvania

"Mother of God."

Claire stood the iron upright, her eyes never leaving the white boxer shorts. Reaching for her glasses, she lowered herself onto the nearby sofa and examined the lipstick stains. Slowly, she ran her fingers over them, then pressed the shorts to her mouth and licked the largest waxy red streak.

The iron, sputtering and steaming, brought her around. Resisting an urge to press her palm against the sizzling surface, she unplugged it and clicked on the overhead light. With disorienting clarity she saw for the first time how stale and tedious this room had become.

Working late again tonight, darling girl. Don't wait up...

From molten ladder to laborer to furnace man to steel pourer, Paddy Sullivan had worked his way up the Porter Steel pecking order. Recently an opportunity had literally fallen his way, when an iron rail holding a massive ladle snapped. The ladle crashed to the ground, landing squarely on the broad-shouldered shift manager, who suffocated before the ladle could be hoisted off his chest.

Paddy was assigned to step in as interim manager, allowing the owners time to consider their options. He meant to prove himself worthy of a permanent promotion. And Claire had been behind him all the way.

You can do it, hon. Go for it.

She reached for the phone, then put the receiver back on the hook. Pauline had enough on her plate, moving into her new house in Arizona.

Thirteen-year-old Joe kept up a solid stream of chatter throughout dinner. Normally hockey was his topic of choice. He and his friends played whenever possible… ice hockey, street hockey, table hockey in the cellar. Between practice after school and weekend games, Claire's son barely had time for schoolwork. But tonight he was all about football. This season, for the first time, games would be televised on Monday nights. Monday Night Football had arrived.

Joe went on about his beloved Steelers – or as the neighborhood kids called them, 'those nice boys from Pittsburgh' – while Claire's mind played a perilous game of chicken. Just when it seemed she couldn't hold on any longer, the pain would back off enough for her to stop herself from screaming at the dinner table. Paddy, *her Paddy*, had betrayed her.

"I'm telling you," said Joe, inhaling tater tot after tater tot as he spoke. "Those 'nice boys' are going all the way this year."

Silence. Joe speared a fish stick with his fork and slowly waved it in front of Claire's face.

"Hello…earth to Mum?"

After dinner Joe helped his mother clear the dishes, and then bounded upstairs to his room, claiming homework.

Moments later, she heard his muffled voice enthusiastically chatting on the telephone. Claire wondered how different her life might have been had she possessed the ability to approach each day with Joe's bare-it-all passion. But that wasn't her. She had always been the 'serious' one – as opposed to Pauline's 'pretty,' and Ryan's, 'good as gold.'

"That's me," she said, squeezing more than enough dishwashing liquid into the sink. "Thirty-seven, solemn, and second-string since the day I was born."

A growing mountain of suds spilled over the sink and onto the floor as Claire scoured the bottom of an already immaculate pot. The background clamor of evening traffic soothed her. When she first moved in, a young bride straight from the safety of her father's house, the roar of the streetcar had jangled her nerves. When had she gotten used to the noise? Did she wake up one day, immune to it all? No, she supposed detachment happened over time, then one day you wake up and everything is different. Like the time she turned around and her little boy had grown two inches, along with a faint suggestion of peach fuzz on his upper lip. Or when out of the blue all of her dresses were too tight around the hips. And when had she stopped looking forward to the sound of her husband's key in the door?

"Oh, Paddy," she whispered.

She could still recall every detail of their first kiss. For the longest time she had disregarded his attention. Not because she didn't like him. Never that. Who wouldn't love his kind green eyes, heart-melting Dublin accent and crazy-curly red hair? No, she resisted Paddy Sullivan because he wanted *her*. Awkward, pimply, warts-on-her-elbows Claire Justus; twin sister to Pauline, the most attractive, popular girl at Saint Xavier's.

Even the girls loved Pauline. Who in their right mind went for the crater-face girl, when there was a skinny, clear skinned, wart-free version standing right next to her? Something was wrong with a boy who would pick the clumsy, thicker twin. Lack of good taste, for starters.

But Paddy patiently persisted, and eventually she began to believe. And then, that Indian summer Sunday, down at the old pond.

I have something for you, Claire Justus...meet me at the bottom...swimming through the darkest murk... wrapping his arms around her...pulling her legs around his waist...his kiss, so tender and soft...you really don't get it, do you...you're the one for me, darling girl...

Her feet were wet. Claire looked down. The sink had overflowed and a thin blanket of suds was creeping its way across the kitchen floor. She turned off the faucet, the overhead light. Untying her apron, she stood in the dark and smoothed her skirt with her hands.

Out of habit she raised her hand to knock before entering Paddy's office. The room had always been off limits unless one was invited in - Claire had insisted on this rule herself. *A man needs his space. A place of his own, where he could get away from it all.* She ransacked his briefcase and upended his desk drawers, while marveling that she had never created such a space for herself. On the middle shelf of the bookcase, tossed inside a tatty cigar box like so much small change from his pockets, she found the barely hidden confirmation of her husband's duplicity.

Uncorking Paddy's Irish whiskey decanter, she poured a shot and coughed as the russet liquor seared its way down her throat. The next one went down trouble-free.

She lowered herself onto Paddy's leather couch to examine the sorry contents of the cigar box. A book of matches with a phone number scrawled across the inside. A handful of unopened condoms, decked to the nines in perky square containers. A small spray bottle of cologne. She squirted some on her wrist and inhaled. Apparently Patchouli was making a comeback. She unfolded a pile of rumpled receipts: restaurants, a movie, a hotel on the North Side. And one slightly underdeveloped Polaroid of Paddy and a pencil-thin woman in a tight short skirt. The woman was beaming at the camera, her arms barely making it around Paddy's thick waist. Paddy wore an uncomfortable smile. He looked tired. Which only made sense, Claire reasoned as she walked upstairs to pack. Adultery must be exhausting.

Careful to avoid the third step from the top – it had an awful squeak – Paddy tiptoed up the stairs and into the dark bedroom. As he did every night of his life, he pulled the covers tight under his chin, smacked his lips and closed his eyes.

"Goodnight darling girl," he whispered, already drifting off. "Sleep tight, God bless."

Up with the sun, Paddy went straight to the bathroom. He scrubbed his teeth and took a shower, vigorously soaping his belly as he belted out a song in his deep rumbling voice. He sang loud enough to wake not only his household, but the neighbors on both sides.

"Can't get her up, can't get her up, and can't get her up in the moooooorning!"

Only after he returned to the bedroom, his naked body pink and steaming from the hot water, did he see the note on Claire's undisturbed side of the bed.

Chapter 3

"Why do insane people always live in dark and lonely houses?" asked William, staring at the flickering television screen.

Farley, William and Pauline lay sprawled across Pauline's bed, eating buttered popcorn and watching *Whatever Happened to Baby Jane*. Bette Davis, as the garishly made-up Baby Jane, was happily tormenting her crippled sister, Blanche. Tonight was their last 'us four' movie night before the first day of school. (Officially, as William pointed out, they were 'us three.' Jack was working on his flight plan at the kitchen table.)

It had been six weeks since Farley's near-debacle on the high dive. For all its spectacle, the day had actually ended well. After dropping Farley and Pauline off at the house, Jack and William had disappeared for a few hours and returned with engraved bracelets for 'their girls.' A shiny strip of silver imbedded in the leather bore the words:

Brave and Daring

Contrary to Farley's fear of living out her time in Arizona as a friendless outcast, she had already made a few friends, and was even weighing the possibility of a potential best friend. Now that she wouldn't be one of those kids who wandered the cafeteria, clutching their tray and trying not to appear desperate for someone to sit with, she was actually looking forward to the fourth grade.

Farley scooped a handful of popcorn and considered William's question.

"The reason insane people always live in dark and lonely houses," she said, "is because dark and lonely houses *make* people go insane. I mean, just look at Bridge Manor…"

She froze. That last part wasn't supposed to come out of her mouth. Fiddling with her bracelet, she glanced at her mother. Thankfully, Pauline seemed not to have heard Farley's wisecrack about her childhood home.

Bridge Manor was a large Victorian surrounded by green trees, winding trails, and a mind-blowing view of the city below. It was also where Farley's grandmother, Abigail, had died young of a 'nervous condition.' When pressed for more details, Pauline would only say that the dear woman was better off with God. *Better off with God?* Farley's imagination took it from there. Clearly, her grandmother had been a lunatic.

"Shhh, I love this part," said Pauline, never taking her eyes off the screen as she scooped a handful of popcorn. She shook her head as she chewed. "I swear to God. Nobody does crazy like Bette."

On the screen Blanche whined, "You wouldn't be able to do these awful things to me if I wasn't in this chair."

They all shouted along with a gleeful Baby Jane: *"But ya AAH, Blanche! Ya AAH in that chaya!"*

"Nothing like the sound of good clean fun," said Jack, sticking his head in the room. "Pauline, your sister's on the phone."

"Something's wrong." Pauline handed Farley the popcorn bowl, rolled off the bed and headed for the kitchen. "I've had a bad feeling all month. I guess she's finally ready to tell me what it is."

Farley ran a piece of popcorn along the salty-buttery bottom of the bowl. The fact that Claire and her mother were twins never failed to amaze her. The two women could not be more different - each seemed to be the reverse of the other. Pauline was lean, tanned, bleached-blonde, friendly, and outgoing. Claire was heftier, prematurely gray, with sallow skin and an off-putting tendency to frown.

Of course, the twins also shared many similar traits. Both were tall, with long legs, a strong nose, and high cheekbones. Their taste in food was almost identical. They even had a mutual best friend in Veda Marie Tendersheets. And, on occasion, Claire and Pauline shared an insight into one another's feelings - they literally felt each other's happiness or pain. They called this rather unique ability their 'twin instinct.'

William fingered his happiness cloak. "Last time Mom had a twin instinct, Aunt Claire called to say Grandfather dropped dead."

"Nobody dropped dead. He just died, like any old person. You worry too much, kiddo."

"I told you not to call me kiddo. That's a mom and dad thing."

The movie cut away to a commercial. Loud music came on and two overly-ecstatic couples kicked up their heels as they walked along the beach, drenching their neatly pressed, haphazardly rolled-up pants. A deep-voiced male announcer declared, 'What a good time for a Kent!'

"If you stood in the living room," said William, "you could accidently overhear Mom talking to Aunt Claire. Just to be sure no one is dead or in a coma or anything."

"I mean it William; you're giving me the creeps."

"Fine." He stared at the television. "I just hope it's not Veda Marie - like a heart attack or an aneurism or something. And I really hope Joe didn't get hit playing hockey and get a concussion or a deep laceration. Most of all I hope..."

"All right, already." Farley rolled off the bed. "But I'm taking the popcorn with me."

Relieved, William turned back to the television. A glamorous telephone operator with impeccably coiffed hair asked the viewing audience to remember, 'long distance is the next best thing to being there.'

"You iron his boxers?"

Phone pressed between her cheek and shoulder, Pauline poured a glass of white wine with her free hand. Jack looked up from his flight plan.

"She irons his boxers?" he mouthed.

"Of course that's not significant, hon," she said, putting her finger to her lips and shaking her head at Jack. "What did Paddy have to say for himself?"

Still holding her wine glass, the phone tight to her cheek, she slid down the wall to the floor and settled in for a long conversation. In the distance, Bette Davis croaked, '*I've written a letter to Daddy.*'

"Get some sleep," said Pauline. "I'll call you tomorrow."

Re-filling her glass, she took a seat at the table.

"I don't get it," she said, "Paddy's been crazy about Claire since...forever."

"What happens now? Did Paddy move out?"

"No. She took Joe and moved back to Bridge Manor."

"You mean temporarily," said Jack, cautiously. "Since we've got it up for sale."

"Claire is asking us to consider taking it off the market. She wants to turn it into a boarding house."

Jack scrubbed his face with his hands. "Pauline, the place is falling apart. We can't afford to keep pouring money into it. We've got to start saving for the future. We still haven't opened a college fund for Farley." He hesitated. "God only knows what kind of money we'll need for William. You know what the doctors say; he'll never be able to live on his own."

"I know." Pauline chewed her bottom lip. "Still, I don't think a boarding house is such a bad idea. There are so many colleges and universities nearby; Claire won't have any trouble finding boarders. She's even going to offer reduced rates in exchange for help with repairs around the house."

"*Repairs around the house?* For Christ's sake!"

"Keep your voice down."

When Jack finally spoke, he kept his voice calm. "Let's be realistic. The roof leaks, the wiring is shot, and kids use the windows for target practice."

Pauline gathered her hair into a ponytail and crossed her legs like a teenager. She filled her cheeks with air and exhaled slowly.

"All I'm asking you to do is think about it," she said. "Any renovations we made would be an investment. Obviously no one wants the house in its current state. We've had it up for sale since Father died, and have yet to receive a single reasonable offer."

"What does Ryan say about all this?"

From the other side of the kitchen door, Farley clutched her empty bowl of popcorn. Don't go down the Uncle Ryan road, she thought. The last time Ryan's name came up, her father referred to him as 'the Christ-child' and her mother responded with a vigorous dose of the silent treatment.

"You know my Mutt," said Pauline. "He's against anything Claire wants. He told her to forgive and forget and go home to her husband."

Mutt was Pauline's pet name for her younger brother. No one else called Ryan Mutt, nor would he have allowed it. After their mother's nervous breakdown, their father seemed to forget he had a family – specifically his baby boy.

This had been perfectly fine with twelve-year-old Pauline. She claimed the child as her own and went about raising him. She cut his food, scrubbed behind his ears, and taught him the importance of manners. Over the years she oversaw his homework, his clothes, even his choice in friends. Pauline made sure he never went to sleep without saying his prayers and he never left the house without a hot breakfast and a kiss.

By her own admission, Pauline was strict with Ryan. She believed someday her brothers flawless man-ners, sports accomplishments, and academic awards would turn their father's heart around. She would often encourage him by saying 'Be the best, Mutt. Then Father will love you.'

"Ryan's not going to go for turning Bridge Manor into a boarding house," said Jack. "He was the first one to suggest we sell the place."

"Don't worry about Mutt. I'll talk to him."

The rigid tone of her mother's voice and the sub-sequent silence made Farley's stomach hurt. She could hear the crinkle of paper as Jack folded his maps and the exhale of yet another count-to-ten from Pauline. After what seemed like an eternity, her mother spoke.

"How about this: we take the house off the market for a year or two. Just until the demand for stately manors picks up."

Jack stacked his maps and connected them with a rubber band.

"We can wait until the cows fly home, Pauline. The demand for a falling-down, decrepit mansion is never going to 'pick up.'"

Farley held her breath. Here we go, she thought. She was pretty sure her mother's cheeks were combusting right about now.

"Jack James," said Pauline, "that 'decrepit mansion' is my childhood home. I do not appreciate your cavalier attitude…"

Exhaling, Farley shoved the door open.

"Guess what! I decided Loretta Vega is my new best friend. She's really cool." She laid a buttery index finger across her forehead. "And she has one great big eye-brow that goes all the way across, like this."

Jack turned off the bedside lamp and reached for Pauline. She tucked her head into his shoulder and en-twined her legs through his. They held each other in the dark and listened to the shrill chirp of crickets outside their window.

"You *do* know cows don't fly," whispered Pauline.

"They don't?" Jack kissed her hair. "Maybe not where you come from."

She raised herself up on one elbow. "Farley thinks Bridge Manor is a dark and lonely house."

"Isn't it?"

"Wise guy." She poked him with her finger. "It wasn't always dark and lonely, you know. For a while there, it was really something."

Jack had seen photographs of the magnificent three-story Victorian before it went to seed. In its day, Bridge Manor had held its own against the mansions of Highland Avenue.

"And yet, you still couldn't wait to get the hell out of there," said Jack. "How many times have you told me Bridge Manor was just another sorry – albeit grander than most – ashtray, filled with the smoke and soot and grime of the city?"

"Too many, apparently." Pauline made a face. "Do you have to remember everything I say?"

He kissed the top of her head. "Only the juicy stuff."

"Such as?"

"Such as…that the rivers back then were black as coal. Sometimes the downtown streetlamps stayed on all day because the pollution blocked out the sunlight. And those 'goddamn white lace curtains.'"

Pauline shivered, despite the warm night. Every Sunday of her childhood, women up and down the hillside would hang their hand-scrubbed white lace curtains out on the clothesline to dry. By the following week those curtains were black again; ripe and ready for another Sunday scrubbing. Back on the line they went.

"God, I hated those women," she said, propping herself up on one elbow. "Out there week after week, clothespins in their mouths while they fought the wind to hang their precious curtains. It was like watching Sisyphus push that goddamn rock up the hill, just to watch it roll down the other side. I used to wonder what the hell they were waiting for. Why didn't they get out? They could start over somewhere else. Somewhere clean."

Jack smiled. How lucky he was to have found a woman with a soul as restless as his. Like him, she thrived on constant change. Each new move was an adventure; a challenge to conquer.

Pauline ran her fingers through his chest hair. "But that's just it…Claire never minded the sooty air or the black water or the pathetic curtain hangers. She *never* wanted to leave Bridge Manor. She even tried to convince Paddy to live there, after they were married."

"The cost of restoring an old place can get pretty steep, Pauline. Not to mention keeping it up."

"Claire is smart. She'll find a way."

Jack traced his hand down the curve of his wife's face. "I suppose if things got too bad, she could sell *The Hobbit*."

"Yea, right." She chuckled. "You know Claire would live in the poorhouse before she'd sell her precious books."

"Especially that one."

The extremely rare first edition of JRR Tolkien's book was part of a large collection of rare books the twins' father had left to Claire. The two of them had always shared a love of books; scouring bookstores together and searching for treasures among the dusty shelves.

"I can't help but feel bad for Paddy," said Jack. "I don't know what I'd do if you left me."

Spreading her legs, Pauline straddled her husband. Jack inhaled the citrus smell of her shampoo as she leaned down to whisper in his ear.

"I'm not going anywhere, lover boy. You're stuck with me..." She nibbled his earlobe as her hips ground into him in a slow, circular movement. "...forever and ever, amen."

He groaned. Wrapping her hair around his fist, he gently pulled her toward him. He sucked and gently bit her nipples until her body began to tremble.

"Promise you'll never leave me," he said, firmer than he meant to.

"I could never leave you, Jack." She moaned, arching her head back. "I'd rather die."

Chapter 4

"Paddy, is that you?" The heavy oak door creaked in protest as Claire pulled it open. "Since when do you come to the front door?"

In all the years he'd been coming to Bridge Manor, Paddy Sullivan had never used the front door. Nobody did. The Justus family had always preferred to use the mudroom entrance around back, which opened into the enormous kitchen. With its massive brick fireplace and high windows overlooking the sloping back yard and the city below, the kitchen was the heartbeat of the house. The front door was for salesmen and formal guests. For strangers.

He removed his hat, clutched it to his chest and took a few deep breaths. "I would have come right away, but you asked for some time. I thought the least I could do was give you a week." He flashed a nervous smile. "Longest week of my life."

"Glad to hear it," said Claire. "Hope it was hell for you."

Although her voice sounded strong and bitter, her heart wasn't in it. Even under the dim porch light, she could see Paddy was suffering. His broad shoulders drooped toward his chest, and his clothes seemed a size too big. His arms – still knotted with muscles from decades in the mill – seemed to have shrunk. At not quite forty, he looked more like fifty. *Jesus, Mary and her husband,* she thought, *it's only been a week.*

"I've come to say my peace, Claire."

She stared him down, a million vicious responses running through her head. Finally, heaving an exasperated sigh, she grabbed him by the arm and yanked him into the house.

"Get in here," she said. "Your peace will have to wait until I get some food in you."

Paddy finished off the last of his pastrami on rye as he watched his wife caress the bottom of her ring with her thumb. He had surprised her with it the morning she started her first job as a librarian's assistant. 'A beautiful ring for a beautiful lady,' he had said, taking her in his arms. After she finally agreed to marry him she insisted there was no need for another ring – or any other jewelry for that. The gold ring with the tiny diamond in the center was the only ring she ever wanted on her finger. Raising his head, he met his wife's clear blue eyes as the clock above the stove ticked.

"So." Claire folded her hands on the table. "Let's hear it; do you love her?"

"No." Paddy shook his head. "It was never about love, for either one of us."

"Then shame on you all the more."

He wiped his forehead with the flat of his hand.

"I don't know what happened," he said, his voice as quiet as a confessional whisper. "I lost my way - and I'm ashamed to admit it to you now. One day I was a feisty mill rat with a mind full of plans and possibilities; a whole lifetime adventures still on the horizon, everything yet to be lived. Suddenly…here I am. Middle aged, with too-late written all over me, and the unemployment line taunting me like a schoolyard bully." He paused, a surprised look on his face. "This morning I wiped the steam off the bathroom mirror, and a balding, fat man stared back at me. A no-body...acting like an old fool."

"A nobody," repeated Claire. The fool part she didn't contend.

She rinsed his plate in the sink, then leaned against the counter and crossed her arms. "Did you ever think to ask me – or your son - if we think you're *a nobody*?"

Joe. Paddy flinched. "He must be pretty disap-pointed in his old man."

Claire's hands instinctively slid down to her hips; her way of wrapping her arms around herself without actu-ally wrapping her arms around herself.

"Do you honestly believe I would burden that child with your sins? Joe is our son; not a tool for revenge."

Paddy smiled gratefully. That was Claire for you. "What did you say? How did you explain the two of you moving back to Bridge Manor?"

"I started by telling him how much we both love him. Then I said you and I have decided to spend some time apart." She paused. "And that his father has gone out of his ever-loving mind."

Paddy coughed.

"I might have left out the last part," she said.

"Thank you, darling girl."

Darling girl. Hearing Paddy's nickname for her made Claire's heart hurt. She had loved this man since he was a teenager fresh from Ireland, with a thick, inner-city Dublin accent. And heaven help her, she still did.

"I would have told you sooner," said Claire, topping off Veda Marie's coffee. "But I needed to wait until I was sure myself."

"I knew what you were up to." Veda Marie raised an eyebrow as she blew on her mug. "I'm not blind, missy. For the last month, you have read everything you could get your hands on about home renovation. Not to mention that fire-trap pile of Bed and Breakfast literature stashed under your bed."

Claire chuckled. "I couldn't find any books on running a boarding house. Those old B&B magazines were the next best thing."

"Perhaps because boarding houses are a thing of the past."

"The term 'boarding house' might be outdated, but people will always need somewhere to live. Particularly in an academic city like Pittsburgh." Claire opened her notebook. "I've worked up a business plan, along with a general budget for getting us up and running. These numbers are rough, of course..."

Veda Marie flipped through the pages. She didn't look up until she got to the last page. "You're serious about this."

"I am," said Claire. "And I hope you'll join me. I need a house manager."

"I've never run a boarding house in my life."

"But you have been taking care of Bridge Manor for more than - what, half your life?"

"No need to do the math."

"I need you, Veda Marie. You make this cold, damp place *warm*. Even in the later years, when we couldn't keep up with the repairs and the squirrels and birds and exotic rodents started nesting in the upper floors." She waved a hand. "You merely closed off the 'bad' rooms and concentrated on keeping the 'good' ones comfortable for us."

Veda Marie tapped her fingers against the table. Her orange-red hair was tied up in a pretty green handkerchief and she wore her signature double coat of Maybelline red lipstick.

"Tell me something," she said. "Is it really Bridge Manor you're trying to rebuild, or your life?"

Claire took her time looking around the massive kitchen. "A little of both, I guess."

Veda Marie lit her first cigarette of the day and exhaled as she leaned back in her chair. Claire was right; she'd been here half her life now. She had barely been twenty when she came to this house, a half-filled suitcase in one hand and an ad for a housekeeper in the other. Having escaped a problematical marriage, she chose Pittsburgh because the rivers reminded her of her home on South Carolina's Pee Dee River, and because she figured Chester would never look for her in a mill town. And for the most part, she'd been happy here.

Barely four years older than the sixteen-year-old girls, Veda Marie had immediately slipped into multiple roles: part-mother, part-older sister, and all friend. After Pauline, Claire and finally Ryan moved out, she cared for Mr. Justus until he died. She then offered to stay on until the house was sold – a time she secretly prayed would never come.

"Are you sure, Claire?" Her South Carolina accent made 'Claire' two syllables long. "You really want to jump back into broken plumbing, hissing radiators, exploding fuse boxes and damp rooms that never get warm in the winter? Do you have *any idea* what you're taking on?"

Claire grinned. "Not a clue. What do you say…are you in?"

Veda Marie blew a tendril of hair from her face. "Oh, what the hell."

Armed with pad, pen, flashlights, and tissues, the two women scrutinized the house, from the dirt cellar to the attic above the third floor. They opened doors and windows, measured holes, checked for leaks, flushed toilets, and examined the fuse box. Claire marked loose floorboards and stairs with orange spray paint. Veda Marie wiggled banisters to test sturdiness. They flipped switches, crawled through crawlspaces, and made list after list after list.

Chapter 5

"Farley, wait up!" shouted Loretta, running across the parched dead-looking grass and dirt of the marching field.

Squinting through the small lens of her Instamatic camera, Farley snapped a picture of her friend. Barring a few minor glitches, their best-friendship had worked out well.

Given the military's affinity for sudden transfers, friendships had to form without delay, from which 'best friends' emerged and were declared. An accelerated getting-to-know-you process consisted of searching for common ground: bases they had lived on, friends they might have in common, mutual experiences of life in other states and continents. Loretta and Farley were both fourth graders, had lived in New Mexico (at different times), and adored cheeseburgers, movies, and Audrey Hepburn, in that order. More than enough in Farley's book - by the time fifth grade rolled around, she would probably be living on another base, anyway.

"Hurry up!" she cried, waving Loretta on. "I have to meet William's bus!"

William attended an off-base school, so his civilian bus was not allowed beyond the gates. Between the Vietnam War and anti-war protests picking up steam, bomb threats were not uncommon on military bases. Anyone entering the base had to show proper ID.

"You are not going to believe this," gasped Loretta, out of breath. "I'm serious; this is big."

She shoved her asthma inhaler in her mouth, pumping twice. Farley resisted the urge to take another picture. With one giant eyebrow covering her forehead and tiny black hairs over her lip, Loretta was sensitive about close-ups. Farley patted her back until her coughing and wheezing was over.

"Major Allen died," she said. "His jet went down in a training exercise."

Farley covered her mouth. "No way! Tammy's father?"

Certainly, Farley had overheard her parents speak of casualties over the years, and fatalities were all over the nightly news. But now something as enormous as death had actually touched someone they knew. Tammy Allen was in her homeroom. She borrowed pencils from Farley. Loretta was in her P.E. class. The three of them had lunch at the same table - although Tammy ate way down the other end, with the popular crowd.

"I heard my mom telling someone on the phone," said Loretta.

Farley listened, horrified, as Loretta repeated her mother's one-sided conversation.

"...Mrs. Allen opened the front door and there they were: the Wing Commander, his wife, and the Chaplain. She tried to shut the door but the Chaplain stuck his foot in the way. Mrs. Allen fainted, flat out."

"Wings at the door," whispered Farley.

That was what the base mothers called it. The mere whisper of 'wings at the door' always triggered knocks on wood, signs of the cross, and prayers for the sorrowful trio to stay away.

Loretta nodded, holding up her finger. There was more.

"Get this," she said. "Tammy and her mother can't live here anymore. They have to move off base. From now on, they'll be *civilians*."

At the main gate, Farley considered the guards with their starched uniforms, serious expressions, and perfect salutes. Her mother liked to say that the armed guards and wire fences at the base represented safety from the civilian realities of traffic, the high prices of supermarkets, anti-war protests, and the god-awful notion of living in one place for too long.

Jack gave Farley a gentle nudge. "Too loud."

"Sorry."

Farley had a habit of reciting prayers at the top of her voice when she was in church. She loved the way everyone turned around, looking to see who knew that prayer so well. But Major Allen's memorial mass was solemn, certainly not the time for showing off.

It seemed like the whole base went back to the Allen's house after the service. Tammy and her mother accepted hugs, words of encouragement and sad smiles through a teary line of neighbors, friends, and classmates. Loretta and Farley inched forward, watching a hugger reluctantly release her grip and wander away to get a plate of food.

"Poor Tammy," sighed Loretta.

"Yea, poor Tammy."

The girls watched as Miss Marks, the cruelest teacher in the school, embraced Tammy. Farley leaned in close to Loretta.

"You have to admit, though," she whispered, "it must be nice to have all that attention and sympathy."

"That's sick," said Loretta, louder than she had to.

"I didn't mean it," Farley mumbled, her cheeks blazing.

She really didn't. Arbitrary thoughts constantly flew straight out of her mouth before she had time to think them through. Her father called it her "Achilles' heel." He said she would outgrow it, once she learned to filter.

On the ride home William half screeched, half sang, *"See, I been through the lettuce on a horse with no name!"*

Farley was not in the mood. "Dad, do we have to listen to him sing?"

"William…" said Jack, never taking his eyes off the road.

William sang louder. *"It felt good to be out of the ra-ain!"*

"Son, modulate your voice."

"In the desert!" he screeched.

Farley slapped her sweaty thighs, leaving bright red palm imprints. She'd had it up to here – mostly with herself. "Mom! Please?"

Pauline turned around and tapped William's knee. "Tell you what, kiddo. If you can keep it down until we get home, your dad and I have a surprise for you."

A surprise. Farley narrowed her eyes. Come to think of it…her mother did seem oddly pale for someone who was constantly working on her tan. She tapped her mother's arm. "We're being transferred, aren't we?"

Silence.

"Perfect timing," muttered Farley. "I'm in dire need of some new friends."

Jack opened his heavy atlas on the dining room table.

"I've been assigned to a base in Udorn, Thailand," he said, turning the oversized pages.

"Thailand!" William clasped his hands together and bounced on the balls of his feet. "We're moving to Thailand! Is Thailand near Disneyland?"

"Not quite, professor." Jack tapped a spot on the atlas. "It's in Southeast Asia...here."

Farley and William moved in for a closer look.

Thailand was oceans away from America. In and around its border were names like Laos, Cambodia and Bangkok. And Vietnam. A sick sensation began to form in the pit of Farley's stomach. She tried to catch her mother's eye, but Pauline was too busy crinkling up her forehead and pretending to be fascinated by the atlas.

"The thing is," said Jack, "this time I have to go alone."

"For how long?" asked Farley, hating the high-pitched whine in her voice.

Jack put his arm around Pauline, who was nodding and smiling like a crazy person.

"A year," he said. "Two at the most."

Outside, the sound of a jet coming in for a landing seemed louder than usual.

"What about the rest of us?" William wrapped his arms around himself. "Will we stay here?"

"I thought we'd go home while your father is away," said Pauline.

"Home to Germany, or home to New Mexico?" William asked, thinking of the most recent bases they'd lived on. "Or do you mean..."

"No, hon," said Pauline, exuding Romper Room enthusiasm. "We'll move back home to Pittsburgh. Won't that be fun?"

While Pauline started dinner, Jack pulled his black leather camera case down from the hall closet and placed it in Farley's hands.

"I know you'll take good care of it."

She caught her breath. "You're giving me your camera?"

"On one condition," he said, ruffling her hair. "While I'm away, I want you to take at least one picture every day. Something you think made the day special. Will you do that for me?"

"Of course."

"Good. When I come home, we can go back through the days together."

William tugged on his father's arm. "What about me? What do I get to do?"

Jack leaned down until his forehead touched his son's. William wasn't a hugger; he and Jack had their own show of affection.

"Professor, you are in charge of putting the pictures together in a book."

William nodded, solemnly. "I do love the smell of glue."

Pauline had insisted on making a special spaghetti dinner, as if they had something to celebrate. Farley kept busy chopping garlic for the bread and trying not to cry. Over the years, her father had been away for weeks, even months at a time. But a year? Two? And Vietnam. She knew what went on over there. Everyone knew.

After dinner Pauline sat in front of the television – which was not on - and stared into space, while Jack got William ready for bed. He made a point of tucking him in extra tight, like a taco. Being tucked in like a taco was William's latest thing; it gave him the happy-hug feeling without having to experience the actual hug.

Farley went to bed early and lay in the dark, sniffing her fingers. Even after a hot bath, the comforting aroma of garlic lingered on her skin. Just as she was finally drifting off to sleep, William cracked open her bedroom door and tiptoed to her bed.

"Are you sleeping?" he spit-whispered. Missing his two front teeth, whispering wasn't William's strong point.

She gave a low moan, pretending to be asleep.

"I heard you sniffing a mile away, Farley," he said, clicking his tongue. "So you can stop faking it."

Lately, William had developed a habit of clicking his tongue on the roof of his mouth when he was worried about something. He said it was a lot like itching a mosquito bite; once he got going, he couldn't stop.

"I think Dad should probably stay home," William said loudly, overriding her pretend sleep. "Malaria is a common ailment in Southeast Asia and it's highly resistant to drugs. He could also come down with dengue fever or typhus. Or leprosy. Even diarrhea can be deadly if it's not brought under control."

"He has to go. He got orders."

"I think he should ask for a different *orders*," he said, his voice rising.

"That's not how it works."

"Then we need to quit the Air Force."

Farley let out an exasperated sigh - as if the same thought hadn't been bouncing around in her head all evening.

"Dad doesn't quit, William. And if he did, we'd have to go to the same school every year, with the same friends, and live in the same house for the rest of our lives, with no guards and no gates to keep us safe. Is that what you want? Do you really want to be a *civilian*?"

William was quiet, except for the occasional click against the roof of his mouth.

"No," he finally said. "I guess not."

Farley pulled back her covers. "Come on, I'll let you sleep with me if you promise to stop worrying."

Click.

"I promise to try."

In the early morning hours of Jack's departure, the flight line had an unreal quality to it. The James family clung together, arms intertwined. They might have been one massive body. Over the roar of the jet engines, they could barely hear each other.

"I love you, Dad." Farley's puffy eyes threatened to overflow with yet more tears. "I miss you already."

"I love you, too," he said. "Don't forget; whenever you miss me, go outside and look up."

"Because we're all under the same sky!" shouted William, giving himself a few substantial yanks.

Jack bent down and touched William's forehead to his. They stayed like that for a long time. Then he stood and took Pauline's face in his hands and kissed her. Leaning back, he pressed his palm against her cheek.

"Pauline, I want you to know that no matter what happens…"

"Don't you dare, Jack James," she yelled over the noise. "Whatever it is, you can tell me when you come home."

Us-four-minus-one, Pauline, Farley and William stood on the tarmac and watched as Jack's jet rose higher and higher across the morning sky. Until he disappeared.

It Burns a Lovely Light

Chapter 6

Pauline rented a three-bedroom walk-up in downtown Pittsburgh. The location was perfect. The Significant Me – highly recommended by William's teachers in Arizona - was two blocks from home. Saint Bridget's, where Farley would attend the fifth grade, could be seen from their rooftop patio. And both Claire and Ryan lived just across the Monongahela River.

Pauline's siblings lived at opposite ends of Overlook Trail, a precipitous cobblestone road. Bridge Manor, Claire's home, sat at the top. Appearing to cling to the hillside, the old Victorian had a commanding view of the city below. Ryan's stone cottage was located near the river at the bottom of Overlook Trail. His house, along with shops, a market, and St. Xavier's Church, formed Grady Square, the heart of the small community of Grady.

True to her promise Farley took at least one photograph a day: her finger pushing a lemon seed into a pot of soil, Pauline unpacking the 'nice' dishes, William eating a picnic lunch on the rooftop patio. Using a tripod, she photographed the three of them pretending to be Sears catalogue models. She captured the crisp leaves of October; Pauline blowing kisses to the camera with Christmas tinsel in her hair; Bridge Manor in various stages of repair; Joe and Paddy teaching William to skate on a frozen pond, and Veda Marie pinching suckers from her spring tomato plants. Somewhere between the leaves and the tomatoes, Farley decided she wanted to be a professional photographer.

She devoured photography magazines. When she wasn't in her school uniform, Farley took to wearing all black and wandering the city, snapping pictures. She tried to act the way she thought a professional photographer would act, all artistic and lost in thought - although she couldn't quite pull off 'moody and withdrawn.'

Pauline deposited a worn-looking cloth bag full of submarine sandwiches on Bridge Manor's massive wooden table.

"I got two meatball cheeses, two Italian with everything, and two tuna salads - toasted, heavy on the onions." She wiped her face with a napkin. "I don't know how you live with this humidity. Give me the dry heat of the desert any day."

"Don't tell me you walked all the way from your apartment," said Claire, not looking up from the bills she was paying.

"It's only a few miles."

"Straight uphill. You're putting us to shame."

"Speak for yourself, Claire Sullivan," yelled Veda Marie from the pantry. "I'm as healthy as a frisky thoroughbred."

Claire grunted. "Then why are you always running to the doctor?"

"Unlike you, I enjoy having my good health confirmed with regular check-ups."

Pauline filled a glass with water.

"Is it me," she said, "or have those steps gotten steeper since we were kids?"

Generations ago, hundreds - maybe thousands – of public steps had been built into the steep hills overlooking the city. Before sturdy roads, inclines, and transit systems, the steps made it much easier to maneuver up and down the slopes. Many of the steps were now in disarray but large sections of them were still in use, including the ones that led from Grady Square straight up to Bridge Manor's back yard.

Veda Marie dumped an armload of paper plates, napkins and cups on the table. "Speaking of kids," she said, "where are your little chickens?"

"They're a few minutes behind me. William saw a frog about halfway up the hill and Farley's friend, Dion, threatened to kiss it." She examined a framed picture hanging beside the pantry. "When did you put this up?"

The photograph was of Claire, Pauline, and Veda Marie. They had taken a break from one of their many renovation projects. Just as they were striking a pose, Veda Marie broke them up with some funny piece of gossip. Farley's camera captured the three of them in a fit of hilarity.

Veda Marie faced sideways with one knee slightly bent, her head thrown back in laughter. Even in her worn denim overalls she was a Barbie doll - complete with a too-tiny waist and impossibly perky breasts – but there was a durability to Veda Marie that made her seem much larger than her small frame.

In the center of the photograph stood Pauline, her hair in a ponytail, an oversized smile on her face. Dressed in tight clam-diggers and an old work shirt of Jack's with the shirttail tied under her chest, she held a similar sideways pose.

Claire faced the camera head-on, eyes shining, mouth partially open. She wore a pair of cuffed dungarees and one of Joe's hockey practice jerseys. Her frizzy salt-and- pepper hair was plastered to one side.

"We hung a bunch of Farley's pictures last night," said Veda Marie. "I'm trying to get the lower level spruced up before my sister Mary comes to visit. Wait till you see the drawing room; we covered up four or five holes in the wall with Farley's masterpieces."

Pauline squinted at the photo. "I'm constantly amazed at how she can take an everyday scene and make it extraordinary."

"I know it."

'I know it' was Veda Marie's favorite expression. She used it often and enunciated each word with without-a-doubt confidence. "Our girl is as good as any big-shot professional."

"Don't encourage her," said Pauline, only partially kidding. "Lately she's become obsessed with this dream of traveling the world alone, taking pictures of pygmies and igloos and creatures from the blue lagoon. I get the becoming-a-photographer part. I mean, look at her work. But *alone*? What's with that? Being alone is my worst nightmare."

"Dreams change on a dime when you're young." Veda Marie opened the refrigerator door. "I seem to recall you wanting to be a nun, back in the day."

Claire looked up from her bills. "I forgot about your Sister Pauline phase. You spent half our junior year on your knees repenting for your evil, domineering ways. Happiest year of my life."

Pauline made a face at her sister. "Ha, ha. Funny."

"At least Farley wants to do something she's good at," said Veda Marie. "Even Ryan commented on her talent, and you know how tight the man can be with the compliments."

"Where is Mutt, anyway? I thought he was going to help us clear out the carriage house."

"He waltzed in the door this morning, ready to work. Then Claire mentioned you wouldn't be here until the afternoon. Suddenly he remembered a pressing engagement and high-tailed it out the door, all sad-eyes and mopey face."

"Now you're exaggerating," said Pauline, laughing.

"I am not."

By the time newly-wed Pauline and Jack boarded the train for their honeymoon, thirteen-year-old Ryan had run away from home. He tried to join the Army, lying about his age and padding his shoes with newspapers to make himself appear taller. One look at his baby face had the recruiters in stitches. They told him to beat it. Go home to mama. He returned to Bridge Manor filthy and dejected - and suddenly intolerant of Claire, for the simple fact that she wasn't Pauline.

"So tell me about Farley's friend," said Veda Marie. "About time she brought someone up to Bridge Manor."

"She's probably afraid we'll put them to work," said Pauline, unwrapping the sandwiches and slicing them into quarters. "The girl's name is Dionna Piotrowski, but she goes by 'Dion.'"

Claire closed her checkbook and capped her pen. "I know a Mrs. Piotrowski from St. Xavier's. Despicable woman. Always on moral patrol."

"Let's hope she's not Dion's mother," said Veda Marie. She tucked an escaped strand of red hair back into her kerchief as she headed for the refrigerator. "Is Dion in Farley's class at school?"

"Yes, but they didn't really become close until Mother Superior caught them arguing in detention. She decided they should spend more time together, and sentenced them to a week of mopping and waxing the gymnasium floor. By the time their sentence was up the girls were inseparable."

"Why were they in detention in the first place?" asked Claire.

Pauline tore off a piece of meatball sub. "Dion flashed her bum during recess."

"A girl with spark." said Veda Marie. "She'll fit right in around here. What was Farley in for?"

"For arguing with Sister Fides."

"Whoa," said Claire. "Never argue with a nun."

"Each student was assigned a poem to memorize and recite. Farley's was *First Fig*, by Edna St. Vincent Millay."

"One of my favorites," said Veda Marie, closing her eyes as she recited the poem.

"My candle burns at both ends. It will not last the night.

But ah, my foes and oh, my friends, it gives a lovely light!"

"Apparently, Farley replaced '*gives*' a lovely light with '*burns*' a lovely light," continued Pauline, "explaining that the candle was clearly doomed from the start."

Claire chuckled. "Doomed from the start?"

"The child is brilliant," said Veda Marie.

Pauline sighed. "Well, the child received a failing mark for her brilliance. I have to say; she did put up a good argument. She said all forms of art should be open to interpretation, and this was hers."

The mudroom door slammed behind William as he stumbled into the kitchen. He juggled his hands in excitement. "You're not going to believe this! Dion saves her scabs in a jar!"

The girls came in behind William, their faces moist with sweat.

"Veda Marie and Claire, this is Dion," said Farley, pointing to the two women.

"Why are you saving scabs?" asked Claire, her mouth full.

"I'm going to be a nurse when I grow up."

Veda Marie handed both girls a glass of iced tea. "Welcome to Bridge Manor, Dion. I'm Veda Marie Tendersheets."

"Wow, that's a really cool name."

Veda Marie patted her hair. "I know it."

Pauline polished off the last of her potato chips as she examined the to-do wall. The to-do wall was actually an enormous black chalkboard the three women had found at a flea market. They all agreed; only the high ceilings of the kitchen could handle such a large board without taking over the room. Suspended with heavy wire and framed by the red brick wall, the effect was both sensible and striking.

Veda Marie had insisted on writing the list - saying no offense, but Claire's handwriting was practically illegible and Pauline's was too fancy to be taken seriously:

Immediate Repairs
Leaks in roof
Un-stick stuck windows
Tape broken windows on east side
Repair steps on second floor main stairway
Throw away anything mildewed
Remove rotten wall-to-wall carpeting
Replace disgusting/broken toilets
Large hole in wall next to kitchen
Patch drip under kitchen sink
Replace washer
Purchase heavy duty dryer
Seal around doors and windows
Increase insulation in attic
Close off fireplaces in bedrooms

Improvements That Will Have to Wait
Paint, inside and out
Wallpaper stripping
Strip, sand, and refinish hardwoods
Have fireplaces cleaned
Repair Carrara tile in bathrooms
Untangle weeds from front and back
Renew old path through woods

Pie in the Sky
New roof
Finish Cellar
Lose weight

"I swear to God," said Veda Marie, talking around her cigarette as it bobbed up and down between her lips, "that list doubles while we are sleeping in our beds."

Pauline ran her finger down the list. "I'll start with taping the broken windows."

She spent as much time as possible at Bridge Manor, insisting that hard work was just the thing to keep her sanity in check. And it seemed to be working, for the most part. She shuddered as she thought about the ring game.

It started by accident shortly after they moved back to Pittsburgh. She had placed her wedding ring on the side of the sink while she washed her hands. As she dried her hands, the edge of the towel flipped the ring into the sink and twirled closer and closer to the drain. She screamed and clawed at the sink, trapping the ring against the side with the palm of her hand. Clutching the ring, she sobbed, euphorically relieved.

Then she began to press fate, giving her ring the occasional, horrific twirl in the sink. Oh, but the rush. The pounding of her heart as she watched the symbol of their love move closer to the gaping drain. The unspeakable thrill each time she saved her precious ring.

It Burns a Lovely Light

Chapter 7

On the last day of school before summer break, the girls were still in their scratchy wool uniforms. Saint Bridget's had seasonal uniforms for the boys; heavy blue trousers and a jacket for cold weather, cool cotton trousers and a lightweight sport coat for the warmer months. The girls had to wear the same plaid skirt all year, along with thick stockings and long sleeved button-down in the winter, and white knee socks and a Peter pan blouse in the fall and spring.

"Come on, you guys." Exasperated, Farley lowered her camera. "Walk like *real* zombies."

Dion slapped her pimply thighs. "That does is it. I quit."

"Me too," said Joe. "It's hotter than the gates of hell out here."

"No shit, Sherlock." Dion fanned her skirt, underpants be damned. "At least you're not in a wool skirt."

As a change of pace from her everyday photos, Farley had proposed setting up some zombie shots. The atmosphere was perfect; still steamy and sticky from a recent rain, yet horribly bright.

"I promise we'll stop after this shot," said Farley. "Remember to keep your arms down. You're a zombie, not a sleepwalker."

She tilted her head and let her mouth droop. "See how my eyes are sort of dead-looking, and my jaw hangs off to one side?"

Lumbering across the lawn, Hockey Player Zombie Joe asked, "How's this?"

"It would be better if you weren't in the shade," said Farley, frustrated. "Everyone knows the scariest scenes take place in broad daylight."

A wood-paneled station wagon pulled down the driveway and honked two quick honks. A frazzled looking woman and a tall, skinny teenage boy emerged.

They heard Veda Marie's excited screams from inside the house. "Claire! Pauline! My people are here!"

"...and *this* is my nephew, Henry," said Veda Marie, one arm around his shoulders.

Henry blushed. "Hi."

William frowned at Veda Marie's sister, Mary. Her brown hair was cut short, pixie-style. She wore a sundress, flip-flops, and clear lip gloss.

"You're not as fancy as Veda Marie," he said.

"I know it." Mary leaned down to be eye-level with him. "I never could hold a candle to Veda Marie when it came to getting up to something and looking pretty doing it." She winked. "So I settled for being the smart sister."

"Why did she call you 'my people'?"

"In the south, 'my people' means family."

William turned to Veda Marie. "Am I your people, too?"

"Of course you are, lovey."

Mary was whisked into the house with promises of Cold Duck, Velveeta cheese squares, and a grand tour of a new-and-on-its-way-to-being-improved Bridge Manor. Henry stayed outside with the zombies but declined the invitation to become one of the un-dead. He sat on the picnic table, watching, pretending not to notice that Farley – of the wild, dark chocolate hair, scuffed-up knees and sweaty Catholic school plaid – was examining him through her camera lens.

He's going to be a tall one, thought Farley. It was nice to look a boy in the eye for a change. At twelve, she was taller than almost everyone in her school. Sixteen-year-old Henry wasn't finished growing, either. Farley had seen enough growth spurts in her day to recognize a late one in the making. His feet and hands were meant for a giant, and his grown-up ears and nose seemed to overwhelm the rest of his little-boy face, complete with dimples that really showed up when he smiled. And when Henry Freeman smiled, everything in the whole world seemed a little bit better.

"Farley's an interesting name," he said, looking directly into her lens as she fired away.

"Beats Henry by a mile." She moved closer. Click. "Are you really going to New York to look at *cooking* schools?"

"Culinary schools," he corrected. "I'm going to have my own restaurant someday."

"How do you know?" She zoomed in on his dark brown eyes. She liked the way Henry spread his words out; smooth and relaxed, like he had all day. Like Paul Newman in *Cat on a Hot Tin Roof*.

"Well, that's what I want, anyway. Which is funny, because I can't stand the sight of food being chewed. Makes me weak in the knees."

Farley peeked around from behind her camera. "There's a cool scene in *True Grit*, where everybody is eating around a big table. No dialogue, just a bunch of people masticating like crazy. Most disgusting scene in the history of movies."

"Thanks for the warning."

"No problem." Click. "I can't believe you're going to be a senior this year. Are you old enough?"

Self-consciously, Henry touched his hairless chin. "I'm sixteen. I skipped a few years. So, are you going to be a photographer when you grow up?"

"I *am* a photographer." Click. "I'm going to wander through every continent, photographing things most people would never otherwise see."

"Then you should know you can't take pictures from that angle," said Henry, poking her lens with his index finger.

"Why not?"

"Because the sun is directly behind me." He paused. "I'm pretty sure it's a rule."

"A rule?" She lowered her camera. "Where is your sense of adventure, Henry?"

"I happen to have a wonderful– albeit prudent– sense of adventure."

Farley tried not to smile.

"What?" he said.

"In my whole life I'll probably never use the words 'albeit' or 'prudent.'"

He grinned, his dimples going deep. "Then you're missing out on some perfectly good words."

The mean woman from St. Xavier's was indeed Dion's mother. Mrs. Piotrowski picked her daughter up after dinner, wearing a housedress and a permanent puss on her face. She could be heard screaming at poor Dion before the car even left the driveway.

After dinner the kids walked down to Grady Square for ice cream. Joe and William took their cones to the river. Farley and Henry sat on a bench to eat theirs.

"Your aunt brags about you all the time, you know," said Farley, licking her cone.

He covered his eyes with his non-ice cream hand, pretending nervousness. "I'm afraid to ask."

Farley imitated Veda Marie's Carolina accent. "An absolute *angel*, that Henry. Never gave his parents a *day* of worry! And a regular Chef Boy-Ar-dee in the kitchen. A hoot! Sweet. Honor student, top of his class." Giggling, she reverted back to her own voice. "It's enough to make you sick."

Seeing Henry laugh made her flush with pleasure.

On the way back up the hill Farley shared her dream of photographing the world. She liked the way Henry really listened to her - and treated her like a real person instead of a goofy kid. After a while she realized she'd been doing all the talking and asked him about his restaurant plans.

"I want all of my ingredients to be fresh," he said, using his hands to accentuate his point. "Some of the best meals I've ever tasted were good because of the freshness of the food, not because someone found a wild new way to prepare it."

"Do you have a name picked out?"

"I'm going to call it 'Freeman's.'" He paused. "I flipped my first pancake when I was seven years old. I've been dreaming of owning my own restaurant ever since."

She stopped walking, stunned. "Henry, I know exactly what you mean! Photographing the world is so real to me, I can taste it."

Crossing his arms, Henry rocked back on the heels of his feet. "But why do you have to do that alone?"

"I love not knowing which way I'll turn or what's over the next mountain. It's hard to wander free with someone else attached." She raised her chin. "I might only be twelve, but I've seen enough of the world to know I want more."

"All right," he said. "Let's do it. I'll have my restaurant. You'll go out and capture all of the beauty of the world. And we won't let anything stand in our way."

"No matter what."

"No matter what." He stuck out a long, bony hand. "Deal?"

She started to spit on her hand, the ultimate seal of an oath, when she remembered Henry's queasy disposition. Instead, she grabbed his hand and shook it, hard. "Deal!"

Years later, she had to wonder at the innocence of it all.

Chapter 8

"We've been hit."

The Phantom F-4's warning panel came to life.

Jack and his navigator, Rudy, were returning from a combat mission, successfully locating and photographing the assigned missile site. North Vietnamese anti-aircraft fire battered the Phantom F-4.

Both hydraulic power control systems in the lurching two-man aircraft were losing pressure. Once the systems failed, control of the aircraft would be impossible. Jack turned the plane east. He would put it down in the Gulf of Tonkin, where U.S. ships patrolling the sea could pick them up.

"Going feet wet," he told Rudy.

"Roger that."

To prevent seat collision, Rudy's rear canopy would fire first, with Jack's following 3/4 of a second later. As each canopy jettisoned, it would automatically pull the safety pin that catapulted the men out of the aircraft. Jack checked the pressure gauges as the F-4 approached the coastline. Almost zero. Hold on…closer…closer. All right, here we go.

"Eject on my count of three," Jack exclaimed. "One…two…three."

Both men pulled their ejection handles. With a roar, Rudy's canopy departed the aircraft and his ejection seat catapult fired. Jack's did not. He looked up. His canopy was still attached to the aircraft.

His movements were deliberate and calm, in spite of how fast everything was happening. For emergency jettisons, there were limited options; he could recite them in his sleep. Again he pulled the seat handle between his legs. Nothing. Reaching above his head, he pulled the second handle. The canopy failed to fire.

The nose of the aircraft started down. With barely enough hydraulic pressure and manual rudder control remaining, Jack leveled the wings and brought the nose back to level flight. He reached for his final option, the canopy jettison handle located above the instrument panel.

"Pauline!" he cried, pulling the handle.

"Listen to this," said Farley, reading from a book on the French poet, Anatole France. "If the path be beautiful, let us not question where it leads." She let out a dramatic sigh. "I can't wait to follow beautiful paths, no matter where they lead."

Farley and William were sitting on their small kitchen counter, watching their mother put the groceries away.

Pauline unwrapped a new roll of paper towels. "Can't you just talk about boys and pimples like a normal girl?"

"Mom, it's a commendable goal. That's the exact word Henry used. He said mine was a *commendable* goal."

It had been over a month since Henry and Mary's visit and Farley was still talking about the deal she and Henry made. If anything she seemed to be picking up steam.

Caressing his happiness cloak, William touched a spot on Farley's face. "Speaking of pimples, you have a gigantic one on your chin." He squinted. "It might even be a boil."

Farley pushed his hand away and hopped off the counter.

"Whoa," she said, pretending to admire one of her many photographs taped to the refrigerator. "Could this be…a Farley James?"

Pauline leaned in. "By God, you're right. Don't you love her fresh, prickly insight?"

"She really forces you to look," agreed Farley. She nudged her mother with her shoulder. "They say she wanders far and wide with her trusty camera."

Pauline puckered her lips. "That's a vicious rumor. I have it on good authority she still lives with her parents and her brother, happy as a clam."

"Doorbell!" William hopped off the counter. "I'll get it!"

"Hey, fella." Dion handed William a rolled-up magazine. "I brought you an article on Computerized Axial Tomography."

"Hi, hon," said Pauline. "Farley's in the kitchen, planning her career."

"Look, Mom!" William was already rifling through the magazines pages. "Dion brought me an article on Computerized Axial Tomography!"

"A what?"

"*Mom.*" William rolled his eyes. "A CAT scan. Only the most important medical breakthrough since the X-ray."

Pauline glanced at Dion as she dug through her purse. "That's awfully heavy for summer reading. Shouldn't you be reading Nancy Drew or something?"

"Not if I'm going to be a nurse, Mrs. James."

"You kids blow me away. How can you be so sure of the rest of your life? You've barely hit puberty, for crying out loud."

"*Mom!*" Farley appeared, holding two cans of Tab.

"I know I'm going to be a superhero," said William.

"Of course you are," said Pauline. She waved a pair of tweezers in the air. "Whew! Found them. I'll be in the car if anyone needs me."

Farley gestured for Dion to follow her to her room. "Come on."

The girls were obsessed with Don McLean's song, 'American Pie.' They knew every word by heart, and had even worked up a dance routine, which they were constantly modifying behind closed doors. William was painfully jealous. He loved to sing, although he couldn't remember more than a line or two of any song, never mind the corresponding dance steps.

"What's your mom doing in the car?" asked Dion.

"She's plucking her eyebrows. She says the rearview mirror is the only honest mirror."

"She plucks her eyebrows while she's driving?"

"No, silly. She does it in the parking space."

Farley pulled the record out of its album cover and slid it down the thin pole of the record player. After a scratchy start the needle got on track.

"Shut the door," she said. "I want to show you some new moves I made up for this part…"

On the other side of the bedroom door, William hummed along:

"...touched me deep inside, the day the music died."

Pauline adjusted the rearview mirror and examined her handiwork, tilting her face from side to side.

"Hang in there, girl," she whispered. "One more month and Jack will be home. Thirty-one more days."

Sometimes in the middle of the night she would lie awake, haunted by how close she had come to not meeting her husband. Released from West Point for the weekend with no set plans, no family to visit...he might have gone anywhere. What if he had taken a different train, or hadn't sat next to Paddy? What if Claire hadn't been sick, leaving it up to Pauline to meet Paddy's train? And so it went. And then there was her horrible compulsion with the wedding ring.

"You need to come home now, darling."

William sang as he ran toward the car, his voice shrill and wobbly.

"Something touched me deep inside, the day the mewwwwwsick died!"

"What's up, kiddo?"

"A man is on the phone!" He hopped up and down, one hand down the front of his shorts. "I said 'James' residence, William speaking,' and I used my peaceful voice and everything!"

Pauline hurried up the stairwell with William trotting behind her.

"First the man said 'is your mother home' and I said 'she's not exactly *home*, home. She's downstairs in the car pulling her eyebrows out!'"

"Oh, dear," giggled Pauline, opening the apartment door.

Pauline's high heels, Farley's high-tops, and William's Hush Puppies made a discordant racket as they pounded full speed down the hospital's shiny white corridor. Farley and William got to his room first. They stopped at the open door, unused to seeing their father injured, vulnerable. His left leg was elevated and a thick white bandage covered part of his head.

"Jack!" Pauline blew past them and threw herself into her husband's arms.

"Pauline," he sobbed, burying his face in her hair. "When the plane was going down, all I could see was your face. Nothing else; just your beautiful face."

William and Farley watched from the doorway. For a moment, before she remembered that she was the luckiest girl in the world, Farley wondered what happened to the rest of their faces.

Pauline bought her children lunch in the hospital cafeteria. Carrying their trays, they found an empty table next to a young doctor who appeared to be studying.

"Best seat in the house!" exclaimed William, clearly worked up.

Pauline helped William unload his tray. "Let's keep it down, kiddo."

"Sorry, am I getting all shrill again?"

"Shhhh," said Farley.

Using her chin, she pointed to the doctor beside them. His face teetered a few inches above an open notebook.

"He's probably been up for days," she whispered. "Look at him; he's asleep on his feet."

William's foot bounced up and down as he considered this. Technically, the man was sitting.

Inspired by her own – and now Henry's – dreams, Farley was drawn to the idea of fierce dedication. She felt sorry for anyone who didn't have ambition. After all, what was the point of getting up in the morning if you don't have something to go all-out for?

"You two enjoy your lunch," said Pauline. "Do you remember how to get back to Dad's room?"

A group of nurses stared unashamedly after Pauline as she high-heeled it back to Jack. Perhaps to counteract their identical head-to-toe uniforms, each woman's lunch was on a different color tray.

"That is so unfair," said Red Tray, gawking as Pauline weaved her way toward the exit.

Yellow Tray balanced a square of jiggling Jell-O on her fork.

"I'd sell my soul to the devil himself to have a figure like that," she said. "I'd throw in my husband's soul, too."

Blue Tray took a bite of her sandwich and waved it in Farley's direction.

"This one must take after the father," she said, in a weak attempt at a whisper.

"Talk about unfair," said Yellow Tray. "How'd you like to have a mom like that, while you're so…"

William clicked his tongue as Farley turned to the women.

"I'm big-boned," she said, her mouth full of macaroni salad.

Chapter 9

Dear Henry,

I hear you hit the floor during your sauce exam. Veda Marie ran that one up the telephone lines before you had time to dust off your chef-training-pants. To think you almost made it through your first year without a single incident.
Farley

P.S. I took this picture of scrambled eggs and peppers in a dive in Mexico.

Dear Dion,

Thanks for the article on the fine art of French kissing. (Where do you get these things?) I can't believe your mother found your scab jar. On second thought, I believe it. You're lucky she let you back in the house.
Farley

Dear Henry,

Next stop, Travis Air Force Base in California. I'm usually glad to move - fresh start and all. But lately something has been bothering me. Moving a lot means you never really need to face your mistakes.

If I have a fight with a friend, who cares? We'll be gone soon anyway. Not popular in school? Better luck next base. Each time I promise to stay in touch, but then my new life begins and everything about the old base seems to get lost in the move. I'm pretty sure I wouldn't say this in person, but it's easier on paper: I'm worried that I don't know how to be a real friend.
Farley.

PS. Sorry this was all about me. I hope your pastry is improving.

Dear Farley,

I kicked ass on the pastry exam, thank you very much. Regarding your 'real friend' concerns, I can only judge for myself but you've been a good friend to me. I've got a stack of postcards with words of encouragement, and some pretty damn good photos you took the time to send me. So quit whining and go take some pictures.
Your friend,
Henry

Dear Henry,

Congratulations on surviving culinary school! You're a free man, Freeman. (Ha-ha!) Now go get a job. You've got to start saving up for your own restaurant. Just think, you're one step closer to your dream. As I write this I can practically smell the food coming out of Freeman's kitchen. We're moving to Wright-Patterson Air Force Base in Ohio. I know. Ohio. Oh, well. It won't be for long. It never is.
Farley

Dion,

I'm really proud of you for getting straight A's again. You could even be valedictorian next year! So much for my junior year. I've ruined it already. I sort of made a name for myself after giving my so-called boyfriend a tastefully photographed self-portrait of me 'au natural.' Who knew he was such a sharer? I got a major lecture from my parents about the risks I'd taken - not only with my reputation, but with my Dad's shot at an upcoming promotion to full Colonel. Apparently fathers who can't keep their kids in line don't make good leaders. It's not fair that he should pay for my stupid mistake.

Farley

P.S. So what if you didn't make cheerleading. You've got better things to do with your time, right?

Dear Farley,

Thanks for the postcard. I'm sorry I haven't written in so long. My job is insane. The head chef sweats all the time – yes, into the food – and is constantly screaming something in Italian that no one understands. I know kitchens are traditionally frenzied, but this is ridiculous. Everyone runs around like a miserable maniac. At least I'm learning a lot about what I *don't* want in my restaurant. I plan to leave as soon as I can find the time to look for another job.

Your friend,

Henry

PS. Get out of the nudie-photo business. It doesn't suit you. (Sorry, Veda Marie spilled the beans.)

Henry,

    Frenzied?? Are you sure you're American?
I'm sorry your job is insane. According to my dad, it's best to start in the bowels of the mailroom and work your way up. You, my friend, are in the bowels. Dad got promoted after all, in spite of my nudie-photo antics. We're being transferred to Nellis Air Force Base, Las Vegas. I can't wait. I plan to spend my entire senior year making up for my junior year. Fresh start, here I come!

    Mom and I are already looking at colleges. I'm thinking of applying to The New York Institute of Photography. That puts me in your midst. Consider this fair warning.
Farley

Dion,

    Can you believe we're graduating high school? I made it by the hair of my chinny-chin-chin.

    Vegas turned out to be extremely unhealthy for me. My friends and I got in the habit of skipping school to hang out at the casino swimming pools, catching up on our tans and enjoying the ninety-nine cent all-you-can-eat buffets. Highly addictive, let me tell you. But thanks to the quality of my overall education and winning a few local photography contests, I was accepted by The New York Institute of Photography! New York!
Love,
Farley

Chapter 10

"Can we visit the Official MGM Lion again?" asked William, fiddling with his headgear. At first he had been concerned about the new metal addition to his braces. Superheroes didn't wear headgear. Then his father let him in on some top-secret information: Headgear was a superhero's dream come true, as it interfered with the villain's listening devices. Now he only removed the contraption to eat.

"Not this time, professor," said Jack, saluting the guard as he drove off the base.

How they could keep a lion in a casino was beyond Farley. They kept him in a cage with a collar around his neck. The worst part to her was that the animal didn't seem to mind; as if he didn't know any better.

"Tonight's a special night, hon," said Pauline, her eyes unusually bright. She had gotten Farley tickets to see Barry Manilow at Caesar's Palace – supposedly as a graduation gift. She wasn't fooling anyone; whenever Pauline drove the car, her eight-track of Barry Manilow's Greatest Hits played non-stop.

At first they had all been delighted when Jack was assigned to Nellis, but the thrill of the lights and chaos of Las Vegas had long since eroded. Farley's disenchantment began with the discovery - exactly one block from the flashing signs and neon lights of the strip - of multiple pawnshops, each filled with suitcases, watches, and wedding bands. Her photograph of two horizontal shelves that seemed to go on forever, stacked floor to ceiling with luggage, won first prize and front page coverage in the Nevada Times photography contest.

"Dad, can we stop for a second?" Farley pointed toward the mountains. "I want to get a picture of the sun going down."

Pauline, Jack, and William climbed onto the hood of the car and leaned against the windshield, while Farley removed her Minolta and a wide angle lens from her case. Over the years the camera had been updated, but her father's old brown leather case remained the same. She set up the tripod and began photographing the sunset behind the darkening mountain ridge.

"Now take one of 'us four,'" said Jack, patting the hood of his old '69 Buick.

Farley set the timer, then ran and hopped on the hood. Everyone wrapped their arms around each other and smiled for the camera. The timer went off, capturing the James family at their best in mid-laugh, and lit by the sizzling orange glow of the sunset.

As she gathered her equipment, Jack handed Farley a large manila envelope.

"We were going to wait until after the show to give you this," he said, "but your brother is ready to implode. Happy Graduation."

"Happy Graduation!" echoed William, clenching his fists and bouncing up and down on the balls of his shoes.

The envelope contained a round-trip airplane ticket to Paris, five one-hundred dollar bills, and a colorful drawing of a girl with a camera around her neck. At the top, written in red crayon:

Farley and her trusty camera
Ready, Set, Wander Free!

"We've got you flying in and out of Paris," said Jack. "The rest of the trip is up to you. And don't worry; you'll be home in plenty of time for school."

Farley turned to her mother. "Are you all right with this?"

"Why wouldn't I be?"

"No reason."

Because conversations in cinderblock duplexes are easily overheard, she thought, recalling an argument she heard only weeks ago.

'Don't you dare make me the bad guy, Jack James,' Pauline had said, clearly livid. Silverware clanked; Farley pictured her mother tossing it in the dishwasher with the precise deliberation of a circus knife thrower. 'Of course (*clank*) there's nothing wrong with having a dream. But there is no (*clank*) way I am going to allow our daughter to flit across Europe (*clank*) by herself (*clank*), doing God (*clank*) knows what.'

'Spending the summer exploring Europe sounds a lot more wholesome than hanging around Vegas,' said Jack. 'The casino environment hasn't exactly worked out for her. And why do you always refer to her traveling as 'flitting' or 'traipsing'?'

The silverware tossing came to an abrupt halt.

'What is that supposed to mean? Are you implying I'm making light of our daughter's dreams?' Her voice rose to a shrill pitch. 'Maybe I'm jealous... is that what you think?'

They were quiet for a while. The next time Farley heard her mother's voice, it was muffled, as if cocooned inside a great big Jack-hug. So typical.

'She is barely eighteen years old,' said Pauline, apparently having come up for air. 'We are supposed to protect her, not send her out into the world all alone.'

Farley could practically hear her father scrubbing his face with his hands.

'She's not your average naive eighteen-year old,' he said. 'Not by a long shot.'

'Those photographs were museum-quality,' snapped Pauline. 'It's not Farley's fault her juvenile delinquent boyfriend wasn't sophisticated enough to recognize a work of art. She has nothing to be ashamed of.'

Farley groaned. She was never going to live that one down.

'I wasn't talking about...that,' Jack had said. 'What I *meant* was, she's already experienced that world we're sending her into. Strange food, exotic places, odd characters. Our daughter has no roots. She's been a nomad all her life. It's how we raised her. You know that, Pauline. So tell me, what's this really all about?'

Pauline spoke so softly, Farley had to hold her breath to hear.

'She'll be gone for the summer. Then she'll go away to college and we'll keep moving. We'll never all live together under one roof. This is the end of 'us four.''

The sun disappeared and the air grew cool. Still clutching her envelope, Farley embraced her mother.

"We'll always be 'us four,' mom,'" she whispered.

William rolled down the back seat window.

"Can we go now?" he said. "I'm feeling dangerously close to malnutrition."

On the way to dinner all Farley could talk about was her trip.

"First I'm going to Brittany. I can't wait to see Dad's Bigouden."

The Bigouden was a group of people native to Brittany, where Jack's *Grandmere* had lived. As a boy, he spent many happy summers swimming, sailing, wandering through his grandmother's large raised garden beds, and fishing in Brittany's icy waters. His *Grandmere*, his last living relative, died when he was in high school. Jack had never taken his family to Brittany - the place of his happiest childhood memories.

William frowned. "You mean the small people with the twisted legs?"

Pauline gave Jack an I-told-you-so glare.

Years ago, Jack used a loaf of bread to demonstrate the height of the traditional Bigouden woman's headdress. They had all laughed. But when he started in on the Bigouden's physical description, Pauline made him stop. She had seen the wheels in William's brain shift into over-frenzy. Many of the Bigouden were short with large, round heads. Some of the older generation had a twisted way of walking– possibly hip dysplasia from inbreeding. Even now, some of William's drawings were of gnome-like creatures with Charlie Brown heads and shriveled polio legs.

Driving home, the desert was pitch-dark. Windows down, stomachs full. The Buick sped through a universe of jackrabbits and night noises, the pavement rushing below. To Farley, it felt more like flying than driving. She closed her eyes and inhaled, taking in the cool, fresh desert air and the sharp smell of sagebrush. This is what happiness feels like.

"Dad," said William from the darkness. "If you stare at the road long enough, you can get hypnotized. Road Hypnosis. Also called White Line Fever, and Driving Hypnosis."

"I can't be hypnotized." Jack turned his head, a silly look on his face. "Because I'm not paying attention to the road!"

"Very funny," said Pauline, slapping his arm. "Eyes on the road."

Pauline gave her hair a furious spray. Between Farley's upcoming trip and college preparations, the past week had been insane. Jack was flying out at dawn, and the last thing she wanted to do tonight was drive halfway up a mountain to a cocktail party. Never mind that the host couldn't keep his goddamn hands to himself. Ordinarily she would tell Jack and let him handle the situation, but this time the creep was his superior officer. Pauline giggled, imagining what her husband would do to the horny, pink-faced Colonel.

Coming up behind her, Jack kissed her neck.

"What's so funny?"

"Nothing. I'm just happy, that's all."

"You're beautiful."

"Why, thank you." She turned her back to let him zip her white linen dress. She leaned up and gently blew in his face. "How's my breath?"

"Delicious." He checked his watch. "We need to leave in ten minutes."

"I'll be ready. Do you mind tucking William in?"

Jack sat on the edge of William's bed.

"I want you to help your mother while I'm gone, professor," he said.

"Okay." William nodded earnestly. "Dad, will you be back in time for Farley's going away party?"

"Wouldn't miss it for the world."

William resisted the urge to squeeze his penis, a babyish habit he was trying to shake, but fell back on in times of stress. Instead, he rubbed the binding of his blanket against his cheek.

"Jimmy Nott from down the street says he's too old to get tucked in. Does that mean I'm too old to get tucked in like a taco?"

"Let's hope not," said Jack. "Your mother still tucks me in."

William exploded into giggles.

Jack wrapped up his goodnight story.

"…and the man of steel takes a mighty leap and soars through the air, leaving behind mean old Jimmy Nott, who gets smaller and smaller by the second."

William felt better. He loved the way all his father's stories ended up with the superhero flying away, and the bad guys always got left behind.

Jack gave William's blanket an extra tuck. "Time for your prayer, professor."

William folded his hands and closed his eyes.

"Now I lay me down to sleep, I pray the Lord my soul to keep.

If I should die before I wake, I pray the Lord my soul to take."

"Goodnight, professor." Jack kissed him on the forehead. "I love you."

"I love you, too."

Clicking his tongue, William faced the wall. He hated that prayer.

"Have fun," said Farley, flipping the channels on the television.

"We won't be late." Jack kissed her on the forehead. "I have to catch a shuttle in the morning."

Pauline hopped on one foot as she slipped on a high heel. "Oh, that reminds me, Jack. I put your flight jacket on the kitchen counter next to your suitcase, so you're all set for your trip."

"Farley." Jack waited until she looked up. "You take care of your brother."

"Dad…" she said, exasperated. "Go, already!"

"Let's go, Jack," said Pauline, blowing a kiss to Farley. "She'll be fine."

Farley uncapped her parent's crystal decanter and poured two fingers of scotch; neat, Joan Crawford-style. She didn't particularly like the taste of liquor, but something about tonight called for a mature drink. Donning Pauline's floor-length, powder-blue silk robe and diamond hair clip, she turned on the radio. She admired her reflection in the sliding glass doors as she danced around the living room, balancing her highball and waving an unlit cigarette. Finally, sweaty and reeking of Chanel, she stopped and studied her reflection.

"Actually," she said, turning her face this way and that.

Farley loved the way her face looked when she said the word 'actually.' The way her lips started off in a surprised '*Aahk*' then pushed in '*chew*,' back to a softer '*ahh*' and sliding into a smile '*lee*.' Tonight, however, the face smiling back had the slightest hint of panic to it.

Lately an electric current of equal parts terror and excitement would come over her like a lovely admonition. Europe. Romance. College. Sex. This summer she would roam new places and take deep, meaningful photographs. She would eat exotic foods and find romance, inevitably leading to sex. Then…college! She could already picture herself, hair falling over her heavy books as she highlighted critical passages. Then there were the formals and club meetings and dorm parties, sit-ins and the protests-for-whatever-wasn't-fair, all while cramming and pulling all-nighters and bouncing in and out of love. Which would lead to sex.

Farley was used to anticipating the new and unknown. It was the thought of back-flipping out of the family nest that terrified her.

At ten-thirty, she hung her mother's silk robe back in the closet and cleaned up her mini-party mess. Then she popped a bowl of popcorn and searched for an old movie to watch on TV. After all, everything was better in black and white.

Larry Ryder put his truck in gear and started up Sunshine Mountain. What a night. Nine years of shuffling cards, stacking chips, and dealing hand after hand, and it's 'Mr. Boot would like to see you in his office…come on in, close the door behind you, Larry…hate to do this…tough times…nothing personal.'

Nothing personal my pancake ass. He shifted down, careful to keep his eyes on the twisty mountain road, which was barely wide enough for two cars to pass.

I got the boot from Mr. Boot. Larry had to chuckle, in spite of his situation.

He cranked his window down and let the cool desert air fill his lungs. So liberating, after the stale casino air. No more false windows to hide the reality of the sun coming up – or going down again. No more bright lights and constant clanging of bells. No more watching (encouraging them, let's be real) poor suckers scrape the bottom of their wallets because, despite the overwhelming odds against them, there was always a chance they could beat the house.

What the hell. He'd find another job. He was honest and not afraid of hard work. Sure, he'd land on his feet. But Mr. Boot would always be five-foot-four with a voice like Alvin the Chipmunk. Energized, downright hopeful, Larry turned on the radio and sang along with Waylon and Willie and the boys. A little louder than usual.

"Out in Luckenbach, Texas, ain't nobody feelin' no pain!"

Up ahead, a flash of oncoming headlights. The car was flying. Goddamn kids. Larry slowed and brought his truck as close to the edge of the road as he dared. He watched in horror as, instead of turning with the curve of the road, the car went straight through the guardrail and disappeared over the side of the mountain.

"Holy-shit-holy-shit-holy-fucking-shit," he cried, speeding uphill until he found a spot wide enough to turn around. Then he drove back down the mountain as fast as he dared. He threw his truck into park and scrambled down the ravine, dreading what he might find.

Larry would never shake the images of that night. The flattened metal where the driver's side should be. The woman, so beautiful. The man's head resting on her shoulder, his lower body crushed beneath twisted metal, his blood seeping through the white of her dress. Smoke. The searing smell of gasoline.

Larry yanked on the passenger side door.

"It's stuck!" he yelled to the woman. "Push it! Push the door from the inside!"

She ignored him, stroking her husband's hair. Frantic, Larry ran around the car, searching for a way in. As he rounded the trunk there was a dull thump. Then another. Flames burst from under the back of the car. Holy shit. This fucker was going to blow.

Running back to the front of the car, he waved his arms over his head.

"For God's sake, get out!" he pleaded. "Your man is dead!"

That did it. She looked up, straight into Larry's eyes.

"Atta girl," he panted, pointing to the shattered section of the windshield. "Now climb on out, right there..."

Her eyes still on Larry, she whispered something in the hole where the dead man's ear used to be.

Larry backed away as the flames moved closer.

"LADY, GET OUT OF THE CAR!" he screamed.

She gave him a slight, heartbreaking smile and shook her head. No.

It Burns a Lovely Light

Chapter 11

William sat on the counter top, his slippers making a 'thumpada-thumpada-thumpada' against the cabinet as he watched Farley cook. One by one, she cracked the eggs on the side of the skillet and dropped them into the sputtering bacon drippings. She scooped around the edges with a spatula. Hot grease spit from the pan, leaving shiny dots on her hand and forearm. William flinched.

"Farley…"

She scraped the burnt toast with the edge of a steak knife. In the stillness of the morning, with the first light finally emerging, the sound was like a shovel scraping across the sidewalk.

Four plates of eggs, bacon, and toast. Orange juice. Two hot coffees. Jelly. Butter. Catsup.

Neither of them touched their food. William rubbed the hem of his pajama top against the palm of his hand and clicked his tongue. Across the table, Farley shivered, oddly cold, even with her father's flight jacket over her lap.

Outside the familiar whine of the jets warming up… taking off. Silence. The bright green leaves from the lemon plants strained toward the emerging daylight.

"Farley…" whispered William, his lip quivering.

The doorbell sounded different this early in the morning.

"I knew it!" cried William, jumping up from his chair. "They're back! They're home!"

He ran for the front door.

"No," said Farley, unable to move.

William had once described what happened to the body when dread and panic collide. The bowels loosen before the brain registers the terror. Bowels. They had laughed.

As if from the back row of a smoky movie theatre, she watched as they entered the kitchen and took their places on her mother's polished black and white linoleum. The Wing Commander, his face kind. His wife, sunglasses in the morning. People really do wring their hands when they are anxious. The Chaplain, specks of dried blood on his chin – a quick shave before the breaking of the hearts.

Wings at the door.

Farley stood, her legs unsteady. Her mother's diamond clip flopped over one eye, hanging on by a few fragile strands of hair. She looked into the sad, pastel eyes of the Wing Commander.

"I always thought you would be taller," she whispered.

"She's in shock," said the wife. "Get her some brandy."

The floor tilted.

In the movies there is often a pause between waking and remembering. A few precious seconds of innocence before reality comes flying in to devastate all over again. Just a small piece of happiness before the awful truth rips you open. But when Farley woke up in her parents' bed, her pillow was already drenched.

The room was dark, except for thin veins of sunlight bleeding through the drapes. Outside, children played Red Rover. She heard high-pitched voices calling someone – someone who had no idea his whole life could be smashed to pieces with the ring of a doorbell – right over.

In the house, sounds of people softly gathering…"I threw together a casserole…here, let me take that…can't believe it…I know…I know..."

She escaped into the exquisite obscurity of sleep. An occasional cool hand on her forehead…the sweet, overwhelming fragrance of Shalimar.

When she woke, the slivers of morning sunlight had been replaced by the cold bluish light of early evening. The faint odor of this morning's breakfast still lingered in the air. The odd thought came to her; for the rest of her life, the smell of burnt toast, bacon, and the death of her family would be undeniably forged in her mind.

Muffled voices of women in the hall, lining up for the bathroom.

"They were the perfect couple."

"I'm still in shock. I can't stop crying."

"I know; I burst into tears as soon as I heard. We got the first call, after the Wing Commander and the Chaplain."

"Beth said they got the first call."

"Beth is so full of shit."

A toilet flushed. Silence. The sound of running water.

"Did you taste Maureen's dip?"

"God, what a waste of good crab meat."

The squeaky creak of the bathroom door opening.

"Maureen! I love your hair."

"Really? I don't know."

"Such horrible news."

"The worst. Can you believe Pauline wouldn't get out of the car?"

Farley sat up.

Her ear to pressed to the door, she listened to the voices stepping over each other.

"…tragic love story … rather die than be without him…she wouldn't get out…those poor kids…"

The voices continued as Farley slid down the wall and pressed her cheek to the carpet. She wondered, in that calm way shock has of padding the heart until the mind can possibly begin to comprehend, if she could survive this.

"Isn't Farley off to some artsy photography school in New York?"

"I wonder what's going to happen to William. He's a handful."

"I hate to say it, but who wants to take that on?"

Take care of your brother.

Let's go, Jack. She'll be fine.

William.

Making her way through the cluster of the well-meaning, the heavily perfumed hairdos and mournful embraces, Farley found him in the living room, curled up on the floor next to their mother's lemon tree.

"Scotch eggs, my favorite." Joe tossed a hard-boiled egg coated with hot sausage from hand to hand.

"Put that down before you burn yourself," scolded Veda Marie. "Sit. I'll make you a plate."

"No time. I'm already late for the coaches' meeting."

Claire refreshed her coffee. "I hope all this coaching isn't interfering with your studies."

"Never fear, Mummy dearest. I'm only an assistant coach." He tossed the egg high in the air. "When I'm head coach, we might have a problem."

"So you're ready for your Geology exam this afternoon?"

"You bet."

Veda Marie's eyebrows disappeared into her bangs. Lighting a cigarette, she leaned against the counter.

"We need to patch the roof on the carriage house again," she said. "One of Resa's tiny dancers is going to snap an ankle, maneuvering around all those buckets."

Resa Romano taught dance classes in the carriage house out back. She looked the part: bone-thin, hair always up in a messy bun. Her posture was perfect. One wayward eyetooth pushed her lip out, giving her mouth an exotic twist.

"No biggie." Resa waved a hand. "Any dancer worth her leotard should be able to leap over a few buckets."

"You're a good sport, Resa," said Claire. "I already have a call in to a new repair company."

"What happened to the other guys?" she asked.

"They quit," said Claire. "I think they were afraid of me."

As if on cue, the phone rang.

"That's probably the new one." Claire pushed her chair back. "I'll get it."

"Try being nice this time," said Veda Marie.

She stubbed her cigarette in the ashtray and swatted Joe on the arm. "If that exam of yours is so easy, why were you still at your desk at two o'clock this morning?"

"What are you, the bedtime police?" Joe playfully returned her swat. "Get out of my business, woman."

A shrill laugh escaped before Claire clamped her hands over her mouth; her eyes wild. The receiver fell to the floor.

"Mum?"

Veda Marie picked up the phone.

"Who the hell is this," she demanded.

After she hung up the phone Veda Marie pulled Claire into a tight embrace.

"I thought those calls only came in the middle of the night," whispered Claire.

"Tell me, Mum." Joe straightened his shoulders, preparing himself. "It's Dad, isn't it."

"No," she moaned. "Pauline...my Pauline...and Jack. Oh, God!"

"Joe, the car keys are under the seat," said Veda Marie, lowering Claire into a chair. "Run and get your Uncle Ryan."

Chapter 12

"Wake up." Farley's voice was flat. "We're here."

"Are we home?" asked William, rolling crumbs of sleep from his eyes.

Home. Farley stared out the car window. "We're at Bridge Manor."

The screen door slammed behind Veda Marie as she ran toward the car, arms spread wide. Farley fell into her embrace and moaned as they rocked back and forth. With one arm around Farley, she waved for William to come closer. Still so very small, his reddish hair was already turning brown. Braces dominated his pale freckled face.

"May I give you a kiss, lovey?"

He nodded, and she kissed his cheek.

Behind them, Joe's heavy footsteps pounded down the driveway. "Farley!"

Joe's stocky body was all muscle and he had his mother's deep, gruff voice. Yet his face crumbled like a child as he ran toward his cousin. Inches shorter than Farley, he lifted her off her feet and held her tight. Finally, wiping his eyes with the back of his thick hand, he turned to William.

"Hey. How's the superhero?"

Grinning shyly, William clenched his arms Popeye-style.

William put his hands on his hips and made a big show of looking around his bedroom as he tried not to cry.

"Your room and Joe's are connected by a bathroom," said Veda Marie. "Your sister's room is directly above you."

A small hand appeared in the doorway, fingers wriggling. A child giggled.

"I swear, that giggle sounds like Eileen Kane," said Veda Marie.

"It *is* me, Veda Marie!" A girl with freckles on her nose and a head full of golden curls tip-toed into the room. She wore a smiley face tee shirt and dirty pink shorts.

William wriggled his fingers. "Hi."

Eileen waved back. "I have freckles, too."

"I have more."

Silence.

"Eileen is a dance student of Resa's," said Veda Marie, opening William's suitcase. She lives down the hill from us." She turned to Eileen. "Does your mother know where you are, lovey?"

Eileen's bottom lip pushed out in a perfect pout: a Hummel come to life.

"She's not my mother," she said. "She just said be home in time for supper."

Supper. William perked up. "What time do we eat?"

"No particular time," said Veda Marie. "I can make you something whenever you're ready."

Eileen and William shared a bowl of grapes under the gingko tree.

"My name isn't really Eileen," she said, her mouth full. "It's Eleanor Rigby."

William frowned. "That's a lie name."

She wrinkled her nose, changing the design of her freckles. Grape juice trickled down her chin. "I'm seven and a half. How old are you?"

"I turned fifteen on my birthday." He hung his head and sucked on his headgear. "My mom made Superman cupcakes with kryptonite sprinkles and everything."

"I don't have a mother, either." Eileen ran her hand down the shiny fabric of William's cloak. "I like your cape."

"It's not a cape. It's a happiness cloak."

Not to be outdone, Eileen pulled up the back of her shorts, revealing a dark, inch-long scab on her bum. "Look-it. I did it with a paper clip."

"That could get infected."

"I do it all the time." She crowded a few more grapes into her mouth. "Let's play tag," she said, her voice muffled by the fruit. "I'll chase you."

"I know what you are, but what am I!" screamed William, delighted to be playing again.

Sitting on top of the picnic table, Paddy and Claire watched the children run around the back yard.

"Please God, someone wake me up," said Claire.

Paddy squeezed her hand. In the years since Claire left him, their relationship had progressed from cordial-yet-kind to a cautious camaraderie. But recently - thrust forward as a result of the death of Jack and Pauline - they had moved into something reminiscent of the friendship of their youth.

"You should have let me go with you," he said.

"You're probably right. They like you better, any-way."

"Now you're talking nonsense."

Claire waved a tired hand.

"An officer was assigned to help with the arrangements," she said. "The poor man literally held me up when I went to the crematorium. He walked me through the forms and papers, and explained the indemnity compensation process."

"What's that?"

"The process of getting money for William and Farley. A legal representative of the military will come out next week to let us know how much money they'll receive."

"Why can't they tell you now?"

"They have to conduct an official investigation before any funds can be approved." She hesitated. "Apparently Jack started a fight with a fellow officer…a higher up."

"An argument fight, or a *fight* fight?"

"A fists flying, blood all over the place fight."

"Then the officer must have had it coming."

"I'm sure you're right. Still, this investigation may have an effect on how much money is approved for William and Farley."

"Maybe we should talk to Ham."

"I called him before we left the base. He said he'll stop by on his way home from work tomorrow."

Paddy nodded, pleased. "Ham Kane is a fine man and a hell of an attorney."

Claire chuckled, releasing a slightly wet snort. "Shame about the wife."

Ham Kane was Eileen's father and Claire's nearest neighbor. A widower, he had recently married after a six-week romance. His wife, Billie, had a reputation as a somewhat successful realtor and a master manipulator. She drove a flashy car, wore full-length fur coats long after the black winter slush melted, and believed without a doubt that her clients were ignorant fools who would be lost without her.

Paddy gestured toward William, who was struggling to catch up with Eileen in a cartwheel race. "How is he taking all this?"

"He's confused. Anxious. He wouldn't get in the car when it was time to leave the base. He has decided that cars are no longer safe. When we finally got him in the car he hyperventilated. The doctor gave me a prescription for some sedatives. The entire drive, the poor thing was either sound asleep or grinning like a lunatic."

Paddy removed a handkerchief from his pocket and wiped his eyes. "And Farley?"

Claire exhaled. "Beyond devastated. She hardly said a word the whole trip."

"The poor girl."

"She opened up one night, while we were watching William play in the motel pool. She says she's not going away to school, that William has lost enough. And she made it clear that staying at Bridge Manor for long is *not* an option."

"Already calling the shots. Pauline would be proud."

Behind them, the screen door slammed.

"Your mother called, Eileen," said Veda Marie. "Dinner is on the table. Claire, will you walk her?"

Eileen yanked a twig from her shiny gold curls. "She's not my mother."

"Will you come back?" asked William.

"Sure." Eileen swiped the dirt off her shorts. "I come here all the time."

"William!" Paddy slapped the picnic table with the palm of his hand. "Come on up and keep me company, son."

"I probably shouldn't." William rubbed his lips. "It's germy to sit on a table, Uncle Paddy."

"Which is why we never use it as a table. We consider it more of a giant chair, where we can sit and look out over our fine city."

William hesitated, then climbed up and sat next to his uncle.

"Tell me the truth," said Paddy. "Would it help or hurt for me to talk about your parents?"

"Help," he mumbled, rubbing the fabric of his cloak over his cheek.

Paddy thought for a minute.

"They were special, those two," he said. "I loved them very much. We all did." He held his hand out flat. "Did you know I met your mother when she was this high?"

"No." William pulled his cloak tight around him. "It's weird to think of them having a life before me and Farley."

"The best part of their lives was after you and your sister came along."

"I know," said William, sliding his tongue along the metal of his headgear. "I wonder where they are, right now."

"Where do you think they are?"

"Some people said they're watching over us."

"That's what I like to think, son."

As the daylight faded, Paddy pulled his car into the half-empty parking lot of Mick's Pub. He needed a pint. Or two.

"This one's on me." Mick placed a draft in front of Paddy. "I'm sorry for your loss."

"Thank you, Mickey." Paddy took a long swig.

"I hear Claire is taking on the children."

"You know Claire."

"That's quite a load. She's a good woman."

"The best."

"You've had quite a go of things, lately. This tragedy, on top of the layoffs..."

Paddy grunted. When he spoke his voice was so soft, Mick had to lean across the bar to hear him. "All my life I wanted to be a company man, and I finally made it." He nodded. "Only to be given the distinction of dismissing some of the finest, most hardworking men I'll ever know."

"You did what you had to do."

Mick refilled Paddy's mug, then poured a shot of whiskey and dropped it inside the mug. "It's a wonder Porter Steel is still operating at all; what with mills and factories closing all around us."

"You should have seen them, Mickey. One by one, I called them up. Ritchie Flynn. Tommy Sawicki. Stephen Quinn, with eight kids, three in diapers. That Kevin Walsh never missed a day of work in his life. And to a man...each and every one of them shook my hand before leaving."

By the time William climbed into the bathtub it was well after his normal bedtime. He chatted nervously as he watched Joe shave.

"It might be good to have regular seasons again. It's weird having Christmas in the warm."

"You'll be plenty cold around here by Christmas," said Joe.

William walked his Underdog figurine along the edge of the tub.

"I do remember that Bridge Manor can get sort of damp," he said. "I'm a little concerned about that. You never know when a chill can cross over to hypothermia."

Joe tapped the side of his razor on the sink. "No point in worrying about winter right now. It's summer."

William tried to whistle as Underdog dive-bombed under the bubbles. "Probably no point in worrying about itchy winter skin, then."

"You got that right."

"Although I don't like to be hot, either," mumbled William. "Dehydration is a big concern of mine."

"Night," said Claire.

"Goodnight, Aunt Claire." William wished Farley hadn't gone to bed so early. She hadn't said 'goodnight,' either. "You can leave the door open if you want to."

Turning to leave, Claire stopped when she heard a strange clicking sound. "Is everything all right?"

"Yes, thank you, Aunt Claire."

She tilted her head. There it was again. "You're sure you don't need something?"

"No, thank you."

She grasped the handle of his bedroom door. "Goodnight."

"Aunt Claire, are we orphans now?"

God in heaven. Think. She cleared her throat.

"The word 'orphan' typically refers to children," she said. "You're a big boy now."

"So I'm probably too old to be tucked in like a taco," he said, his eyes shining in the dark.

Claire looked back at her nephew, all freckles and metal braces and sad, peculiar statements. "My goodness, you're much too old for that."

She left, closing the door tight behind her. William lay in the dark, running the binding of his blanket up and down the palm of his hand.

"Are you there?" he whispered. "Are you watching over me?"

Claire knocked on Farley's door, harder than she intended.

"Come in."

Farley was curled up in the window seat, wearing one of her father's old West Point tee shirts and a pair of white boxers. She turned to her aunt, then quickly turned away. Claire and Pauline had been far from identical. Still, every time Farley looked at Claire she saw her mother.

"Do you need anything?" Claire clenched her fists, castigating herself for her inability to find the right words. *Do you need anything?*

After hours of tossing and turning in her bed, Claire padded downstairs to the kitchen. Opening the refrigerator, she removed a carton of milk, some chicken, and pasta salad. She grabbed chips, a jar of baby gherkins, and a bottle of hot sauce from the pantry. Lit only by a shard of moonlight, Claire dug in.

Veda Marie flipped on the light. "What are you doing up at this hour?"

"What does it look like?" Embarrassed, Claire slid the unopened bag of chips across the table. "I'm not going to eat those."

"Of course not," said Veda Marie, dryly. "Show a little self-control."

"You don't have to be sarcastic." Her lower lip trembling, Claire pulled the bowl of pasta salad toward her. "I don't know how to comfort them."

"Of course you do," said Veda Marie, her voice softening. "They're half out of their minds with sadness. We all are."

Claire stabbed a tortellini with her fork as a tear dropped into the bowl. "Pauline would have known what to do. She was the strong one."

"Apparently not, lovey."

Claire swallowed a lump of pasta salad.

"Farley knows," she said. "She knows Pauline could have gotten out of that car."

"Oh, that poor dear."

Claire wiped her face with a mangled napkin. "Jack and Pauline's friends gathered at the house that first day. You know, bringing food, making phone calls, commiserating. Farley overheard some of them saying Pauline wouldn't get out of the car." She exhaled, tearing at her napkin. "I tried talking to her, but she didn't want to talk about it."

"Give her some time, then try again." Veda Marie paused. "And next time, take your hands off your hips. It's scary."

"I don't do that."

"You do, lovey. But only when you're nervous." She patted Claire's hand. "Come on, we've got a big day tomorrow."

Veda Marie put her arm through Claire's as they walked upstairs.

"I'm surprised your brother didn't come by, tonight of all nights."

"He called," said Claire. "His new car had the wrong something-or-other. You know Ryan; he had to make sure everything was perfect before he drove it off the lot."

Veda Marie shook her head. "Funny, him being a priest."

At exactly six o'clock in the morning, Father Ryan Justus rose from his bed. He dropped to the floor and did one hundred sit-ups, one hundred push-ups, and fifty squats. Then he showered, shaved, and liberally after-shaved. Sometimes the phrase, "that stings in a good way" would come to him as he slapped his cheeks with the faint citrus tonic. But not this morning.

This morning Ryan was on auto-pilot, going through the motions and praying for the wisdom to guide his grieving flock through this dark tempest. He prayed for the words to ease their sorrow and encourage their faith. And he prayed for the strength not to curl up in the fetal position and wail, flock be damned. Oh, God.

Wrapping a towel around his waist, he padded through the living room into the kitchen. He sliced strawberries into a bowl of bran cereal and washed a multivitamin down with a glass of tepid lemon water. Then he dressed for the long day ahead.

For their day-to-day work, priests were encouraged to wear the black clerical shirt with the white collar and black pants. Today he would wear his cassock. Truth be told, Ryan preferred his cassock and wore it whenever possible. The long-skirted, close-fitting black garment made him feel closer to God.

Bullshit, Mutt. You like the way it compliments your long legs and lean build.

He froze. After a moment, he lowered himself into a chair and covered his face with his hands.

"How could you leave me, Pauline?" he moaned.

He couldn't bring himself to say out loud what his mind immediately added: *Why couldn't it have been Claire?*

There comes a time when the mind and the heart can no longer bear the pain. For Farley it was the day her parent's ashes were scattered over the side of the Smithfield Street Bridge and into the river below. The old timers called it the kissing fish bridge. Where Farley and William's parents shared their first kiss. Where Jack tried to propose and Pauline interrupted his stammering by asking him where he stood on the name Farley for their first child.

"Farley James." Pauline had said. "Works for a girl or a boy, and it's got an illustrious ring to it, don't you think?"

In the back of her mind, Farley had hoped that the act of scattering their ashes might bring some small sense of relief. She pictured the ashes, brilliant in the morning sun, dancing and drifting their way down to the Monongahela River, where they would blend with the river and glide with the current. The background music would come in, slowly. A farewell so devastatingly beautiful it would live in her soul forever, and ease the pain that pressed on her heart.

The faint odor of fish and the stifling smell of exhaust on the bridge were embellished by the morning's humidity. Against the backdrop of streetcars, cars, trucks, and curious pedestrians, Father Ryan delivered a solemn prayer and raised the urn above his head.

After a final "Amen,' he unfastened the urn and poured the ashes over the railing. They blew underneath the bridge; a few small dark clumps clung to the ironwork along the bottom. And that was it. No dancing or drifting. No devastating beauty.

Beside her, William pressed his head against the railing and looked down at the water.

"I guess they really aren't coming back," he said. "No one comes back from ashes."

No longer able to stand, Farley slid to her knees on the warm sidewalk. The suffocating devastation of their death and the overwhelming shame of being the one not chosen closed in, threatening to crush her. Oblivious to pedestrians and the clamor of traffic, she shoved all of the terror and shame deep and deeper down inside of her until she felt nothing at all.

William placed a small hand on her shoulder and squinted at the skyline.

"The city looks different when you're not just visiting."

Dear Farley,

I wanted to write something that would make you feel better, but there are no words for that right now. My heart breaks for you and William. Hold each other close. Farley, your enthusiasm and excitement for the future has been an inspiration to me since the day we met. Remember your dreams. They will carry you through.
Love,
Henry

Farley spent most of that summer in her room, sleeping or staring out the window. Everything hurt. Walking downstairs exhausted her. She smelled. She had difficulty keeping food down, carrying on a conversation, or caring about anything at all. Even William. She knew she should comfort him, tell him everything would be all right, press foreheads like their father used to do. But that would involve opening her heart; exposing her feelings. And she couldn't do that. The pain would be too much to bear; it would crush her.

Chapter 13

"It's about time things warmed up around here," said William, raising his face to the sun. "All that snowing was getting on my last nerve."

"You're spending way too much time with Veda Marie," Claire mumbled as she and William maneuvered their way along the crowded city sidewalk.

In the nine months since he and Farley moved to Bridge Manor, William had fallen into a routine of school, snack, and following Veda Marie around the house. If she wasn't available, he would follow one of the boarders. He and Joe took a streetcar to the occasional sporting event - he still refused to get in a car. But it was Farley's company William preferred, and she was either at work or holed up in her room.

Tired of Farley's self-inflicted confinement, Dion had appeared one morning with her arms full of job applications. A week later, Farley accepted a waitressing position, which she came to enjoy. As she told Claire, the frantic pace left her no time to think. Order in...hot food out...refills...complaints...more bread...check, please. By the end of the day she was too worn out to do anything but fall into bed.

Claire shifted her shopping bag and took William's hand as they approached the intersection.
At sixteen, his body was still fragile and childlike, but his long, ill-proportioned feet seemed predisposed to tripping.

"Can I have extra chips in my lunch, for Marcus Shultz?" asked William.

The light changed and they stepped onto the crosswalk. "We'll let Marcus's mother take care of his chips."

William's voice was somber. "Marcus's mother doesn't believe in chips."

Half-way across the street, an elderly man smiled and tipped his hat. "Good afternoon, Mrs. Sullivan."

Raising her chin, Claire walked on. William tugged on her hand.

"Didn't you hear that man? He said 'good afternoon' and he took off his hat and everything!"

She continued walking.

"Aunt Claire, you have to say it back! That's not nice!"

"No more talking," snapped Claire.

Veda Marie emptied a load of warm, clean laundry onto the drawing room table and turned on the TV. For three peaceful hours a day, she washed, dried, folded, and ironed to the leisurely pace of *All My Children*, *One Life to Live*, and *General Hospital*. A feeling of tranquility came over her as she worked. The walls could be falling down around her, as long as her linens were folded into neat piles and her towels smelled like sunshine. September called it her personal way of meditating.

September Rose was by far the most interesting boarder at Bridge Manor. Initially, Veda Marie would have put money on Resa Romano, given that she was a recovering alcoholic and an ex-anorexic, to boot. And no one knew much about Mr. Winston, their most recent boarder. He seemed nice enough, although a bit standoffish for her taste.

September was Bridge Manor's official indoor house painter and clandestine – or so she thought – resident pot smoker. Her first project had been the old playroom - now Farley's room - on the third floor. After applying a light buttery color, she distressed the walls to give them an aged look. Then she finished off the room by trimming it in an eggplant color, blended with tiny flecks of gold. The result was breathtaking.

But the best part about September was how she was with William. Veda Marie smiled, recalling the first time the two met. A few days after he and Farley arrived, Veda Marie asked him to help gather tomatoes in the garden. Returning from a weekend with friends, September floated down the yard to greet William. He had immediately taken to the girl with the long, free-flowing skirt, peasant blouse, and bare feet. September was a poster child for healthy living, with her silky strawberry blond hair, and shiny, clear skin. Although, thought Veda Marie, she could do with a little color on her lips. Everything about her - down to the bump on her nose - seemed…true.

"Is September Rose a lie name, too?" asked William.

"It's not the name my parents gave me. My real name is Samantha Rosenstein. I liked September Rose better; so I changed it."

William hugged himself and twisted from side to side as he stared at her feet.

"Walking in bare feet is an invitation to ringworm."

She checked the bottom of her feet. "All clear."

"Are you a hippy?"

"I don't think so. I just got tired of being the penny-loafer, cookie-cutter, Magna cum laude type. After college, I decided to be more…carefree."

He put a finger in his ear. "You *decided*?"

"It took some practice, but I was determined. I even moved to a commune in Vermont for exactly three days. Commune's weren't for me." She placed a gentle hand on William's cheek, a gesture that usually made him flinch. "I guess you could say I'm trying out a different lifestyle."

"I'm trying out a different lifestyle, too."

Veda Marie busied herself yanking weeds, her heart in shreds.

"I know," said September. "I'm sorry about your parents."

"Me too." William pushed his glasses up on his nose. "My sister won't come out of her room."

"She's doing what she needs to do." September pulled a large ripe tomato from the vine and held it under William's nose. "Smell."

Closing his eyes, he took a long, deep whiff. It smelled like sweat, grass and summer.

"Are you a vegetablarian?"

September laughed. "No. I'd die if I couldn't have a rare, juicy steak once in a while. But I do love a tomato still warm from the sun. Want a bite?"

"Maybe after we wash it."

He watched, fascinated, as she opened her mouth and sunk her white teeth into the tomato. Juice squirted down her blouse. She closed her eyes and let out a long, sensual moan. William giggled.

"Sorry," he said, covering his mouth. "I'm extremely immature."

September wiped her chin with her wrist and smiled. "Never apologize for being yourself."

Chapter 14

The slam of the mudroom door startled Veda Marie out of her thoughts. William stomped into the kitchen, dropped his package on the table, and stormed out of the house.

A tired-looking Claire appeared in the doorway, her arms full of packages.

"What in the world?" said Veda Marie, folding a warm sheet.

"William is upset that I didn't bring my best manners to town."

Veda Marie raised her eyebrows. "Because you usually do?"

Claire scowled. "I don't know how you ever played poker with those eyebrows."

Meanwhile, William ran down the back yard, through the trail in the woods, and down the hillside steps. When he got to the place where the houses were closer together, he sat. He watched a man try to light a grill on his back deck. The man's wife set the small picnic table and chased bees away from the condiments. Two girls practiced cheers in the grass. Down here on these steps, there was a lot more happiness for William to watch.

Veda Marie handed Claire a basket full of folded sheets. "You can tell me all about it while we make up Mr. Winston's bed."

"Since when do we make up our boarders' beds?"

"Fitted sheets can be tricky. I can't stand the thought of the old man struggling with them."

"He's not old. I'd put him at late sixties, tops. You're going to be fifty soon." Claire bumped Veda Marie as they walked to his room. "Who knows? The two of you might hit it off."

"Now you're talking crazy, Claire Sullivan."

"Why? I see more and more interracial couples…"

"You know I don't give a damn what color Mr. Winston is. But I have a strict policy of only dating men who can keep up with me. The man uses a cane, for crying out loud!"

Initially, Claire and Veda Marie had decided not to accept any more boarders. September, Resa, and Farley filled the third floor and Joe, William, Claire, and Veda Marie took up the second floor. The only room left was the one behind the kitchen, and such close proximity to the kitchen might lead to privacy issues.

Then along came Mr. Winston, a distinguished gentleman with blue-black skin, a perfectly groomed white beard, and a slight hearing loss. The retired professor of architecture had an old-world manner that had appealed to both women. Besides, as Claire pointed out, they could use the extra money.

Veda Marie spread a clean sheet over Mr. Winston's bed.

"All right, back to you," she said. "Tell me why you misplaced your manners."

Claire tugged on the sheet. "William and I ran into Mr. Franco, the owner of The Novel Hovel."

The Novel Hovel was a used bookstore Claire and her father used to frequent. They'd often spend their Saturdays in that dark little store, going through mountains of used books, searching for treasures.

"That old man is still alive? He was old twenty years ago."

"Still kicking." Claire grimaced as she tucked in the corners. "So today he tipped his hat and said 'hello.' I ignored him and kept walking, which upset William."

Veda Marie was surprised. Claire could be crotchety, but she had a good heart and was never *intentionally* rude. "Why would you ignore an old man's greeting?"

"Because he's a liar and a cheat. And I don't want to talk about it anymore."

On her way through the kitchen, Claire slipped an oversized chocolate bar into William's lunch bag.

"Enter if you dare," said William, making a beard out of the bubbles in the bathtub.

Farley waved the steam from her face and addressed the Superman shower curtain. "Morning, kiddo."

Silence.

"Claire told me what happened," she continued. "She feels bad for snapping at you."

Nothing. Not even a splash.

"Listen, I know I haven't been around a lot, but I got a new…"

"Ever," interrupted William.

"What?"

"You haven't been around *ever*."

Farley closed the toilet lid and took a seat. She glanced up at Superman, who seemed to be glowering at her. She looked away.

"I got a new job," she said. "I'm still waiting tables, but at a new restaurant called Uncle Salty's. Of course the uniforms are asinine and the shoes are hideous... but you'll like the restaurant. The inside of the building is stuffed from floor to ceiling with really cool antiques."

"Like the antiques Mom found in London?"

She pressed her lips together. *Sorry, kiddo. Can't go there.*

"They have these old cash registers," she continued, "and brass instruments and sports memorabilia, and black-and-white photographs..."

"You mean like the pictures you used to take?"

She put her head in her hands and addressed her padded white waitress shoes. "So, Uncle Salty's has this management training program. They said if I worked hard I could be a manager in no time."

"Go for it. Work away." His thin arm appeared between Superman's spread legs. "Can I please have a towel?"

Farley pulled a Mighty Mouse towel from the rack. Turning to place it in his outstretched hand, she froze. "Where did you get that?"

"What?" The arm disappeared.

"That thing on your arm."

"I found it in one of our boxes, from back when," he said, his voice thread-like.

Once, feeling cruel, Farley had asked him what 'back when' meant.

He had shrugged and replied 'You know, back when we were a real family.'

The object flew over the man of steel and bounced off the wall, sound ricocheting off the old Carrara tiles.

"Take it. It's yours, anyway," said William. "I thought you didn't want it anymore."

The leather and metal bracelet slid to a stop at Farley's feet, the words "Brave and Daring" clearly visible through the steam.

It Burns a Lovely Light

Chapter 15

Claire sat on the edge of Ryan's stiff sofa. She had never liked the decorations in his house, the plastic plants, floor-to-ceiling mirrored walls, and the monochromatic alarmingly-beige-colored carpets and drapes. It wasn't right for a priest to have such a vain house, and it was downright criminal to force all that beige-ness on an otherwise innocent historic stone cottage.

"More coffee?" asked Ryan.

"No, thank you." Claire put her cup down on its matching china saucer. The man could use some mugs. "Now, why don't you tell me what is so urgent on a Saturday morning."

Ryan stood in the center of the room, arms folded, pelvis forward. He pointed toward the kitchen where William, having already worked up a sketch of a human leg, was sitting at Ryan's small table, filling in the veins with a red crayon.

"Do you have any idea what that boy has been up to?"

Claire didn't answer. There was no good answer to a question like that.

"He's been looking into people's windows," said Ryan. "Peeking into their homes."

Clicking his tongue, William tried to concentrate on his coloring.

"To make matters worse," Ryan continued, "I have to hear about it from one of my parishioners."

"William isn't *peeking* at anyone," said Claire, straightening her spine. "He likes to sit on the hillside after school. It makes him happy. And as far as I know, those steps are still public property."

Ryan paced the room, taking slow, deliberate steps.

"Apparently he's been doing this since…" he swallowed. Almost a year and he was still unable to mention Pauline's death. "That's not the point and you know it, Claire. You'd hit the roof if a man in a cape was lurking around, peeking in the windows of your precious Bridge Manor."

"Cloak."

"What?"

"William wears *cloaks*. Not *capes*. And he doesn't lurk."

"Damn it, Claire!"

William put his crayon down and rubbed his happiness cloak against his cheek.

Ryan whispered through clenched teeth. "I'm only thinking of the boy, here. One of these days, someone's going to call the police."

Standing, Claire willed her voice not to shake.

"The boy's name is William," she said, "And this has nothing to do with him; it's about you. God forbid a member of your precious flock…"

"Aunt Claire?" William appeared around the corner, his eyes round. "Why are you talking like that?"

"It's your Aunt's sorry attempt at sarcasm," said Ryan, glaring at his sister. "Not very attractive, is it?"

"Father Ryan is mad at me," said William, as he and Claire started up the road.

"Don't be silly. You shouldn't listen to private conversations."

"I didn't listen. I just heard."

That evening, Farley heated a glass of warm milk to bring up to bed with her.

"How was work, lovey?" called Veda Marie, searching for a hammer in the pantry.

Yawning, Farley stuck her head in the pantry. "They want me to wear zany buttons on my suspenders. Apparently zany waiters are all the rage."

"Who knew?" said Veda Marie, hooking the hammer in her belt loop and turning off the pantry light. "Hey, *Psycho* is the Creature Feature tonight. Want to watch it with me?"

She wasn't a fan of being scared to death, but she had to do something before Farley went back up to that hidey-hole of hers.

"Not tonight. I'm too tired."

Holding her glass of milk, she turned to go upstairs.

"Farley, wait." Veda Marie paused, then pushed on. "Unfelt feelings don't go away, you know. They stay down inside of you, working themselves up into a frenzy." She pressed her hands together. "You've got your whole life in front of you, lovey. But you've got to acknowledge your pain before you can move beyond it."

Farley held her breath and tried to calm the pounding in her chest. Her voice was calm, but Veda Marie could see the anguish in her eyes.

"Goodnight, Veda Marie," she said. "I'll check on William."

Cracking William's door, Farley peeked in. He wasn't in his bed. And his open drawers were empty.

Careful not to trip in the dark, Farley made her way down the hillside steps. As she drew closer, she heard her brother singing quietly to himself.

"You don't tug on superman's cape; you don't spit into the wind..."

Her brother's undersized frame began to emerge in the darkness. He had his legs pulled up and his cloak wrapped around him. Beside him sat his suitcase and a brown paper bag with a roll of toilet paper sticking out of the top.

"It's awfully late," said Farley, sitting next to him.

Silence.

"You hate the dark, kiddo."

He raised his chin and pulled his cloak tighter around him. "You're not allowed to call me kiddo anymore. That's Mom and Dad's word."

"Okay."

They watched as someone wandered through a house, turning off the lights. First the cellar went black, then the main level...then upstairs.

"I hear Saint Ryan got his collar all up in a twist," said Farley, still staring at the now dark house.

William's eyes watered, the corners of his mouth puckering downward. "*Father* Ryan was being cruel and unusual."

"Maybe we should go back to Bridge Manor and talk about it."

"Maybe we *shouldn't*," he said, tears spilling onto his cloak, "since I don't want to live there anymore. Everybody is too busy for me. Nobody tucks me in like a taco or sits down to dinner. And lots of times I have to eat by myself."

Farley felt her heart catch. "Oh, honey..."

He buried his face in his cloak. "I'm trying so hard to be good. I modulate my voice whenever I remember and I say all my prayers, even the bad one about dying before I wake." His voice grew louder and his tiny shoulders heaved. "Nobody even checks to be sure I have a well-rounded lunch. Someone keeps putting *candy bars* in my pail." He gasped. "And you don't like me anymore!"

"Of course I like you! I *love* you."

He shook his head. "People don't hide from people they love."

For a moment Farley couldn't speak. She could hear the blood pounding in her ears. "I swear to God, I'm not..."

"Yes you are, too!" he screamed. "If you're not working, you're up there in your room with the door closed up tight. You're so busy hiding and not eating and getting all skeletal you forgot how to be a sister. I know it's not 'us four' any more, but what about us *two*? What about me? I'm still here!"

"William..." Farley reached for him.

"Get off of me!" He sobbed, shoving her hand away. "I might not be smart when it comes to real life, but even I know nothing good comes from *being mad forever*!"

The lights from the houses threw shadows across the hillside as he wiped his glasses with his cloak. Tears continued to drip from his chin.

"I'm sorry." Farley could barely breathe. "I'm trying to shut out all the hurt, and I don't know any other way to make it stop. I'm barely hanging on, William. I'm afraid…"

"Afraid of what?" he said, hiccoughing. "What's left to be afraid of? Everything bad already happened."

Farley unrolled a stretch of toilet paper and wiped her eyes. Not everything, she thought. I'm afraid for you and for me and for the emptiness in my life. The aching in my heart terrifies me because it never stops. Every hour of the day I want to scream because it isn't fair. It isn't fair.

"It's like all of the happiness in the world went over that cliff, William. In that one moment, my childhood ended and my life became completely unsprung."

"I'm unspring too," he mumbled.

"I know." She blew her nose. "We used to fit in anywhere, us four. We belonged. I don't know how to move on anymore, William. I'm like an interloper, pretending to be alive."

"You're not doing a very good job with pretending. And you could start moving on by being my sister again."

Except for with the occasional back-deck light, the houses had all gone dark. Standing, William wiped the dirt off his cloak and picked up his suitcase.

"I guess we might as well go back," he said. "You can still call me 'kiddo' if you want to."

Farley hoisted the paper bag onto her hip. "Are you sure?"

"I'm sure. My heart was already starting to miss it."

The following morning there was a large note on the chalkboard wall, written in Claire's messy handwriting:

From now on dinner will be served family-style
At 7:00 p.m.
If you are here, please try to attend.

Chapter 16

"I must say, you look awfully distinguished with that walking stick."

"Why, thank you, Veda Marie," said Mr. Winston, bowing slightly. "I find slipping on a public street to be quite humbling."

Tapping his cane on the first stair-step leading to the upper floors, he hesitated, "Thank you for another delightful meal this evening. I hope we'll be continuing with the 'family style' dinners."

Veda Marie was pleased. Only a few weeks of sitting down to dinner together, and she could already see a change in the camaraderie of the residents. "We'll definitely keep it going."

"Good." He clutched the railing and slowly began his ascent. "You know what they say: 'A sit-down dinner can take an average meal and turn it into a feast.'"

"An *average* meal, can you believe that?" said Veda Marie as she helped Claire bail out the clogged mudroom sink. "He's a hoot, that one."

"I just hope he doesn't break his neck on those stairs."

"Still. It's nice of him to reach out to Farley." They bailed the sink in silence for a while.

Tomorrow would be the first anniversary of Jack and Pauline's death. One year since their ashes were sprinkled over the Smithfield Street Bridge. Claire had to smile as she pictured the two of them, kicking up their heels and shrieking with laughter as they rode the Monongahela to the Ohio… hell, all the way to the ocean.

Mr. Winston had never been to the upper floors. He adored his room on the first floor, just down the hall from the kitchen. He loved its hardwood floors and deep windows, the faded quilt on the old mahogany bed, and the ancient cool blue painted wardrobe in the corner. There was even a freestanding claw foot bathtub in his private lavatory.

His room was extremely private, since the wall separating his room from the kitchen was made of solid brick. Sometimes when the house was quiet, though, he heard footsteps on the floor above him. Claire and Veda Marie each had rooms on the second floor. Now and then he wondered which woman's footsteps he was hearing as she prepared for bed. He rather hoped they were Veda Marie's.

When he finally reached the top of the third floor landing, he stopped to rest for a few moments.

"Man on the hall," he said, tapping his walking cane against an open door as he shuffled passed September's room.

He found it interesting that September – the painter – had chosen plain whitewashed walls for her room, which gave the room an instant sense of cleanliness. Only the wooden, slatted closet door was painted a faded green. A green and white quilt covered the bed.

Next to the bed stood a small nineteenth century table, and there was a colorful braided rug in the center of the room. September was sitting in the window seat, reading a book and smoking a rustic looking cigarette. Looking up from her book, she smiled.

"Hi there, Mr. Winston."

He gave his 'man on the hall' warning again as he neared Resa's open door. She was on the floor doing some sort of stretching exercises, legs spread, nose pressed against one knee. She waved as she switched knees. Her entire bedroom was black. Black painted walls and a black dresser. It might have been cave-like, except for the large windowpanes, a stark white rug, and a white-framed photograph of Resa and an attractive blonde woman, grinning at the camera. From a radio on the nightstand, Mick Jagger wailed, *'Look at me! I'm in tatters!'*

If Farley was surprised to see Mr. Winston at her door, she didn't let on.

"Hi."

"Miss Farley." He held out his elbow. "I was hoping you would be so kind as to accompany me on my evening walk."

There was a sweet breeze in the air as they approached Grady Square.

"Did you know that Grady was named for the steep slope on which it was built?" he asked.

"I never knew that."

"This community was originally a series of shanties and tenant shacks," he said, naturally falling into his lecturer's voice. "Mostly Irish and Polish immigrants that worked in the mines and factories."

They stopped to watch two young boys in pajamas wrestling on their front lawn. Their parents watched from the porch, laughing and clapping.

"William thinks you should be a radio star," said Farley. "He says your voice sounds like thunder."

Mr. Winston laughed a deep belly laugh, his white teeth gleaming. "That brother of yours is an extraordinary young man. I envy his innocence."

"He'll never grow up. No matter how old he is, he'll always be a little boy."

"Like Peter Pan."

"That's right." Farley smiled. "I never thought about it like that."

They approached Rosemary's Market.

"Are you up for a Nutty Buddy?" he said.

"Now you're talking."

They chose a bench facing St. Xavier's. The full moon hovered above the church's stately stone bell tower. Mr. Winston took his time unraveling the paper wrapping on his ice cream cone, as if he found enjoyment even in that most insignificant act. For a while, they enjoyed their cones in comfortable silence.

"Imagine," he said, "that church was constructed by immigrant mill workers over a hundred years ago. Those limestone blocks probably came from the ground beneath our feet. Look at those windows. They're massive, and yet beautiful in their simplicity."

"Simplicity. That's what I used to look for in my photographs."

"Do you miss your photography?"

Farley thought of her camera, gathering dust in her closet. She hadn't touched it since the night she and William arrived at Bridge Manor.

"I miss a lot of things."

Farley took his arm as they made their way up the steep hill.

"Do you have family around here, Mr. Winston?"

"I have a brother."

She waited for him to go on, but he didn't.

"Why did you come to Bridge Manor? I mean, why not a nice apartment, or a condo?" She covered her mouth. "I'm sorry. My dad used to say things flew out of my mouth before my brain had time to run a safety inspection."

"It's quite all right, dear. I consider unfiltered annotations to be an admirable trait." He winked and patted her hand. "I came to Bridge Manor because I don't do well alone. I have a tendency to dwell."

After a long soak in the tub, Mr. Winston buttoned up his pajamas and poured himself a half glass of merlot. He tried to read, but his mind kept returning to Leonard. His brother. The one he worshiped and emulated as a boy, and cursed as a man.

Everything had seemed so important back then, he thought. Differences had to be fought over. Someone must be right. Someone must be wrong.

Chapter 17

Farley rolled over and pulled the covers over her head. "I'm asleep."

Veda Marie opened the door. "Sorry, lovey. I just got a call from The Significant Me." She held up William's hamster cage. "William forgot Scribble."

"So?"

"So, it's share-a-part-of-my-day, day. There's a party in it for the class that shares the most. His teacher said he went to pieces when he realized he forgot Scribble. I thought you could take him on your way to work."

Farley growled. "Okay."

"I'll leave the little critter on the picnic table, so you won't miss him on your way out."

"Where have you been?" Dion adjusted her pickle hat. "Your boss is going to kill you for being late again."

"I know," said Farley, panting. She scrutinized Dion's costume. "What the hell are you wearing? Have you no pride?"

"I'm a wiener." Dion raised her chin; dignity in a hot dog bun. "I'll never have enough money for nursing school if I choose my jobs based on pride." She grabbed Farley's arm. "There goes our bus!"

The girls ran alongside, yelling and waving their arms until the driver stopped. As they boarded, Dion flashed the driver a smile and a healthy dose of Frankfurter cleavage. "Thanks, hon."

Aside from her over-blown lips, Dion had what could have been described as a plain appearance: average height, one hundred forty pounds, and shoulder length black hair. But there was also an almost primal sensuality to Dion; she exuded 'come hither'.

By the time they got off the bus, the rain had stopped. Steam was drifting up from the asphalt. Farley waved goodbye to Dion, who would spend the day travers-ing the city as a hot dog, doling out coupons for Franklin's Five and Dime. She pulled on Uncle Salty's heavy doors and trudged into the restaurant.

"Farley?" Her manager called from his office. "May I see you for a minute?"

"Sure, Mr. Chabon."

His smile was crooked and horsy. "What did you call me?"

"I mean, Nat."

His office was decorated in the typical Uncle Salty's style of highly organized, zany, haphazard, patriotic, base-ball-playing, fishing, brass instruments, and apple-pie mementos.

Nat crossed his arms and pressed his chin to his chest. "Would you consider yourself a happy member of The Uncle Salty's family?"

"God, yes," she said, still trying to catch her breath. Sweat trickled down her back. "I'm so happy, I whistle while I work."

He gestured toward the window overlooking the dining area. "Tell me what you see out there."

Farley pressed her forehead against the cool window and stared down at the wait staff. They seemed happy, joking and laughing as they buffed and dusted and shined away. "I see waiters and waitresses."

Nat leaned forward, a teacher coaxing the answer out of his pupil. "Doing…?"

"Sparkle and Shine."

"Very good," said Nat, as if he were praising a puppy. "And would you agree that Sparkle and Shine is an essential part of your job?"

"Yes."

"Do you think it's fair that you can waltz in here after Sparkle and Shine is almost over?"

"When I was hired, they talked about a management training program. They told me I'd work my way up to manager. I've been here for two years, and I'm still waiting tables."

He put on a Mister Rogers frown. "Unfortunately, your demerits outnumber your gold stars."

"Demerits and gold stars are for kindergartners, Nat."

Nat frowned. "Beg pardon?"

"Nothing. Can you at least increase my hours?"

"Then we'd have to pay you overtime. A forty-hour work week should be plenty of time for you or any waiter worth his-or-her salt to earn generous tips."

"Except that half those hours are spent in the tip-free time zone, polishing brass and dusting antiques. So we're basically cleaning for minimum wage, which doesn't seem fair to me. Nat."

His frown reorganized itself into a scowl.

"Actually," said Farley, "I'll tell you what I see down there. I see grown men and women wearing candy cane shirts and kiddie suspenders covered with asinine buttons, pretending that they're in the throes of Sparkle and Shine because they love it - not because they have bills to pay and groceries to buy."

For some reason - probably to punish herself for shooting off her mouth again - she took the Smithfield Street Bridge home. She stopped halfway across and leaned against the railing. Mr. Winston said that Jack and Pauline's kissing fish bridge had been designed by the engineer who later designed the Hell Gate Bridge. How ironic, she thought. A small tugboat pulled a barge along the river. In the distance a steamboat's horn sounded. What she wouldn't give to be on one of those boats, going anywhere. Just take William and go. She had some money saved, but not enough. Too bad; it's not like she had a job anymore, and she wasn't in school…

School. She jerked her head up. Her college fund! College was expensive; there must be thousands of dollars in that fund! Claire would know; she was the trustee. Despite the heat, Farley broke into a trot.

By the time she reached the back yard she was drenched in sweat. When she reached the back lawn she saw a flash of sunlight glinting off something metal on the picnic table. Scribble! She had completely forgotten. The poor thing was probably dying of thirst. Picking up the cage, she burned her hand on the hot metal and dropped it onto the lawn. The door flew open and a stiff, lifeless Scribble bounced onto the brown grass.

She found Claire mopping the third floor hallway, a bucket of lemon oil soap next to her.

"I'm still William's guardian," said Claire, not looking up, "and I believe that staying here is the best thing for him."

"That's another thing. When can I become his guardian?"

"We'll have to talk to Ham about that. I do know you'll need to show financial security, first."

Farley's chest tightened; her breathing began to speed up. She swallowed, forced herself to calm down. Maybe Claire was right. The daily consistency of Bridge Manor probably was best for William - at least until she could get a handle on her financial situation.

"I don't know what's happening to me," she said, wiping her forehead. "I need to get away for a while - to pull myself together. Do you think I could use some of my college money?"

"It's a *college* fund," she snapped, shoving the mop from side to side.

Perhaps it was Farley's overactive imagination, but Claire's mop strokes seemed to become more violent.

"You don't have to yell," said Farley.

Claire stopped mopping.

"I'm sorry," she said. "You have every right to ask about your own money. What I meant to say was; the fund can only be accessed for college."

"What if I never go to college?"

Claire seemed to have to think about this. "Then you get the money when you're twenty-five."

Farley stayed in the bathtub until her fingers pruned up and the water was chilly. Finally she climbed out and reached for a towel. Mid-reach, she caught sight of her naked reflection.

There was a time when she would have been thrilled to be this thin. But now all she saw was a worn-out young woman with blotchy skin, unruly hair and sad shadows under her eyes. A woman awfully close to going off the deep end.

She rummaged through the cabinet drawer. As the heat of the day finally surrendered to evening, she raised the scissors to her hair, calmed by the sound of each crisp 'snip.' Tufts of hair flew in every direction, creating a wet dark mat on the sink and floor.

When she was finished, she turned her head from side to side. Hideous. Yet, for some reason, she felt better. She needed to think - a feat practically impossible in her sweltering bedroom. Changing into an old tee shirt and cut-off shorts, she headed back down the yard.

"Get a grip," she said aloud. "Pull yourself together!"

"You're absolutely right," said Veda Marie. "I'm quitting after this pack."

Looking up, Farley could barely make out Veda Marie's form on an outcropping of rock. The glowing tip of her cigarette zigzagged as she patted the boulder.

"Come on up here and keep me company."

Listening to the sounds of the night, they watched airplanes glide across the skyline, red taillights flashing above the sparkling lights of the city.

Veda Marie pointed down the hill with her manicured toe.

"Another office tower going up. It's amazing how fast..." Her voice wandered off as she narrowed her eyes, taking in Farley's new haircut. Farley pulled her knees up to her chin and stared out at the flickering lights of the city.

"Want to talk about it?" asked Veda Marie.

Farley was quiet for a while, gathering her thoughts.

"I thought we were so special," she whispered. "I used to feel sorry for anyone outside of our little foursome. But the reality is, Jack and Pauline were the special ones. William and I were just the lucky spectators, along for the ride."

"We're all special, lovey."

"I don't know what I'm doing anymore." She choked out a laugh, trying to catch her breath. "I lost my job, killed Scribble and mutilated my hair, all in one day. I'm afraid of myself." Wincing, she ducked her chin to her chest. "I can't even breathe right anymore."

"Deep breaths," said Veda Marie, her voice calm as she rubbed Farley's back. "I believe you're having a good old-fashioned panic attack."

"Turns out she's been having these attacks for *over two years*," said Veda Marie, refilling her coffee mug, then Claire's. "All that unacknowledged pain she's got tamped down inside of her is making her sick."

Claire gnawed on a stubby fingernail. "What if it's not a panic attack? What if it's her heart, or…something else?"

"We'll know soon enough; last night I called my favorite doctor. He said he'll squeeze her in this afternoon."

"You must have called him awfully late," murmured Claire.

That evening, the residents of Bridge Manor walked to the edge of the property to gather around Scribble's final resting place. September carried the shoebox she and William had decorated with small pebbles and shiny buttons. Joe held Scribble, swathed in a white hankie. In a sullen voice he led the prayer.

"Scribble was a plain hamster. A little on the boring side. Yellow, ugly teeth. But he was our Scribble, and we loved him. And Farley didn't mean to kill him."

Farley punched him in the arm.

"Owww! Amen."

Joe handed the hamster to William. Horrified, he dropped the stiff hamster and ran for the house.

"There goes all the hot water," murmured Claire.

Veda Marie, Claire, and Farley followed the rest of the group up the lawn.

"The doctor wants me to work on controlling my anxiety," said Farley.

Claire nodded. "Which is what we want to talk to you about."

Veda Marie put an arm around Farley's shoulders. "I gave my sister Mary a call while you were having your check-up. I mentioned a little something about your panic attacks."

"Oh, God," groaned Farley.

"Hush your mouth; Mary is family. And she happens to have a place on Kiawah Island, right off the coast of South Carolina. She hardly ever uses it anymore. It's yours for the summer, if you want it."

"I can't accept her beach house..."

"Of course it's hardly bigger than a shack, but you can swim and walk the beach. We need to get that chopped up head of yours pointing in the right direction. I'll drive you down myself. I could use a few days visiting my sister."

"That's so nice of her, but I just lost my job. I can't afford..."

"We already have a plan," said Claire. "We'll rent your room out for the summer, and you can keep any money that brings in. You won't need much if you're frugal. Between the rent money and your social security checks, you should be fine."

"Although I'm not going to lie to you." Veda Marie ran a hand through Farley's butchered hair. "A few hours in the beauty parlor would be time well spent."

"Claire Sullivan," said Veda Marie, "you circled that parking lot five times to save us walking twenty feet to the beauty parlor."

"Mind your own business." Claire eased the car into a parking space.

In the brightly decorated salon, Veda Marie tucked a roll of folded dollar bills in Farley's hand.

"You always want to take care of your shampoo girl," she said. "Bring the tip directly to her lest there be some confusion of where it came from."

Claire snorted. Veda Marie snapped her purse shut.

"Laugh all you want. There is nothing like a good head-scrubbing. Hell, I'd tuck the cash in her bra myself if I thought she'd rub my head longer."

"Mrs. Sullivan?" A scrawny young woman in a black smock held out her hand. "I'm Suzanne. I'll be doing your hair today."

"I don't think so. Anne does my hair."

"Anne no longer works here. Don't worry, I have your file." Suzanne waved the file in the air. "I promise, I'll do your hair just like she did."

"A change is what you need," said Veda Marie, elbowing Claire. "No crime in taking care of yourself. You're too young to be 'old lady gray.'"

Claire was hurt. "I am not gray."

"You're just a bit snow-capped." Veda Marie turned to Suzanne. "Give her some color and a fresh new cut, and put it on my tab."

Suzanne dusted the hair off Claire's neck and spun her chair around, so she could see the back of her head.

"You look a decade younger!" cried Veda Marie, clapping her hands.

Claire's hair was now a shiny auburn, cut in a classic bob. Her face appeared thinner; even her skin looked brighter. She blushed and touched her hair, more pleased than she would admit.

Farley leaned forward in her chair and caught her breath. She had been worried that her aunt's new cut and color would make her look more like her mother. Instead, she was just a younger, prettier Claire.

"Thank God that's over," said Claire, as they walked to the car. "I need a nap."

"Farley James, that pixie cut is absolutely adorable on you," said Veda Marie.

Farley grinned as she mussed up her hair. Short pieces stood straight up.

"If this isn't a new beginning, I don't know what is." Veda Marie closed her passenger door. "Claire, swing the car down by the river. I've got a surprise for us all."

Veda Marie removed a small athletic bag from the trunk and handed Farley a pair of sneakers.

"I took the liberty of stealing them out of your closet," she said. "Tie them up tight, so you don't trip over yourself on the way up the steps."

Claire frowned. "What steps?"

Veda Marie looked over at the steep slope across the road. "*Those* steps, leading up that beautiful hill and ending up in our back yard." She handed Claire a pair of Converse high tops. "I couldn't find any sneakers in your closet, so Joe lent you his. Put them on."

Claire stared at the high tops. "I'm not putting these on."

"You most certainly are - and I'll tell you why." Veda Marie pointed to Farley, who had found a bench and was tying up her sneakers. "Those panic attacks of hers are a warning. She needs to work off her stress. You need to work off your midnight refrigerator raids. And I need to hang onto my girlish figure."

"What are we supposed to do about the car?"

"Joe is picking it up after practice. So stop shaking that sassy new hairdo at me, tuck your lower lip back in, tie up your Chuck Taylor's, and get your rear-end up that hill."

Chapter 18

William carried Veda Marie's overnight bag to the car, ring-bearer style. Joe heaved Farley's suitcase into the trunk. Claire placed an overstuffed picnic basket in the back seat. Mr. Winston checked the oil and tire pressures for the second time that morning.

"You're good to go," he said, wiping his fingers with a rag. He opened the driver's side door for Veda Marie. "Now remember, keep an eye on your gauges."

Veda Marie raised one eyebrow. "I *know* how to drive, Mr. Winston."

"Don't forget to lock your doors," said Claire.

Farley turned to William, who had been unusually quiet all morning. He stared at his shoes.

"Give me your hand, kiddo," she said.

Pulling the 'brave and daring' bracelet out of her pocket, she fastened it around his wrist. Then she leaned down and pressed her forehead to his.

"I'll be back."

His lower lip quivered. "You promise?"

"I promise."

As the car pulled out of the driveway William wiped his eyes with his arm. So gentle he almost didn't feel it, Claire laid a hand on his shoulder.

"Pig tails!" cried Farley, as a massive pig truck came up next to them.

Veda Marie laughed. "Welcome to South Carolina. Pigs and cotton and endless South of the Border signs."

They kept pace with the truck for miles, delighting in the rows of squiggly pink bums pressed against the truck's side. When the truck pulled off at a rest stop, Farley rolled her window up and sat back in her seat.

"When I travel, something inside me comes alive. It's like…a spark in my soul goes off." She smiled. "Do you miss South Carolina?"

"I miss Mary. And Spanish moss, and the Pee Dee River."

Over the years, Farley had heard bits and pieces of Veda Marie's past life. She used to have a gambling problem and had married young; that was about it. Her mother used to say life was Veda Marie's private business - which always struck Farley as odd, given Veda Marie's gift for gossip.

"You never talk about your life back then."

"What do you want to know?" said Veda Marie, steering with her knees while she lit a cigarette.

Farley looked out at the acres and acres of cotton fields. "More about you, I guess."

Veda Marie's chuckle sounded far away. "I was barely fourteen when I fell in love with our hired hand. Chester was twenty-three. He had a way of staring off into the sky that reminded me of Fabian. The poor guy didn't stand a chance. For Valentine's, he carved my name in his arm in black ink. By my sixteenth birthday I was Mrs. Chester Broke."

She was quiet for so long, Farley decided she was finished.

"Turned out," Veda Marie finally said, her cigarette bouncing between her lips, "my Chester was as dumb as a squirrel in the road. Those dreamy stares of his? Poor thing was merely trying to think straight. Still, I would have stayed with him, but for one thing. One day I took the long way home from the store. He was standing in the doorway with his arms all folded up. Hit me right in the kisser. That was the beginning of a whole new relationship for us."

"So you left?"

"Not right away. I made a plan. From that day on, I rummaged for coins. Not that there were many to find - no one had money to throw around. But if you look hard enough, you will find a penny in the grass, a nickel in the laundry, a dime between the sofa cushions. I pulled my mother's old handbags out of the attic; you'd be amazed at what all I found in those bags."

She finished her cigarette and smashed it in the ash tray.

"Suddenly I was Mrs. Clean; 'airing' sofa cushions, rearranging the cellar. I went through every drawer and cabinet, under the seats in the truck and the tractor. I even crawled under the front porch, petrified as I was of snakes.

If Chester noticed my new cleaning habits, he never said a word. Saturday and Sunday mornings, I scoured the grass behind Rooster's bar on my hands and knees. I swept the gutter in front of the church and let everyone remark on what a saint I was." She drove the next few miles in silence. "What's in that basket Claire worked so hard on?"

Farley unwrapped a sandwich and passed it to Veda Marie.

"How did you get away?" she asked.

"Rooster's announced a big poker tournament. Chester and a buddy of his decided to win themselves a fortune by cheating. Peabody had a knack for cards, and he came by every night to drink beer and teach Chester the finer points. I kept my ears open. I knew their cheating plan was never going to work, but I sucked up Peabody's poker lessons like a sponge."

"The next time Chester's moods got a hold of him, I decided my odds on winning at poker were higher than my odds on surviving him. I grabbed my savings and took off for Las Vegas, under the made-up name of Mrs. Tendersheets."

"Weren't you afraid he'd come after you?"

Veda Marie flashed a wicked smile.

"I called him from a roadside motel," she said. "Told him I'd panicked, since I found out I had gonorrhea in the most painful way. I worked up some tears and cried for him to please come and carry me home. He didn't even ask where I was. He just hung up the telephone."

They had arranged to meet Mary in Charleston, about a half-hour from Kiawah Island. If she registered any shock at how different Farley looked, she didn't blink. In her white cotton sundress and short brown hair, Mary threw her arms around Farley and squeezed, Veda Marie style.

The three women shared a late lunch of razor sharp crab legs and two dozen massive oysters on the half-shell. Farley loved hearing about Henry's life in New York. Although they still exchanged the occasional postcard, they hadn't actually seen each other since the first time they met. She tried to picture him as a man, but the best she could do was put a chef's hat on the gangly boy with the dark eyes and brilliant smile.

After lunch, Mary led the way in her car and they headed out for Kiawah. Trees lined the narrow roads as they got closer to the island; the tops of their branches met in the middle, forming a tunnel, with Spanish moss dripping down the center like Christmas tinsel. They stocked up on groceries at the Piggly Wiggly and picked up Mary's beach bike from the local gas station, where she had had the tires filled with air. At the house, Mary showed Farley the hiding place for the spare key (under the headless gnome, outside the back door), and gave her another loving squeeze.

Veda Marie was not so quick to leave. She had things to say.

"I want you to work on something while you're here, lovey. You need to get in touch with all those smothered feelings you've got inside. When they start to surface, let them come. Don't fight it. Don't be afraid. It'll feel like hell but it won't kill you. Roll around in it. And then let it go."

Farley waved goodbye, half relieved, half scared to death. Unconsciously, she adapted her mother's custom of making the house her own. She put away the groceries, made up the bed, unpacked her clothes and toiletries and wandered through the small house, touching everything. Then she put on the navy blue one-piece bathing suit September and Resa had presented to her as a going-away gift. (They had also given her an obscenely thick joint and a book titled 'Learning to Shag.')

Directly out the back door was about a hundred yards of sand dunes and wild grass, leading to the ocean. She ran along the wooden footpath all the way to the beach.

The sun had already begun to set as she dug her toes in the wet sand. Unbroken sand dollars, empty horseshoe crab shells, smooth pebbles and shells seemed almost too perfectly placed, as if a set-dresser was trying to imitate the perfect beach for a movie.

She ate her dinner of grilled cheese and green beans on the screened-in porch, enjoying the gentle sound of waves in the distance. For the rest of the evening she worked on a jigsaw puzzle under the dim light of a hanging bulb, finally crawling into bed and drifting into the most peaceful sleep she'd had in years.

It happened about six weeks into her stay. She dreamt she was in a darkroom, waiting for a photograph to reveal itself in the chemical tray. The image began to materialize...she could almost see it...

...this must be a Farley James...those images... lemon trees...old and new...here and gone... unfelt feelings don't go away...take care of your brother...she wouldn't get out of the car...

She sat up, the sheets sweaty and tangled tight around her legs. Heart pounding, she covered her eyes with the palms of her hands. Something was loosening deep inside of her, rising perilously close to the surface. Oh, God, she couldn't breathe.

"Let it come," she gasped, squeezing her eyes shut. "It won't kill you."

In blinding waves of sobbing and cursing and hatred and love, all the grief, longing, and rage that she had so vigilantly kept in check broke free. As the white morning light crept into the room, the oppressive weight within her heart began to dissipate, and in its place rose the slightest, most magnificent sensation of hope.

Dear William,

I'm sorry it's taken me so long to write. For some-one who has nothing pressing to do all day, my days are awfully full! I've been running, riding my bike, fishing, crabbing, swimming and exploring the island. I'm taking some serious alone time, as you would say.

I've fallen in love with Loggerhead Turtles. Oh kiddo, they are beyond adorable! Unfortunately the rest of nature seems to like them, too. If the hatchlings survive the shell stage, they dash from their nest in the sand dunes to the ocean.

Meanwhile, blue heron, egrets, crabs and other predators lurk around with lunch on their mind. I volun-teered to be a part of the local nesting program and I love it. We monitor the nests and check for emerging hatchlings, while trying not to disturb anything and stay out of the way. I'm sending you a book on Loggerheads. I was hoping we could read it together when I get home.

Speaking of home, it looks like Bridge Manor will be home for a while longer. We can't access our trust fund for five more years. But don't worry, we won't have to wait that long! As soon as I get home, I'll get a job and work hard and save every penny. In no time at all we'll be back in business - moving on, like we used to.

And now my sweet William, I need to tell you something. I want to apologize for the way I've treated you since we moved to Bridge Manor. I'm sorry for hiding away and feeling sorry for myself. Most of all, I'm sorry for leaving you to fend for yourself. You were right, that night on the steps. 'Us four' is gone, but we're still here.

But you were wrong about one very, very important thing. You said you might not be smart when it comes to real life. Kiddo, you see life through eyes that are true and honest. You react to life with a heart loaded up with love. When it comes to real life, William Justus James, *you are brilliant.*

Your loving sister,

Farley

Dear Claire and Veda Marie,

I hope you don't mind sharing this letter, but I wanted to say something to you both. Thank you for the love and care you've given William and me. You took in two lost souls without a second thought. I'm only now beginning to realize what a mess I've been. Thank you for helping me to get away when I so dearly needed to.

I feel myself growing stronger, inside and out. I try to experience each breath as it fills my body, chipping away at the heaviness in my heart that has become too familiar. (I know - how September of me!) You were right, Veda Marie; hurt and pain does diminish when I allow myself feel it.

I doubt I'll ever understand why Pauline did what she did. (Sorry, Claire, it seems easier if I don't call her 'Mom.') I don't know if I can ever forgive her for leaving us when she had a choice. But I am starting to believe that I can move past all that and get on with my life.

Love,

Farley

P.S. One of the best things about this beach house is the outdoor shower. I think Bridge Manor could use an outdoor shower, don't you?

In her dream a phone was ringing and she had to go to the bathroom in the worst way. The ringing went on and on…and on… she had to *peeeeee....riiiiiinggggg.* Opening her eyes, she threw out her arm and knocked the receiver to the floor. A man's voice drifted up from the floor.

"Hello?"

Sizing up the distance to the bathroom door, she groped for the phone.

"Farley? Is anyone there?"

"Hang on," she said, her voice groggy.

Half-way across the small room the telephone cord reached its limit. Crossing her legs, she kept her eyes on the bathroom as she brought the receiver to her ear.

"Sorry. This is Farley."

"Farley, its Henry." Silence. "Henry Freeman."

She spun around, wrapping her ankles in the cord. This wasn't Henry. This was a man.

Dion,

You will never guess who called me this morning. Henry Freeman. It's wild; his voice is really deep now and he sounds so masculine. I guess that makes sense since he must be around twenty-five. He and a friend are planning a trip down south in three weeks, and wanted to know if they could stop by Kiawah a few days. I thought it was nice of him to ask, since this *is* his beach house. Of course, I said yes.

I know you said you couldn't come down this summer, since all of your money is going toward nursing school. But I beg to differ. You need to take the occasional beach-beer-crab-picking-break to reenergize yourself. Any health professional will back me up. Plus, you'd be doing me a big favor.

I'm nervous about having my long-lost-friend-visitor come to stay. Even though we were post-card friends for a while there, face-to-face is…real life. Not to mention I'll be a third wheel if this 'friend' is a girlfriend. Just think about it. You've been working so hard; you really do need a vacation.

Love,

Farley

P.S. All begging aside, no pressure. And I promise I'll understand if you can't come. But please try!

Farley,

Henry of the big ears? The guy who refused to be a zombie? I wonder if he grew into those ears. All right. Enough with the begging. I'll come.

Love,

Dion

Farley had fallen asleep on the beach, apparently rolling on to her side at some point. Half of her body was sunburned, including an exposed breast that must have slipped out. There was sand in her mouth. She spit a few times and wiped her tongue with the towel, which merely deposited more sand into her mouth. She spit again as a shadow fell over her.

"That's attractive."

Covering her breast with her hand, she looked up; straight into the sun.

"It's about time," she said.

The familiar ease Farley and Henry fell into as kids was still there. They took their time walking back to the house, talking and laughing.

"I'm glad you're still you," said Farley, dragging her towel behind her. "You're just a taller, hairier, you. With big muscles and a deep voice."

"You haven't changed a bit," he teased, his dark hair partially concealing his brown eyes.

Henry was handsome in the most perfectly imperfect of ways, she noted. In addition to his six-foot-four height, he had a sturdy nose, dark brown eyes with thick eyelashes, and an understated cleft on his chin. The slight scar on his forehead added a rugged touch, which balanced out those deep dimples when he smiled.

The porch door swung open.

"How's our favorite non-zombie?" cried Dion.

Henry laughed. "I wasn't about to compete with 'Catholic School Zombie and 'Hockey Player Zombie.'" He gave her a hug. "Did you meet Colette?"

"She's sampling the boxed wine. I love her already."

"Hello!" The voice sounded far away, like a tiny, French mouse.

A pale girl in her mid-twenties with shiny black hair stepped through the small doorway. She wore cut-off shorts and a white tee shirt, and had long legs and an endearingly toothy smile.

"Farley, meet Colette D'Aubigne." Henry put his arm around her shoulders. "The best sous-chef in New York City."

"Get out of here, Henry," said an obviously delighted Colette. "So nice to meet you, Farley. We picked up some fresh seafood. I hope you like lobster."

Farley loved the way Colette's 'Henry' was '*on-ree,*' 'hope' was '*ope,*' and each word was enunciated. So French.

They dined on boiled lobsters, steamers, corn on the cob, and red potatoes, and a great deal of beer and boxed wine. In the background, beach music competed with the rhythm of the ocean. Henry entertained the table with stories of kitchen disasters. He and Farley compared the best crabbing and fishing spots, which led to Farley's concern for the Loggerhead turtles, which led to a slightly drunk Colette bursting into tears.

"I love your little turtles," she sobbed. "I'm sorry, wine makes me gentle."

Later, Dion and Colette tried unsuccessfully to dance the shag while Farley and Henry picked at the empty lobster shells.

"Did you two meet in school?" asked Farley.

"Colette was a year behind me. We re-connected at our current restaurant." He grinned. "Which leads me to why we're here."

Farley gasped. "You're getting married!"

Dion and Colette stopped dancing.

Henry choked as his wine went down the wrong pipe. When he recovered he shook his head.

"No, we're here because I'm looking to open a restaurant of my own." He waved a lobster claw at Colette. "That courageous woman has agreed to come on as my Sous-chef."

Farley noticed that Colette's cheeks had gone from wine-shiny to blazing red.

Henry dumped the shells into a plastic bag while Dion filled the sink with hot soapy water. Colette had snuck away; Farley found her asleep on the pull-out sofa and spread a light blanket over her.

"I'd like to stay in New York," said Henry. "The problem is, I can't afford much more than a cardboard box in the city. We looked at some properties in Maryland and Virginia, on the drive down here."

Farley grabbed a rag to wipe down the table. "See anything you like?"

"Not yet. I've got a few places lined up to see in Charleston. But so far nothing seems right."

"Because they're not in New York," said Dion, her mouth pulled down, drunk-sad. "If you want to stay in New York, the right place will come along. Keep looking."

Or, find a city *like* New York, thought Farley, with less expensive real estate...a city like Pittsburgh.

"What do you mean you don't know if they're an item?" asked Veda Marie. "It isn't too hard to spot romance. I can smell it in the air."

"I don't *know* because it's none of my business," said Farley, frustrated. Henry and Collette were due back from Charleston any minute.

"Where did they sleep?"

"What?"

"Did they sleep together?"

Farley exhaled a long breath. "All right, Veda Marie. You got me; they slept together. We all did. We all got naked and had wild, raunchy, horny, sweaty sex. I'm so exhausted I can't think straight."

Silence.

"I'm sorry, Veda Marie. I'm not feeling very well today."

"I guess not. Orgies can take a lot out of a girl."

Pressing her fingers to her eyes, Farley counted to ten. "Back to Henry's restaurant. What do you think?"

"I think you're on to something. Claire and I will get started in the morning, scouring the city for empty buildings."

"Not just empty buildings; empty *restaurant* buildings. So he'll already have something to work with. And don't say anything to Mary. If this gets back to Henry, he'll just tell us we're wasting our time."

Chapter 19

"There is no way in hell I'm getting out of the car in this area," said Claire, peering through the dirty window.

"Its broad daylight, for crying out loud," said Veda Marie.

Turning down Baum Boulevard, they searched for address markers on the mostly empty warehouses. Some of them had been turned into rock clubs, others were in the process of being torn down. She and Claire had decided against calling in a realtor; they would have had to use Billie out of respect for Ham.

"These buildings are going for a song," she said. "We're bound to find something for Henry."

Claire decided against mentioning the obvious; buildings were going for a song because the city was in the midst of the collapse of its great steel industry. Something, despite all the signs, nobody believed would happen. Empty mills and factories were sprinkled throughout the city like coal-black confetti. Paddy's mill – one of the rare hold-outs - was closing down its continuous strip and sheet department. Hundreds of steelworkers would be out of a job.

"I know, Claire. The buildings are going for a song because the economy is bad. But our Caliguiri is making progress. There are signs of life all around us. Every time I look down at the city from Bridge Manor, the skyline has changed."

"Here we go," mumbled Claire.

"I heard that."

It was no secret Veda Marie admired their long-standing mayor. She loved to spout specifics about his efforts to renovate the city, as if no one else ever read the newspaper or watched the news.

Claire grunted. "I loved this city long before you ever stepped off the train from South Carolina."

"Don't get snippy on me; all I'm saying is Pittsburgh is perfect for Henry."

They drove in silence for a while.

"Remember that summer Henry and Mary stopped here on their way to look at cooking schools?" Veda Marie smiled. "He was all ears and elbows. Seven years...hard to believe."

"Eight."

The memory pinched Claire's heart; Pauline had been there. Instinctively she lowered the passenger mirror and examined her face, searching for signs of her sister. She had never minded being the 'less attractive' twin. Not much, anyway. Growing up, Pauline's world of peroxide, Saturday night dates, and 'I'll just have a bite of yours' was as foreign to Claire as kissing games and permanent waves. She tilted her head to catch the light. Pauline never would have taken these crows' feet lying down.

Dear Farley,

I'm so happy you're feeling better, lovey. We all are. William is doing fine, although he misses you more than he will admit out loud. He is really getting into this back and forth letter writing. We'll have to get him a pen-pal when you get home.

Sounds like the four of you had a wonderful time during Henry's visit. Mary told me all about the lunch you treated her to, and said she's never seen Henry so happy. (By the way, she is of the opinion that Colette and Henry are *not* romantically involved. Not that it's any of our business.)

Now for the big news. I scotch-taped the article below:

> "Yet another landmark is about to be lost. With the steel industry imploding all around us, the ripple effect is in full speed. Railroads, factories, stores and restaurants are calling it a day at a heart-wrenching rate. The South Side is the latest victim of our dismal economy. The Fingerling Restaurant is closing its doors."

So you see, after scouring West Liberty, Squirrel Hill, Polish Hill, Bloomfield and all corners in between, we found the perfect building *two blocks from Grady Square*! I'll tell you all about it when we talk this weekend, but I wanted to send you the article from the Post-Gazette that started it all.

Love,

Veda Marie

P.S. You'd think I would have found the article first, being that I am the only true 'morning person' around this place. But Mr. Winston has taken to putting the coffee on before I come down, so I guess he gets the credit.

"Henry probably drove in from New York just to humor me," said Veda Marie, during her weekly call to Farley. "But I could tell the moment he stepped through the doorway we found the perfect place."

Farley swept the floor of the beach house as she talked. "You really think he'll make an offer?"

"He had to go back to New York, but he's already set up meetings with an inspector and someone from the bank for a week from Monday. If all goes well, he said he'll make an offer. As we speak; Henry's dream of owning his own restaurant is being rerouted to Pittsburgh."

"I can't believe it's really happening!"

"He said to tell you he'll call you tonight and fill you in."

"I can't wait to hear every detail. Is William around?"

"Claire had a meeting with Ham. William went along to play with Eileen." She paused. "The summer's over, lovey. Come on home."

Instinctively, Farley turned to gaze out the window. The ocean was calm. Peaceful.

"Would it be all right if I stayed a little longer?"

Chapter 20

Billie Kane lay in her hospital bed, dressed in a flowing blue satin robe. The top buttons were undone to reveal her pale, unlined neck and a modest yet impossibly sexy hint of bosom. She glowed with fever; her hair was perfect. All of her loved ones gathered around her bed. Everyone - even the handsome doctor - fought back tears...

"Billie." Eileen poked her stepmother's arm. "Get up. You said to wake you up in an hour."

She groaned. "How many times have I told you to call me Mommy?"

Eileen pouted as Billie hooked the necklace around her neck. At the center of the necklace dangled a heavy silver #1. It was the most butt-ugly thing Eileen had ever seen.

She stomped her foot. "Why can't I cut my hair? Farley cut her hair short."

"She most certainly did," said Billie. "And now she looks like a lesbian." She clenched Eileen's chin, hard. "Aren't you the lucky girl, going to Patty England's birthday party and getting to wear my special 'best realtor in all the land' necklace?"

Eileen glared, but held her tongue.

"Hands up." Billie rotated her finger to indicate that Eileen should twirl.

Miserable, Eileen lifted her arms above her head and rotated. The lace from her pink blouse itched, her pink tights sagged at the knees, and Patty England was a goddamn bossy bitch. And Billie was a big fat, butt-face bitch.

Ham shuffled through the papers in his briefcase. "A lot of fuss for a child's birthday party."

"Not when the child's father is one of the richest men in the state," sang Billie.

"What does that have to do with Eileen?"

Billie crossed her arms and gave her husband a sarcastic smile.

"I'll be outside," Eileen mumbled.

When Billie did that smile with her mouth but not with her eyes, it was time to get a move on.

"Let me remind you," said Billie, checking her purse for her business cards, "of the three most important qualities of a successful realtor: networking, networking, networking. As the mother of an invited guest, it would be rude for me not to introduce myself to Mr. and Mrs. England and make polite conversation."

"Politely promoting yourself."

Billie sniffed. "A successful realtor is not afraid to toot her own horn. If Mr. England wants to look at purchasing or listing real estate, do you think he is going to call a *strange* realtor?"

I'm sorry Eileen isn't here," said Ham, pouring William a glass of lemonade. "Believe me, she would rather play with you than dress up and go to a birthday party."

"I know." William began sifting through Eileen's crayon box, enjoying the waxy smell.

"I'll only keep your aunt a few minutes. Are you sure you don't want any more ginger snaps?"

"No, thank you. I don't like the feeling of being full."

"I wish I didn't like the feeling of being full," said Ham, closing his study door.

Claire chuckled. "You and me, both." She picked up a framed photo of Billie and Ham on their wedding day. "This is a lovely picture of the two of you. Look at those smiles."

Leaning back, Ham pressed the palms of his hands against his eyes. I deserve this, he thought, resisting the urge to giggle hysterically.

He had wanted – no, needed - someone to take away his fear of raising Eileen on his own, and Billie fit the bill. She was smart, attractive, and successful. She brought fancy, girly gifts for Eileen and charmed his partners at dinner parties. She wore tantalizing red panties with matching bras 'just for him' and was athletic and willing in the bedroom. Check, check, check. So he married her.

William's voice called from the kitchen. "Aunt Claire?"

"Sorry, Ham." She held up a finger. "Give me one second."

Ham's heart beat double-time as he watched her cross the room. How different his life might have been if Claire hadn't turned him away. He recalled his painfully awkward advance, made after she moved back to Bridge Manor. Why had he rushed her? If he had waited….

"All right," said Claire, closing the door. "Let's get started."

Forcing his thoughts to return to the present, Ham removed a thick file from his bottom drawer.

"I don't want you to be discouraged," he said, unfolding a single white sheet of paper. "There are still a few things we can..."

"Just spit it out," said Claire, reaching for the document. She read aloud.

> "The original investigation determined that the accident was due to personal misconduct on Colonel James' part. The airman was found to have initiated a dispute with a fellow officer. The reckless manner and speed of the car that Colonel James was driving was found to have been the primary cause of the accident. Nor was Colonel James acting in the line of duty at the time of death. Since the original investigation, no new evidence has surfaced to contradict these findings. Therefore the appeal for Colonel James' government benefits, specifically VA dependency and indemnity compensation, is denied."

Fifteen screaming seven-year-olds bolted around the England's back yard, intent on staining their party clothes. Billie Kane stood in the shade, disgusted. Mr. England was nowhere to be found. The wife - Tami with an 'i,' of all things - had greeted her warmly enough. But she had cut Billie off, too wrapped up in her little party to hear about Billie's third year in a row as a member of the Carter and Wilder Realtors Million Dollar Club. Selfish bitch.

Preoccupied with her thoughts, she didn't notice the dumpy man in a multicolored clown costume until he was right in front of her, twisting a long balloon into a wiener dog. He bowed, presenting the balloon dog with an exaggerated grin, as if the warped balloon was actually worth something.

"Get that repulsive thing away from me, you moron," Billie hissed, slapping the balloon.

One more look around the yard, and she headed for the door. On her way out, she placed a small stack of her business cards – the new ones with her latest glamour photo - on the table in the foyer.

Chapter 21

Henry handed Farley a can of Iron City.

"Here's to you," she said, raising her beer. "You did it."

"Strictly speaking, *you* did it. You and your cast of characters."

"Strictly speaking, you could have at least waited until I got back from Kiawah to buy the place."

"Who knew you were going to stay so long? It's practically winter. Mom thought she was going to have to evict you."

She smacked his arm.

"Seriously," he said, "I'm glad you're feeling better. We all are."

Farley returned to Bridge Manor in early November, as the first snow threatened. She'd been sad to leave Kiawah, but was excited to get on with the rest of her life.

"In all your dreams," she teased, "did you ever think your restaurant would be just down the hill from your auntie?"

"Don't jinx me; it's not mine until I sign my life away tomorrow morning."

"Everything will be fine."

"I know it," he said, sounding very Veda Marie.

He licked the foam from his upper lip. "I have to say, I couldn't have found a more perfect place. The Strip District is just across the bridge, so I can buy fresh seafood and produce. We've got vineyards and farms nearby, and a greenhouse out back. It's full of junk right now, but eventually I'll grow vegetables and herbs in there. I can't wait to show you everything."

"Why wait?" She grabbed his hand. "Come on, let's go."

They parked in the empty lot and stared at the two-story wooden building.

"I wish I could show you the inside, but I don't get the keys until tomorrow."

Farley opened the passenger door. "I'm sure we can find a way in."

They walked around the back of the building. A nervous Henry kept watch as she tried the doors and windows. Almost immediately, she found an unlocked window.

"I don't think this is such a good idea, Farley."

"Don't worry," she said, slowly working the window up. "And quit looking over your shoulder. You look like a bad spy. No one can see us; nobody drives by here anymore. Which reminds me, you're going to need a tall, well-lit sign that people can see from a distance. You're only a few blocks from the waterfront, but you're off the main road."

"Still as bossy as ever, I see."

"I am not." She grabbed onto the window ledge and bent her leg. "Boost me up."

"Stay here," said Henry. "The flashlight is in the kitchen."

They took their time touring the building, discussing everything from bathroom mirrors to walk-in freezers. Henry was impressed by Farley's extensive knowledge of even the most minuscule details of the food service industry.

"You learned all this waiting tables?"

She shrugged. "I used to drive my manager crazy coming up with ways to do things better."

"I'm sure he appreciated it."

"Not as much as one might think," said Farley. "He fired me."

Laughing, he opened a door that led to a narrow stairway. "Come on, I'll show you my apartment."

"Your apartment?"

For some reason, she had assumed he would live at Bridge Manor.

Pulling in the driveway, Henry put the car in park and turned off the ignition.

"I'll never forget the day Mom and I drove up." He pointed to the lawn. "You were right there, taking zombie pictures with your hair all Medusa-wild."

Farley smiled at the memory. "I was so impressed that you – a teenage boy – treated me like a real person."

"I make it a point to talk to anyone who smells like fried chicken."

"I mean it, Henry. You were the first person to ever take my dream seriously."

He twisted in his seat to face her. Sometimes he was struck by how much Farley resembled her mother. Of course, Veda Marie had warned him long ago to keep that tidbit to himself.

"I believe we all need something to strive for," he said. "Even if that something changes along the way."

For the next hour she didn't hold anything back; from standing in their Las Vegas kitchen that horrible morning, to her suffocating grief that became an almost comfortable obstruction for her to hide behind. She spoke of her disregard for her brother's needs and her emotional and physical deterioration, which led to her healing trip to Henry's own family beach house. She shared her conservative optimism for the future.

"Ham Kane offered me a job typing and filing. It's only temporary, but it will give me time to find a 'real' job. If I work hard and save my money, William and I should be able to move on in a year or so."

"Would you ever consider staying in Pittsburgh?"

"We've already been here longer than we've ever lived anywhere," she said, as if that explained everything.

"So moving on is still in your plans, even if you won't exactly be wandering free." Henry scratched his chin. "Any hope for the 'trusty camera' part?"

Farley looked at her hands. "The day we moved into Bridge Manor, I buried my camera case in the back of my closet. I haven't touched it since."

Later that night, Farley stood in front of the open closet. She pushed aside an old suitcase, a box, a pair of boots. Slowly at first, then faster, she began tossing things - digging her way toward the back of the cavernous closet until she found her camera case. Carrying the dusty case to the window seat, she unhooked the latch and pulled out her Minolta, lenses, filters, and film kit, and lined them up side by side on the bench. Then she buried her head all the way down inside the case and inhaled the smell of her youth.

"I'm not even going to ask," said Resa, passing by Farley's room.

Two months later, Farley pushed open the front door of the restaurant. "Hello?"

She had to yell against the roar of the snowstorm. Winter had come late, and more brutal than normal.

"Back here!"

The dining room was a mess. Floors covered with paper, boxes, boards, tools, drawings, and tables and chairs stacked to the ceiling. Henry's desk was piled so high with papers, only the top of his head showed.

"I thought you were getting some filing cabinets," she said.

Grinning, he spread his long arms. "They're around here somewhere."

Only the large kitchen was partially organized. On the far end, the floor-to-ceiling bookcases were lined with row after row of preserved foods: large jars of tomatoes, beans, garlic, onions, and pickles, which provided a vibrant backdrop against the shiny, stainless steel appliances.

"You were right about the main dining area," said Henry, coming up behind her. "The acoustics are bad and there's not enough light. I've got a meeting with the contractor on Thursday. Do you think you could come?"

"I can't; I have to work. Besides, I don't know anything about construction."

"You knew enough to spot the sound and lighting problem."

"Those were obvious."

"Not to me. I've got a meeting about the new ventilation system, and I can't find my receipts."

"You need help. When does Colette get here?"

"Not for a few months." He looked at Farley, his brown eyes pathetic and pleading. "I've got a proposition for you. Help me through this first part, and I'll help you become the best restaurant manager in the city."

"Me? The only experience I have is waiting tables."

"You've worked in the industry," said Henry, reeling his points off on his fingers. "You learned it from the ground up...starting in the bowels. You know what it takes to run the front of the house. You're smart as hell, you've got great ideas, and I trust you. Come on, Farley. I need you."

"I'm still planning to leave, Henry."

"Fine. Can I have you until then?"

She blushed. "I don't know...."

"I'm begging you. Help me with this ludicrous paperwork. Help me decipher the permits and inspections. I need a schedule and a master checklist so nothing falls through the cracks." He threw up his hands. "And you know...any other stuff that comes up along the way."

She laughed. "Oh, is that all? I thought you meant, like, something hard."

Chapter 22

"Okay, Mr. Winston." Henry slid three small plates across the table. "Veda Marie tells me you have impeccable taste buds."

Mr. Winston tucked a napkin under his chin. "I do hope she meant that as a compliment. I must admit to a particularly sensitive palate."

"Fair enough. I'd like your palate's assessment of my cinnamon-almond cake."

Mr. Winston took a small bite, then a drink of milk. "Moist."

Henry nodded. "Try the second plate."

Picking up a new fork, Mr. Winston took a bite. "The texture is different."

Farley consulted her notes. "Henry eased up on the ground almonds."

Using his napkin, Mr. Winston wiped the corners of his mouth. "By all means, bring back the almonds."

As Farley scribbled in her notebook, Henry tapped the third plate with his pencil. "Last one."

This time Mr. Winston closed his eyes as he chewed. "Cinnamon butter glaze." He waved his fork. "There's your winner, Freeman."

Mr. Winston wasn't the only Bridge Manor resident to be recruited by Farley. By the time spring arrived she had gotten everyone in on the act. September took over the gardening. Before long, pots containing plants in various stages of growth covered the wooden tables running the length of the greenhouse. Tiny signs in each pot read: thyme, oregano, parsley, basil, tomatoes, squash, zucchini, and peppers.

In the spring, shoots of lettuce, peas, and radishes were moved to the large bed behind the property, followed by tomatoes, peppers, cucumbers and zucchini as the days heated up. Small buds of snapdragons, alyssum, marigolds, black-eyed Susans, daisies, and lavender were spread about the property, from which flowers would be cut for table decorations.

William helped September with the gardening after school. He could pretty much count on having a nocturnal emission whenever he spent the day with her. Sometimes he helped out in the office as well, humming to the radio or bursting into song as he filed the burgeoning mounds of paperwork. Not counting the day he got a paper cut and bled all over the laundry receipts, William was an excellent filer.

Veda Marie slipped into the role of Freeman's team mother, cheering each new improvement, making sure no one went too long without food, and washing and folding Henry's laundry. She kept Mary updated on Henry's progress, sending photos and writing long, descriptive letters. Resa planned to wait tables whenever her dance schedule allowed. Even Ryan came down periodically to bless each new stage of construction, claiming 'better safe than sorry.'

But it was Claire who turned out to be Farley's most valuable resource. As a former librarian, she could put her hands on anything; inspection checklists, employee forms, and contact information for local business associations. Farley would leave questions for her on the kitchen chalkboard before she left for work. Often by the time she got home that evening, the answers were on the board and any materials relating to Farley's questions were on the counter.

"It's all here," Claire had said, brandishing her library card as if it were a police badge. "You just have to know where to look."

Veda Marie was determined to walk through her cramp. She and Claire had been hiking for less than ten minutes, but for her, getting started was the hardest part. Her breath heaved in and out, sharp pains ran up her legs, and her feet throbbed. A level-headed person would turn around and head straight home to a cool bath and a tall glass of iced lemonade. But she couldn't. Not after finally getting Claire into a daily exercise routine of hiking the hills below Bridge Manor.

"Eight in the morning and it's already warm," said Claire, wiping beads of sweat from her upper lip. "Suddenly I'm not so opposed to Farley's outdoor shower idea."

Veda Marie grunted in response.

Unlike Veda Marie, Claire tended to be talkative and energetic at the beginning of their walks. Later, as the humidity of the morning threatened to suffocate her, she would begin to wear down – usually around the time they were making their way back up the slope. By the time they reached Bridge Manor she would have to practically drag herself up the lawn.

"Joe's been offered the job of head coach for the Frosty Devils hockey team," said Claire.

Veda Marie waited until her breathing evened out before she tried to talk. "What about school?"

"He says he'll have more time to study because the rink is nearby - right behind South High. Paddy's going to hit the roof."

"Speaking of Paddy, was that him on the phone last night?"

"As if you didn't know. He wanted to take me out to dinner Sunday." She glanced at her friend. "Pull your eyebrows out from under your bangs, Veda Marie. I invited him to join us for Sunday dinner, instead."

The women had recently added a traditional Sunday Dinner to Bridge Manor's meal schedule, for those who might be available. Based on the laughter, the endless stories, and everyone's reluctance to get up from the table, the Sunday afternoon gatherings were already a hit.

"I'm glad to hear it," said Veda Marie. "The man looks like he could use a good meal."

"I'm worried about him; he's under a lot of stress."

"More layoffs?"

"Yes. And I'm afraid it's only going to get worse."

Chapter 23

Henry ducked his head as he stepped through the small greenhouse door. He started holding his staff meetings in there over a year ago, when the dining room floors were being re-finished. It had quickly become the staff's favorite place to meet. The air was damp, thick with the aroma of soil and vegetation, and the room had an organic, calming atmosphere.

He clipped off a limb of rosemary and swept his hand up the branch, giving it a little pressure to release the oil. Cupping his hands to his face, he inhaled the invigorating aroma as he looked around the room.

September Rose, looking like Mother Nature personified, was in the far corner. She had her hand in a mound of rich, black soil as she spoke to some of the waiters. Dion and Farley were going over the latest schedule. He tucked a sprig of rosemary in his shirt pocket and headed toward them.

"Okay, everybody, listen up!" yelled Farley, passing out a stack of papers. "These are our revised schedules. Our days of hosting banquets and fraternity parties are over. The countdown to opening night has officially begun. The big day is scheduled for August 3rd."

There was an outburst of applause.

"Just when I was getting used to the morning-after smell of beer and cigarettes, and the drunken renditions of 'Build me up, Buttercup!'" yelled a waiter from the back, followed by laughter.

"Hey," said Henry. "Those parties and banquets have been paying your paychecks for the past year."

"Study your menus, including the back-up pages," continued Farley. "You'll be expected to know the ingredients of each dish, where the ingredients came from, and what wines are recommended. Colette and Henry gave me their final comments on the handbook, so you should each have your own copy by the end of the week. And finally…" She put her arm around Dion. "Dion has been accepted to the West Penn School of Nursing."

"Part time," said Dion, blushing with pleasure as applause and congratulations filled the room.

After the meeting, Henry grabbed the back of Farley's shirt and tugged. "Want to go to the Strip District with me, tomorrow? There's a new vendor I want to meet."

"Sure," said Farley. "Mind if I bring William?"

They wandered the stalls and side markets, examining vegetables, smelling fruit, and sampling fresh cheese. Henry bought paper-wrapped packets of goat, chevre, and bleu cheese, along with grapes, walnuts, and green onions, carefully packing each item in his cooler.

The colors, excitement, and the commingling odors of the Strip District thrilled William. The meat stalls he wasn't so sure about.

He had no problem with the impaled dead rabbits and chickens on hooks at the entrance of the shops - he had drawn their skinned bodies in his notebooks hundreds of times. But the men in their bloody aprons made the hair on the back of his neck stand up.

"All I need is one more thing and we're ready to go," said Henry, pointing across the street to a seafood stall. "I'm making Veda Marie's favorite dish for Sunday dinner - Shrimp and Grits, the delicacy of the South."

"Maybe you should have searchlights for Freeman's opening night," said William as they rumbled along in the streetcar. "Superheros always show up at those kinds of events."

"You're the only superhero I want at opening night," said Henry, pretending to hit William on the arm.

They got off in Grady Square. Henry heaved the cooler onto his shoulder, while Farley and William carried bags.

Half-way up the hill William began to limp.

"I told you not to wear your new shoes, kiddo," said Farley. "Stop for a second."

Henry put the cooler down and sat on the step, admiring the tender way she helped her brother off with his shoes.

"Lately Joe's been picking up William from summer camp," said Farley. "Yesterday they stopped on their way home and Joe bought them each a brand new pair of penny loafers."

"And we didn't even need new shoes!" said William.

Henry took one of the loafers and began working the back to soften the leather. "Tell me about this store."

William frowned in concentration. "Well, the store smelled like foot powder and new carpet all in one. The air inside was nice and cool because of the air conditioner, so I worried about my sinuses. Extreme hot to cold or cold to hot can cause sinuses to become inflamed."

"By any chance was there a pretty girl helping you?"

William pushed up his glasses and stared at Henry. "How did you know that?"

"Lucky guess. What's her name?"

"Sylvia. She's very clean. We keep visiting her store so Joe can ask her on a date, and he keeps not asking."

Henry softened William's other shoe while Farley snapped pictures of the deserted glass factory below. Under the gathering clouds, the contrast of dark shadows against the occasional sunbeam was dramatic.

"These empty mills and factories are depressing enough," said Henry. "But seeing them in dismal weather makes it so much worse."

Farley smiled. "Dismal days don't bother me. It's the bright, sunny ones that you have to watch out for."

Sitting at the table, William unfolded his napkin and placed it on his lap.

"Did everyone wash their hands?" he said.

"You should know," teased Joe. "Always standing over the sink like the germ police."

Henry ladled the piping hot mixture of cheddar cheese, garlic, onion, and grits onto the center of each bowl, then topped the mixture with steaming pink shrimp and sprinkled chopped bacon and circles of green scallions.

Soon the only sounds in the kitchen were the clinking of forks against bowls and the ticking of the clock over the stove.

"I never thought I'd be eating shrimp with grits," said Paddy.

He had come to Sunday dinner with a handful of flowers, a smile on his tired face, and his pants belted high above his round belly.

"Christ Almighty, if I ate like this every day, I'd be as big as a house," said Resa, glancing at Ryan. "Sorry, Father."

Claire grunted. Nothing like a skinny girl making a disparaging weight joke.

"I could do without taking the Lord's name in vain, Resa," said Ryan, scooping another bite into his mouth. "But you're right on about the shrimp." He waved his fork at Henry. "You're going to be bad news for my physique."

"Best shrimp and grits ever, lovey," agreed Veda Marie.

William frowned. "Veda Marie, is 'lovey' a nick-name?"

"It's more of a term of endearment, because I use it on everyone."

"My dad used to call me Professor," he said, tapping his fingers together nervously. "But I was thinking of starting a new nickname."

"Not allowed," said Joe, talking around a mouth full of food.

"Why not?"

"A nickname has to happen naturally," said Ryan.

"But, what if it *doesn't?*"

Joe swallowed as he winked at William. "Then you're out of luck, pal."

"That's right…pal," said Paddy.

Pal. William's face was one big grin.

The conversation flowed in currents, combining with the contented sounds of an appreciated meal. After Mr. Winston shared a few hilarious stories of his University days, Paddy asked him if he missed teaching.

"Absolutely," said Mr. Winston, spreading a thin layer of butter over Veda Marie's homemade biscuits. He put the knife down and leaned back in his chair. "But newness holds excitement, too. Like any other new stage of life, retirement is a great adventure."

"Ohhh, I know!" William raised his hand. "You could be a train conductor, or an artist, or a farmer."

"Just don't be a dairy farmer," said September. "My uncle was a dairy farmer, and he could never go anywhere. He said it was like breast feeding your whole life."

Veda Marie tapped her knife against her wineglass. "I will not hear such filth at this table."

As dinner was winding down, a woman in a loud print dress and red hat knocked on the mudroom door. Claire saw the woman first.

"Jesus, Mary and her husband," murmured Claire, sliding back her chair and hustling for the door.

"I'm sorry to bother your delicious smelling meal, Mrs. Sullivan," said Mrs. Scott, looking over Claire's shoulder. "I just wanted to drop off a list of a few more documents we will need before we can process your request."

Claire kept her voice low. "You didn't have to do that. I was planning on picking them up tomorrow."

"Oh, it's no trouble at all." Mrs. Scott wriggled her fingers, flirty style, at Henry. "Well, if it isn't Mr. Henry Freeman!"

Embarrassed, Henry stood and shook hands with Mrs. Scott. He had applied for a loan with her company, until Ham - who insisted on reviewing the loan documents at no charge - advised Henry to go elsewhere.

Mrs. Scott removed a tissue from the sleeve of her blouse. "I've been meaning to send you a note, Henry. I have a valuable tip for your restaurant." She unraveled the tissue and inserted it firmly into both nostrils.

"Paprika," she said, in a nasal voice. "I put paprika on everything, particularly meat and spaghetti. Gives it a zing."

"I...I..." He stuttered, staring in horror as Mrs. Scott buffed the inside in her nose in quick thrusts. She removed the tissue and examined it. Henry fell straight back, knocking bowls off the table on his way down.

Chapter 24

At the Second Savings and Loan, Mrs. Scott tottered across the floor in shoes so tight, her feet resembled sausages.

"Right this way, Mrs. Sullivan," she said, showing Claire into her office. "I meant to call and ask about that poor young man, but, what with so many people looking for loans, business has been…" she wagged her tongue and panted like a dog, "…wild!"

"I'm sure," said Claire, taking a seat. She gazed around the walls of the office, trying not to appear nervous.

Mrs. Scott folded her hands on her desk. "How is Mr. Freeman? Does he do that often?"

"He is fine, he was just…dizzy."

"I don't see how he can run a restaurant if he's going around dropping all the time."

"It rarely happens."

Mrs. Scott waved her hand as if to dismiss the subject, then opened the thick file on her desk. "*Anyhoo*, let's talk about your loan application…"

Caressing the bottom of her ring with her thumb, Claire held her breath. She sat up straight as she forced her lips into a smile.

The brakes squealed as Claire pulled into the parking lot of a small diner. In an obscure booth in the back, she salted her double bacon cheeseburger and onion rings and thought about her meeting with Sausage Feet.

"Mrs. Sullivan, I must congratulate you for the *impressive* progress you've made on your property. I for one would have written Bridge Manor off as a loss."

Claire's heart had soared. The loan was going to be approved! What a relief. Why hadn't she done this earlier?

"However," continued Mrs. Scott, "the cost of repairing Bridge Manor to any substantial level would be much more than the value of the house." She tapped an expensive looking pen against her desk. "You understand, it's not my..."

"To whom?"

Mrs. Scott raised her chin; pen tapping away. "Beg pardon?"

"The cost of repairing Bridge Manor would be more than the value of the house *to whom*?"

"Let me be frank, Mrs. Sullivan." Mrs. Scott's tone was disdainful - no more Mr. Nice Guy. "Bridge Manor in its current condition cannot be used as collateral for a loan. Should your situation change, the Second Savings and Loan would be more than happy to revisit your application."

"That doesn't make any sense," Claire had said. "If my situation changed, I wouldn't need the Second Savings and Loan."

Claire took her time on the last onion ring, chasing catsup streaks across the empty plate. As she slid out of the booth, she considered ordering another meal to take with her. After all, the waitress would assume it was for someone else.

She decided to walk the three blocks. Entering the dark store, she caressed her ring. Paddy had paid too much for the gold ring with the tiny diamond in the center.

A beautiful ring for a beautiful lady.

She smiled, remembering how pleased he was with himself. And rightfully so; the ring was as precious to her today as the day he presented it.

My lady. My darling girl.

"Can I help you?" said the clerk, elbows resting on the dusty counter.

"Oh," said Claire, startled out of her daydream. After some creative wriggling and tugging, she removed the ring. She placed it on the counter and raised her chin. Proud and confident, she was. "How much will you give me for this?"

The announcer introduced the Steelers as Joe and Farley finished putting condiments on all six hot dogs. Knowing he would soon be too busy for football games, Joe had surprised everyone at breakfast by offering to treat them to a Steelers game. Although the actual season didn't start until September, but a pre-season game was enough to get Farley, William, and Mr. Winston to go.

"Come on," said Joe, licking yellow mustard off his wrist. "I don't want to miss the kick-off."

Farley dressed her last hot dog and they started up the stands.

"Joe! Joe Sullivan!" someone called. "Over here!"

Joe stopped abruptly, causing Farley to spill lemonade down her shirt. He scanned the crowded stands. His face flushed to a deep scarlet when he saw who was calling. Sylvia Stowe climbed over set after set of knees until she was standing in front of him.

"Hi, Joe."

"Hi."

Joe stared. She looked like an angel, complete with a light that seemed to shine only on her. Tiny flecks of sunlight lit up her hair. Her skin was as clear as spring rain and her cheeks had a dewy glow.

"I can't believe you're talking to me," he said. "I'm not even pretending to buy shoes."

Used to such responses, Sylvia tossed her glossy blonde hair over one shoulder and let out a good old-fashioned, untainted, just-had-my-teeth-cleaned-homecoming-queen laugh. "You are too funny, Joe." She touched his eye. "What happened there?"

"Where?" He stared, his mouth slightly open.

Farley leaned around him. "Joe's a hockey coach."

Sylvia gently touched his forehead. "Does it hurt?"

"Huh-uh." He shook his head.

"That went well," said Farley as she and Joe continued up to their seats.

"Shut up."

"Where have you been?" William never took his eyes off the football field. He gave his penis a few quick squeezes. "I've been perspiring at a disturbing rate. I think I might be dehydrated."

Mr. Winston helped settle William with his hot dog and lemonade, then he clapped his hands together. "Who's going to win tonight?"

"Those nice boys from Pittsburgh, that's who!" cried William.

Chapter 25

Seventy degrees and a blue suede autumn sky for Freeman's opening night. Cocktails were served in the garden area. Resa tended bar while Dion, September and Farley mingled among the crowd, encouraging guests to stroll among the raised beds of vibrant flowers and tour the greenhouse.

At the end of the hour Henry welcomed everyone and thanked them for coming, then directed them inside.

Waiters and waitresses, sharp in their crisp navy shirts and khaki pants and skirts, led the diners to their tables.

The Bridge Manor party was seated at the largest table, along with Ryan, Paddy, Joe, Ham, Billie, and Henry's mother, Mary. A tastefully engraved sign on the table read:

Reserved for
Special Guests of the Chef

Tapping his glass, Father Ryan rose before the first course. He thanked God for the glorious weather and asked Him to bless the bounty, the guests, the restaurant, and the staff. As he prayed, Farley was struck by the unfamiliar look of pure joy on his face. It occurred to her that her uncle was a tremendously unhappy man.

"It's a pleasure to finally meet the mother of such a delightful child," said Mr. Winston.

Smiling modestly, Billie draped her napkin across her lap. "Eileen is my stepdaughter, but I do go out of my way to treat her as if she were my own."

"Hello, Mrs. Kane," said Farley, helping a waitress unload a full tray of appetizers.

"Hello, Ferber."

"Her name is Farley," said Mr. Winston, once she was out of earshot.

Billie shrugged. "Tall girls shouldn't try to pull off unusual names." She raised her vodka glass to beckon a waiter, tapping it with her freshly French-manicured fingernail. She winked at Mr. Winston. "I swear by the 'Vodkin's Diet. Whoever said losing weight couldn't be fun?"

For the next ten minutes, she managed to endorse her realtor skills while simultaneously ordering another double-vodka.

"Quite impressive," said Mr. Winston. "And I hear your husband is a talented attorney."

"Just between you and me," said Billie, "he spends too much time on his charity clients." She pretended to stick a finger down her throat. "Suddenly, he wants to save the world."

As their guests enjoyed coffee and dessert, Henry and Colette emerged from the kitchen. Wholehearted applause and cries of 'Bravo!' filled the room. While Henry introduced his staff, each diner was presented with a gift bag containing a small bouquet of herbs and flowers from the garden, along with a jar of preserved tomatoes bearing the Freeman's label.

After the guests went home Henry opened the bar for the staff. Farley and Dion tucked themselves into a table, slipped off their shoes, and quietly polished off a half bottle of scotch.

Dion leaned in, conspiratorially. "Did you notice the man at table six?"

"Table six." Farley squinted. "You mean the guy with the hair? What about him?"

"He asked me out."

"But he was on a date."

"Give the man some credit; he waited until she went to the ladies room."

Overtired and slightly smashed, that set them off. They laughed, that out-of-control belly laugh you wish would never end. Finally, wiping her eyes, Dion leaned back in her chair. Across the room, Henry and Colette shared stories with a group of waiters.

"Don't you love seeing him so happy?"

"I sure do," said Farley, her tongue thick.

She rested her chin on her fists and watched Henry. Happy Henry. Happy, happy, happy Henry. With his own restaurant and his name on the menu and on a big sign you can see from the highway. She closed her eyes.

Let's do it. I'll have my restaurant. You'll go out and capture all of the beauty of the world. And we won't let anything stand in our way. No matter what.

A few days later, Farley pulled a baby blue dress from her closet and handed it to Dion.

"Try this one," she said. "We have to hurry, though. I told Veda Marie I would bring some cookies to Resa's dance class."

Slipping on the dress, Dion admired the fine linen fabric and the cool feel of the lining. "It's beautiful."

"It looks great on you."

"Thank you. I promise I'll take good care of it."

"You can have it; I can't remember the last time I put on a dress."

"That's because all you do is work." Dion spun away from the mirror. "Hey, why don't we double date? I could ask Duncan to bring a friend."

"No thanks; I can get my own dates."

"They why don't you?"

On the way to the carriage house, Dion couldn't let it go. "Seriously, wouldn't you like to have a real relationship?"

"Right. It's going to be hard enough to leave as it is. The last thing I need is for some romance to make matters worse."

"That's the spirit, Farley. Ever the optimist."

They arrived just as Resa was excusing the class. While the rest of the dancers crowded around the cookie tin, Eileen sulked in the far corner, arms crossed self-consciously over her belly.

"Eileen is growing up so fast," said Dion. "I used to think she was Resa's daughter."

"She should be," said Farley, biting into a cookie. "She practically lives here."

The doorbell rang as Dion was brushing her teeth. She grinned a toothpaste grin into the mirror. Duncan Kennedy, the most beautiful man she had ever seen, was downstairs. Standing on her doorstep. Ringing her bell.

"Dionna!" her mother yelled from the bottom of the stairs. "Door!"

She spit toothpaste into the sink. Her mother could not be more than four steps from the front door. "Can't you get it, Ma? Please?"

"Excuse me, Your Highness," said her mother, sarcasm oozing from her mocking, singsong voice. "Oooh, look at me. I have on a fancy dress. I'm too good to get the door."

"Shut up," Dion whispered, her hands shaking as she turned off the faucet.

She prayed that the traffic from the street would block out her mother's taunting. Running her fingers through her hair, she hurried down the stairs.

Dion plopped down on Farley's bed. "Wake up!"

Farley opened one eye. "What time is it?"

"Who cares, it's our day off. Guess where I slept last night?"

"What are you doing here?"

"I can't go home yet. Ma thinks I spent the night with you."

"How old are you?"

"Back off; I can't afford to move out *and* pay for nursing school." Dion hugged a pillow to her chest. "So guess."

"Give me a hint."

"Duncan Kennedy."

Farley raised herself up on her elbows, smiling.

"Jezebel," she said.

Dion bounced excitedly on the bed. "I wanted to call you last night, after he fell asleep. But I figured it's rude to talk about someone in their own apartment."

"By all means, have a little class. Wait until you get home to talk about him."

"And, he wants to take me to dinner at Freeman's on my next day off!"

"How romantic for you, dining where you work."

Dion hit her with a pillow.

"Sorry I'm late," said Farley, tossing her purse in the office. "Veda Marie had to tell me something she heard from the girl who cuts her hair."

"Also known as gossip," said Henry. He checked a pot on the front burner as he stirred the rosemary potato stew.

Farley never got tired of watching Henry cook. There was a definite rhythm to his movements; his own sort of culinary choreography as he flowed from sauté to sear to blanch and back again.

"It's about Duncan Kennedy," she said.

"Who?"

"Duncan Kennedy…Dion's Duncan? She hasn't gone five minutes all week without working his name into every conversation. He's bringing her here for dinner to-night, by the way."

"So, what did our Miss Tattletale find out this time?"

"Apparently the man has a nasty habit of forgetting his wallet on dates."

Colette, Farley and Henry peeked through the kitch-en door as a waiter led Dion and Duncan to their table.

"There's no way that man could fit a wallet into those skin-tight pants," said Colette. "Which look sharp on him, I must admit."

"The man can *wear* a pair of pants," agreed Farley.

Duncan removed his jacket and placed it over the back of his chair.

Henry lowered his voice as a waiter hurried by. "Maybe the wallet is in his jacket pocket."

"Maybe." Farley straightened. "Let's go find out."

Duncan sat with his chair pushed away from the table, leaning back, legs spread. Dion had to lean almost all the way across the table just to hear him talk. Farley took her time bussing a nearby table so she could listen in.

"So tell me, Dion," said Duncan, looking around the room, "are you planning to go to school full-time?"

"I can't afford to go full-time for a while. But I don't mind; I love working here."

Dion stared as he used one finger to push his hair aside.

He smiled. "What?"

"I love your hair."

"Really?" Tossing his head, his hair flipped and cascaded back into place. "The girls at the office think it makes me look like Robert Redford. I think they're just saying that..."

"No, they're right! You *do* look like Robert Redford."

Approaching the table, Farley complimented Dion on how lovely she looked and insisted on hanging up Duncan's jacket for him. Henry shook hands with Duncan, who remained seated.

"I'm impressed with what you've done to the place, Freeman," said Duncan, in a not-so-subtle superior tone.

Henry presented the couple with a bottle of wine, compliments of the house. Duncan ceremoniously sniffed the cork, wrinkling his brow as he examined it, and then sniffed again. Henry snuck a glance at Farley.

She shook her head. No wallet.

Back in the kitchen, Farley and Henry argued over how to handle the situation.

"We have to tell her," said Farley.

"Not here. You can tell her anything you want tomorrow, but tonight they're in my restaurant. That makes them my guests. Please tell them that dinner is on the house."

"You're really going to help that sleazy cheapskate out?"

Henry put on a fresh apron.

"What I'm doing is avoiding a scene," he said. "Let me know when they're ready to leave."

After dinner Duncan had three on-the-house cognacs and two slices of apple pie, 'to go.' Finally, the waiter informed Henry that the couple was preparing to leave.

"Thanks for giving the old piggy bank a break. I won't forget it." Checking to be sure Dion was out of earshot, Duncan winked at Henry and held out his hand. "And that, my friend, is a promise from yours truly."

Henry gripped Duncan's hand and squeezed – hard.

Duncan gasped, knees buckling. "What the..."

"You ever pull that stunt on her again," Henry squeezed harder, grinding Duncan's knuckles together, "and I'll break more than your piggy bank. Got it?"

Squeaking in pain, Duncan nodded frantically.

"Good." Henry winked and patted Duncan's arm. "And *that*, my friend, is a promise."

Chapter 26

Farley unlocked the petty cash drawer and counted out five one-dollar bills.

"Here you go, kiddo," she said, handing the money to William. "I'm proud of you, earning your own money."

"Thank you." William folded the bills and pushed them deep into his pocket. "I'm proud of me, too."

"Thanks again for the present. What a surprise."

"You're welcome."

He'd gotten the idea a while ago, after watching Farley blow out the candles on her twenty-third birthday. For the next few months he secretly researched aging, sun damage, and average weight gain. On her way out the door that morning, he had presented her with an intricate drawing of what her face would look like when she was fifty.

William bought two scoops of rainbow sherbet at Rosemary's Market. The rest of his money would go straight into his ticket jar. One of these days he was going to treat everyone to the cheap seats, the way Joe did. Eating slowly to avoid an ice cream headache, he started up the hill. He still wasn't over his fear of riding in cars. If anything it had gotten worse. But he rarely had to ride in one; he took the bus or a streetcar from the square to the library, or to school and back. Everything else – Freeman's, Rosemary's Market, Joe's hockey rink – was within walking distance.

On the path between the steps and Bridge Manor he found a shiny black, perfectly round pebble. He polished it with his shirt and put it in his pocket.

"This is a *positive* thing," he whispered.

September told him that positive thoughts helped push negative thoughts aside. Lately though, the negatives were winning.

William knew he was different. And until recently he'd been fine with his uniqueness. Proud of it, even. Not having many friends was something he understood and accepted. After all, a superhero must bear the burden of loneliness. But lately a dark feeling had begun to creep over him, invading his happiness. His body, forever small, had begun to seem less extraordinary…more peculiar.

"Does William seem all right to you?" asked Farley, folding a towel.

"Depends on your definition of all right." Veda Marie looked over at the chalkboard. "If drawing a set of human lungs for us to look at while we eat is all right, I'd say he's fine."

Claire dumped another load of clean laundry on the table. "I've noticed it too, Farley. He's been moody lately. Maybe it's puberty."

Veda Marie chuckled. "Our boy might look young, lovey, but he's twenty."

"Still," said Farley. "He's usually pretty open with me, but not this time. Maybe it *is* a man thing. I'm going to ask Joe to have a talk with him; man-to-man."

Joe tucked William in and sat on the edge of his bed.

"Why don't you start coming to practice with me, Pal? I sure could use some help."

William tucked his arms under his head and stared at the ceiling. "You already have an assistant coach."

"Unfortunately, he thinks he's too good to hand out towels."

"And you *drive* to practice."

"You know, pal, one of these days you're going to have to get used to riding in a car. But I don't mind walking. The rink is just a few blocks over from Freeman's."

William was quiet for a moment.

"I'm tired of not being normal," he said. "I want to be like everybody else."

Joe rubbed his chin. "I know what you mean. I'd love to be like everybody else."

"You?"

"Sure. On some level we're all trying to fit in." Joe tapped William on the chest. "Let me tell you something, pal; you are so much better than everybody else."

William bit the insides of his gums to keep from smiling. "You really mean it?"

"I swear on those nice boys from Pittsburgh."

"Would I get to wear a Frosty Devils jersey with PAL on the back?"

"Of course. You'd be an official member of the team."

William clicked his tongue. "I guess, if the team needs me, I should probably do it."

Veda Marie poured coffee while Claire pulled out sections of the Sunday newspaper.

"I'm surprised Mr. Winston isn't up yet," said Claire.

"He probably found a hair out of place."

For some reason it aggravated Veda Marie that the man showed up completely groomed and fresh smelling first thing in the morning.

"You're just jealous that you have fresh-as-a-daisy-at-breakfast competition," teased Claire.

"I'm not listening to you. It's too early in the morning for crazy-talk."

"Good morning, lovely ladies," said Mr. Winston, pulling up a chair.

Feeling guilty, Veda Marie filled his coffee mug.

Mr. Winston scooped a spoonful of sugar into his coffee and stirred.

"Tell me, William," he said, "how are you finding life as an assistant coach?"

William smacked his hand on the table. ""The Frosty Devils are the best. The guys are always hitting each other in the arm and popping each other on the bum with wet towels." His voice began to rise. "And they have so much hair…Peter Gaglio had a full beard when he was sixteen years old!"

"Voices…" said Veda Marie.

William covered his mouth and leaned toward Mr. Winston.

"Peter Gaglio isn't as big as the other guys, but he has the fullest beard and the biggest muscles. He spits all the time and he skates so fast nobody can catch him. And he knows more curse words than anyone else in the whole wide world!"

"Is that so?"

"Yes that is so." William raised his hand to high-five Joe as he entered the kitchen. "Joe, my man!"

"This Gaglio sounds like a real winner," said Claire.

"Peter Gaglio chaps my ass," said Joe, pouring himself a bowl of corn flakes.

Veda Marie shot him a look.

"Sorry," he said. "What I mean is that the kid's got more talent than he deserves. He's amazing. He's got ice vision - he can sense the way the puck's going to glide. You either have ice vision or you don't. Gaglio's got it, big time. He'll go up against men twice his size and *they'll* back down." He tapped his temple with his spoon. "Nothing going on upstairs, though. On top of that, he's lazy and he's got a bad attitude."

"Why would you want someone like that on your team?" asked Claire.

Joe shoveled a spoonful of cereal into his mouth. "The kid can score."

Mr. Winston tapped his stick on the cobblestones as he and William started down Overlook Trail. "What's the word for the day?"

"'Myriad.'"

"Myriad." Mr. Winston scratched his beard. "Impressive."

"I know, but do you like it as much as piccalilli?"

"That's a tough one. I don't know if I can let go of piccalilli."

William covered his mouth, trying to control his wide smile.

"Myriad," Mr. Winston repeated. "What progress you've made. Miss Kelly will be proud."

After William became too old to be a student at The Significant Me, Claire hired his former teacher to continue working with him. Miss Kelly was currently encouraging William to explore words outside of his "safe" medical zone.

A pickup truck slowed to a stop.

"Good morning," said the driver. "Can you please tell me where Bridge Manor is?"

Opening the door, Claire found a small bald man wearing a short sleeve blue shirt. He had a row of what appeared to be patches of hair sewn into his scalp. His neck was indiscernible; his head seemed to rest on his chest.

"Good morning, ma'am. My name is Sherman Lowe," he said, handing her a business card.

Sherman Lowe
Lowe & Son Restoration
Quality Home Repair and Maintenance
We offer payment plans!

"My company, Lowe & Son Restoration, is doing some work in the area. I happened to notice that your roof is in need of repair."

Claire snorted. "Don't remind me."

Normally she would have shut the door by now, but she felt a little sorry for this man with his painfully polka-dotted scalp.

"Winter will be here before we know it." He examined the roof. "A sturdy nor'easter will blow that baby right off."

"I'm afraid you've wasted a trip, Mr. Lowe. Money's a little tight right now."

He tapped the bottom line on the card, in case she had missed it the first time:

We offer payment plans!

"To be honest," he said, leaning in, "I think you'll find that our payment plans are particularly attractive."

Claire took another look at the card. "How attractive?"

Chapter 27

Eileen bounced her bike down Overlook Trail's bumpy cobblestones. On the steepest part, she let go of the handlebars and made herself count to ten before gripping them again. Her heart pounded with the terrified glee of it all. She pulled her baseball hat down low over her eyes, enjoying the surge of power that started in her crotch and ran up and down her body. There was only the sound of the rattle of her tires on the narrow, winding road.

She reached the bottom and peddled like crazy across Grady Square. As she sped past St. Xavier's her thoughts turned to school. Mainly because, for the first time in her life, she didn't hate it. Sure, the boys still acted nice one day and mean the next, and the girls were still clique-bitches. Her sixth grade teacher was already making noises about a parent-teacher conference, where she would inevitably ask if Eileen had 'been tested' - thank God her dad wasn't big on that. Still, she didn't mind school anymore because, over the summer, something significant had occurred. Eileen Kane had become a Bad Ass.

She soared along the smooth pavement past Freeman's, past the playground and the junior high, until she saw the small wooden sign for Hogg's Pond. She turned her bike onto the dirt road and peddled to the end, then screeched to a stop and looked back to admire her skid marks.

Crouching down, she slipped through two broken boards in the fence and walked toward the pond. The closer she got, the louder the chirping and whirring of frogs and insects sounded – until it was all just one giant, pulsing screeching noise. The ground was wet and warm water squished into her sneakers.

She sat on a log and unwound a pack of Benson & Hedges and a mangled book of matches from the elastic of her underwear. She lit the least bent cigarette and coughed as the stale smoke found its way to her lungs. Plucking a hair from her head, she watched it curl as she touched it to the cigarette's glowing tip. She burned a few more hairs and a few holes in her shirt before pulling Billie's 'best realtor in all the land' necklace out of her pocket.

"Bite me, Billie!" she yelled, and chucked the necklace as far as she could into the middle of the pond.

Claire hired Lowe & Son to repair the roofs on Bridge Manor and the carriage house. The payment plan was so reasonable she decided to go ahead and replace the old dual-basin kitchen sink with a large, single-basin sink. And on a whim - although she herself would not be caught dead using it - she had an outdoor shower installed, complete with insulated pipes.

To enclose the shower, Farley and Veda Marie found three old wooden doors in the cellar. They propped the doors against the fence at the bottom of the property, then recruited Joe and September to help sand and paint.

Farley looked up from her sanding. The weather was mild for November. She was dressed in a blue jeans and a short-sleeved tee shirt with no bra.

"Hey, Claire!" she yelled, pointing to the doors. "Look what we found!"

"Tell her to get down here and grab a piece of sandpaper," said Veda Marie, wiping her forehead.

Claire walked down the lawn and admired the doors.

"I'll help in a second," she said. "I need to talk to Resa first."

"Why do I have a feeling this is about Eileen?" said Resa, wobbling toward the group with a bucketful of soapy water.

Eileen had developed a nasty habit of lifting things that didn't belong to her: William's hockey puck, a perfume bottle of Veda Marie's, a rawhide hair tie of September's. Now, Claire had seen her with an awfully familiar scarf tied around her waist.

"It's a phase," said September. "When I was little I used to take trinkets from people I loved and admired so much, I wanted a piece of them. I even had a name for it: 'steal longing.'"

"I can't imagine you ever stealing anything," said Farley.

"I did, but only for a little while. I started to worry about repercussions from the universe. I was afraid I'd come back as an ant or a flea in my next life."

Veda Marie whispered in Farley's ear. "Apparently the universe missed the pot plant thriving under a heat lamp in her closet."

"The child needs help," said Claire.

"I've already talked to Billie," said Resa. "Although she didn't seem too concerned."

Veda Marie lit a cigarette. "Billie is probably the cause of Eileen's new hobby. I say we continue to overwhelm the child with love, the rest will take care of itself."

"Why, Veda Marie Tendersheets," said Farley, giving her a playful nudge. "Underneath that Southern smoke-screen, you're a flower child."

"That's me, all right." She picked a piece of tobacco off her lip and flicked it. "Mia Farrow in a panty girdle."

"I don't get it; now they're calling for snow," said Farley as she unbuttoned her coat. "What happened to fall?"

Henry poured a bag of shelled walnuts into a mixing bowl. "We were too busy to notice. Dion called; she'll be a few minutes late."

"Hopefully because she's studying. She's failing some of her classes."

"I don't think Mr. Wonderful likes her focusing on anything but his Robert Redfordness."

"What a loser." Farley picked a shell out of the bowl. "I can't believe he lied his way out of his wallet-forgetting habit."

"In retrospect, we should have anticipated that one."

Farley chuckled. In retrospect.

"Are you making fun of me?" he asked.

"Not at all." Her smile was genuine. "I love the way you talk."

Dion danced into the kitchen, patting her shiny new platinum-colored hair. "What do you think?"

"Oh!" Henry put his hands on his head.

"Your hair…you…" stammered Farley.

"You look magnificent!" cried Colette. She kissed Dion once on each cheek. "*Très chic*!"

"Really?" Dion's face was beaming. "I wanted something special. Duncan invited me to his family's cabin. We're leaving after work tonight."

After a particularly hectic night Dion took a bird-bath in the ladies room and changed her clothes. She stepped into the empty dining room in a tea-length red dress, belted with two thin orange patent leather belts. Her hair was parted on the side, bangs pulled back with a small orange clip in the shape of a daisy.

"What a gorgeous dress," said Farley.

"It better be." Dion flounced the skirt playfully. "I had to dip pretty far into next semester's tuition to pay for it."

"Hey, I thought you left an hour ago," said Henry, untying his apron and tossing it into the laundry bin. "Is everything all right?"

"Not exactly," said Farley. "It's Duncan."

"What did Prince Charming do this time?"

"He was late picking up Dion for their special get-away."

"How late?"

"He never showed up."

"Henry's warming up the car," said Farley, handing Dion some tissues. "Look, I know you don't want to hear this, but maybe it's best that this happened. You know, before you got any more…involved."

"Thanks a lot," mumbled Dion. "That makes me feel so much better."

"I'm sorry, but it's the truth."

"Like you know so much about getting *involved*."

Farley threw her arms up. "Look at yourself, Dion. You're miserable. You fried your hair. You're failing your classes and you blew God knows how much money on that dress. It's three-thirty in the morning and you've been waiting around for this guy for hours. And it's not the first time he's stood you up…"

"All right, I get it. You make me sound like an idiot."

"I don't mean to, it's just…"

"Like hell you don't." Dion pressed her lips together. "Let me tell you something, Farley James. It takes courage to fall in love. To put yourself out there, vulnerable and exposed. That's not for the faint of heart."

Farley started to speak, but Dion held up her hand.

"You know what? You're right. I *am* miserable right now. And I've been stood up *again*, as you so kindly pointed out. I'm bleached and broke and behind in my classes. But at least I took a chance. I tried. I'd rather have my heart broken ten times over than to be a pathetic coward like you."

"I'm not a coward," said Farley, stung. "Just because I don't stand by and let some loser walk all over me…"

"No, of course not." Dion swallowed, her cheeks burning. "You just prance around with your head tucked up your ass, pretending not to see what's right in front of you."

"What the hell is that supposed to mean?"

"Will you *come on*!" yelled Henry, leaning in the door. "It's freezing out here!"

Chapter 28

"Shit!"

Farley jumped out of bed. She was late for work; she'd slept through her alarm again. For the past week she'd been waking up in the middle of the night and ruminating over the painful sting of Dion's words. Because Dion had been right, of course. Farley *was* ignoring what was right in front of her – specifically, a very tall, sweet, loving man with dark eyes and a huge heart - because there was nothing in the world she could do about it.

Slamming a toothbrush in her mouth, she brushed while she dressed. She slipped her sneakers on without tying the laces, stuffed a knit hat on her head and skipped every other step as she ran down the back stairs. She tripped over her laces as she entered the kitchen and barreled head-first into Ryan's stomach. Books flew from his arms.

"For crying out loud," he mumbled, scooping up the books.

"Sorry." She bent to help.

He studied Farley as she threw on her coat.

"You look like you lost your best friend," he sneered.

"Ryan…" warned Veda Marie, slicing a ham on the kitchen counter.

"Bye, Veda Marie," said Farley, ignoring him.

The mudroom door slammed behind her. She stood outside for a moment, catching her breath, then slammed back in.

"Why do you do that?" she demanded.

"Do what?" he asked, all piety and innocence.

"You know what. It's like you get off on other people's misery."

Veda Marie's eyebrows went straight up, but she remained silent. Farley put her hands on her hips.

"What's with you, Ryan? My mother used to say you were the closest thing she knew to God."

His upper lip curled into a perfect snarl. "Take it from me, toots; you didn't deserve to have Pauline for a mother."

Farley was momentarily stunned. That was a low blow - even for Ryan.

She snorted. "You got that right."

Now it was Ryan's turn to slam out of the house. Driving down Overlook Trail, he had to remind himself to slow down. It would not do for a priest to run over someone.

Claire pulled the car up next to Farley and rolled down the window. "Hop in. I'll drive you to work."

"Thanks," said Farley, shivering as she slammed the car door. "It's freezing."

"It's not much warmer in here. So help me, our next car will have a heater that works." Lightly pressing the gas pedal, Claire continued down the hill. "Veda Marie tells me Ryan is on a tear."

"You mean as opposed to his usual, perky self?" Farley blew on her hands and rubbed them together to warm them. "What's with him, Claire? He didn't used to be this mean. The way Pauline used to talk, he was practically a saint."

Claire grunted. "I wouldn't go *that* far. But your mother's death hit him hard."

"And here the rest of us are doing so well," mumbled Farley.

At the bottom of the hill Claire put the turn signal on.

"Ryan actually grew up to be a fairly well-rounded kid, thanks to your mother," she said. "She certainly raised him better than Abigail ever could have." She chuckled. "Of course, he's always had an attitude when it came to me. He considered me competition - being Pauline's twin."

Farley blushed, recalling her own similar feelings toward her aunt.

"For the most part," continued Claire, "Pauline single-handedly raised Ryan. She preferred it that way – and she was good at it. She instinctively seemed to know when to let him learn from his mistakes, and when to protect him. Even the fact that your Grandfather blamed him for our mother's illness never seemed to touch him."

"But Ryan was just a baby. How could anybody blame a baby?"

"Easier than blaming himself, I guess." Claire wiped fog off the windshield with her glove. "Your mother never said much about Abigail, did she?"

"Only that 'Abigail was better off with God.'"

Claire sighed as she turned into Freeman's parking lot. "Way to build the drama, Pauline."

From the kitchen came the animated sounds of Henry and Colette preparing for the day. Farley closed the office door and sat on top of her desk. "Okay. Tell me about Abigail."

Claire took a sip of her tea, clutching her mug with both hands to warm them.

"After Ryan was born," she said, "our mother became a different person. It was as if a switch went off. She cried constantly. She slept all day and refused to hold her baby. Her doctors decided she was suffering from 'melancholy' and prescribed bed rest. The poor woman rested on and off for the better part of three years. Finally, Father agreed to have her committed to Dixmont Insane Asylum. There, the doctors recommended an increasingly popular cure for undesirable qualities in women - moodiness, violent tendencies, alcoholism, promiscuity, hysteria. A lobotomy."

Farley was stunned. "You mean, a *'One Flew over the Cuckoo's-Nest'* lobotomy?"

The procedure took mere minutes, explained Claire. Just long enough for a sharp, ice pick-like instrument be inserted through the eyelids and given a slight jiggle, severing the part of the brain that managed mood and temperament. Their father was assured that Abigail would have no memory of any discomfort. And better yet, she could still function well enough for household and wifely duties.

"I remember the morning she came home," she said. "The house smelled like syrup and pine soap. Pauline and I nearly tripped over ourselves, racing downstairs to welcome her. Mother's hospital stay had seemed like forever to us."

"What was she like?"

Claire was thoughtful for a moment. "She was like the walking dead in those movies of yours. Her sweet, melodic voice was now flat and disinterested. She no longer raged, or cried, or laughed, or dreamed. She literally hadn't a care in the world. They cut out her soul."

Farley shivered. "How old were you then?"

"We were twelve."

The two women sat in silence for a few moments, barring the occasional clanging of pots and pans.

"Poor Grandfather. He must have felt awful."

"He did, at first." said Claire. "But it wasn't long before his sorrow shifted to anger. He began to avoid Ryan, sometimes physically pushing him away. He clearly hung the blame for Mother's affliction solely around Ryan's neck. He was more than fine when Pauline, who had always considered Ryan her own little doll, stepped in as both absentee mother and father." She sighed. "She believed if Ryan was good enough - did well enough in school and stayed out of trouble - Father would come around. She used to say, 'You have to be the best, Mutt. Then Papa will love you.'"

"Why didn't Pauline just tell me about Abigail?" asked Farley, walking her aunt to the front of the restaurant.

"Your mother was a firm believer in putting the past behind her."

"Burying the past is more like it." Farley placed a hand on the front door. "What about Abigail; how did she die?"

Claire zipped up her parka and stuffed her hands in her pockets.

"Your grandmother died with dignity," she said. "They may have severed most of her reason and emotion, but the slightest light still burned deep down inside of her. Not long after her operation, she walked down to the river in the dead of night and threw herself in."

For the next few weeks, Dion and Farley bobbed and weaved around each other, the memory of their cruel exchange hovering over them like a sinister shadow. They perfected the art of awkward politeness, fake smiles and otherwise subtly avoiding contact whenever possible.

"Goodnight," said Dion, opening the kitchen door.

Farley didn't look up from the potato she was peeling. "Night."

"Careful going home," called Henry from the walk-in refrigerator. But Dion was already gone.

"We need to hire a new bookkeeper," said Farley.

His arms full, Henry kicked the refrigerator door closed behind him. "Can't you just say you're sorry?"

She looked up at the ceiling. "I'm *sorry* we need to hire a new bookkeeper?"

"You know what I mean, Farley. Apologize to Dion."

The blush started in her chest and crept up to her cheeks. "What for?"

"For whatever it is that's making you both so miserable."

"It's complicated." She picked up another potato and pretended to examine it. "The night Duncan stood her up...I might have said some things I shouldn't have."

Henry feigned surprise. "No...*you*? I don't believe it."

He ducked as a potato flew past his head.

"Halleluiah," breathed Dion, lowering herself into the bathtub.

Her feet were throbbing. She had been on them since she woke up that morning, already late for her eight o'clock Anatomy lab.

Today was cadaver day, and she'd had to wait to have her turn at the liver. By the time she took a much needed shower – the odor of formaldehyde still lingered, but at least it was manageable – she was late for her job at Freeman's. She closed her eyes and sank into the soothing warmth of the water.

"What is this obscenity doing in the bottom of your trash can?"

"Ma!" Dion screamed and sat up, using her hands to cover her breasts.

An empty cardboard container splashed into the bath water, the words Home Pregnancy Test printed in black. Mrs. Piotrowski yanked a towel off the rack and tossed it on the floor near the tub.

"You're nothing but a filthy slut," she hissed. "Get out of my house."

Farley gasped as Henry pulled up to the front of Dion's house. In the glow of the headlights with her breath rising around her, Dion looked like a stricken angel. She rushed toward Henry's car, her wet hair plastered to her face and her arms filled with clothes.

From the porch, Mrs. Piotrowski emptied another drawer of her daughter's belongings onto the wet cement. Farley threw open the car doors. Dion flung her armload into the back seat. They worked fast, scooping up anything in their path. Slips and underwear blew across the lawn. Pantyhose clung to the bushes.

Farley salvaged a soggy white nursing shoe from the neighbors' bushes. If Mrs. Piotrowski tossed it from the second- floor window, she thought, the bitch had one hell of an arm. Behind her, she heard Dion groan.

"Don't, Ma. Please…"

"Henry!" yelled Farley, as Mrs. Piotrowski hoisted a bundle of white nursing school uniforms and scrubs over the railing. Henry caught the bundle inches before he hit the ground, his elbows skidding on the cement walkway.

Henry slammed the trunk and hopped in the car. Dion and Farley slid over to make room for his long legs.

"Let's get out of here," he panted, reaching for the gearshift.

"Wait," said Dion, shivering and trying to catch her breath. "My school books…"

"Henry, find something to put on her feet," said Farley, her teeth clicking together as she opened the passenger door. "I'll get the books."

Henry looked down. Dion's bare feet were covered with blood.

"Mrs. Piotrowski, we need the nursing books!" screamed Farley, pounding on the front door with her frozen hands.

Dion rolled down the car window. "And my notebooks, next to the nightstand!"

"And the notebooks next to the nightstand!" cried Farley, adding steady kicking to the mix. "I'm a big girl Mrs. Piotrowski. I can keep this up all night!"

Books flew from the second-floor window.

Tires screeched as Henry finally pulled away from the house. They rode in stunned silence. After a while, Dion rested her head on Farley's shoulder.

Farley sighed. "I guess that answers the age-old question of 'Whatever Happened to Baby Jane.'"

Dion played with her straw. "Anyway, the pregnancy was a false alarm."

After buying bandages for Dion's feet, Henry had driven straight to Primanti Brothers, famous for their oversized deli sandwiches and late night hours.

"It's funny," she said, wiping her tear-stained eyes. "All I ever wanted to do was be a good nurse. That, and knock somebody's socks off. Now I don't know if I'll ever do either."

"You're going to be a terrific nurse," said Henry.

"That's right." Farley reached for his pickle. "And you can knock your own socks off."

Henry scraped his chair back. "I should probably give Claire and Veda Marie a heads-up."

The girls watched him weave his way across the crowded restaurant.

"What if they don't want a new border?" asked Dion.

"They'll be thrilled." Farley didn't mention that Claire would also be glad for the extra income. She reached for Dion's hand. "Listen, I feel really bad about what happened between us. I should have kept my mouth shut. I had no right…"

"You had every right. You're my friend."

Farley checked to be sure Henry was well out of earshot. "You know how you said I don't see what's in front of my face?"

Dion flinched. "Sorry about that. Not one of my finer moments."

"But you were right. I've been thinking about it ever since." She rubbed her eyes. "In fact it's all I seem to think about anymore – I haven't slept in weeks. I know how Henry feels about me. I feel the same way. I've probably always loved him; I just didn't want to admit it to myself."

"Why not?"

"Because I won't be here much longer. I'd say a year at the most. That's not exactly conducive to a long-term relationship. It wouldn't be fair to Henry – or to myself – to start something that is doomed from the start."

Dion sucked on her straw. "Any chance you're getting a little ahead of yourself, hon?"

Joe dragged an old dresser up from the cellar. Claire and Veda Marie made up the extra bed in Farley's room.

"What kind of a mother turns a daughter out into the world like that?" said Veda Marie, reaching to answer the phone on Farley's nightstand. "Hello? Bridge Manor."

She glanced at Claire.

"No, Mrs. Sullivan *cannot* come to the phone. What's the matter with you that you can't take a hint? Mrs. Sullivan might be too polite to say this, but I'm not. She is not interested in you."

"Give me that," said Claire, yanking the phone from Veda Marie's hand. "Hello? This is Mrs. Sullivan... Yes, I should be able to pay you soon...I'm working something out with my bank...That's right; you'll be the first to know...Goodbye."

"You mean the man with the unfortunate neck isn't trying to win you over?"

"If he is, he's certainly going about it the wrong way. He's a bill collector."

It Burns a Lovely Light

Chapter 29

After intense deliberation Claire decided the Christmas tree should go in the library. Joe and Ryan dragged in the giant fir and set it up in the corner. September, Farley, and Henry unpacked ornaments and hung them on the tree, while Claire directed from her armchair.

"Isn't that always the way," she said, purposely loud enough to be heard two rooms over. "Everyone loves a Christmas tree, but no one wants to take the time to decorate it."

Veda Marie's voice rang out from the drawing room. "Claire Sullivan, that's not fair and you know it! William, Dion and I are in here slaving away on the gingerbread house. One of our walls is treacherously close to caving in and the sugar plums won't stick to the roof."

"And they're watching their soaps," said September.

"I heard that!" yelled Veda Marie, winking at William.

On the flickering television screen, Erica looked thoughtfully at her daughter. *'You look familiar. Don't I know you?'*

"It's about time Erica recovered from her amnesia," said William.

He loved the soaps almost as much as Veda Marie did. The stories dragged along, which gave him time to understand what was going on, and the characters were constantly coming down with strange, exotic diseases. And he loved the way supposedly dead characters constantly returned – through outlandish schemes, tragic hospital mix-ups, or as an evil twin.

Veda Marie pulled her chair closer to the television. "Watch yourself, Erica. That fur collar can't help you now."

"Don't you worry about Erica Kane," said Dion. "She's had more husbands than I've had boyfriends. The girl can take care of herself."

"Is Erica related to Billie Kane?" asked William.

"Somewhere down the line, she must be."

The Christmas tree stood against a background of leather-bound books in floor-to-ceiling bookshelves. Rich with silver icing and colorful ornaments, the effect was magnificent.

"Hold on," said Claire, getting up from her seat in a worn leather library chair. She had a shiny red and silver metal star in her hand. "We almost forgot the most important ornament."

Henry positioned the ladder and nodded to Farley.

"I'll hold it while you climb."

Farley hesitated, then decided she was being silly. It's just a ladder, she told herself. Held by Henry, at that. She climbed.

"Careful," said Claire, standing at the base of the tree.

Nearing the top, Farley experienced a familiar feeling of unsteadiness. She squeezed her eyes shut.

Don't worry, I won't let go.

As she stepped onto the next rung, her foot slipped. She grabbed onto a row of books to steady herself, knocking some of the books off the shelf. Claire threw her arms up as heavy books pounded her head and back.

Farley scrambled down the ladder as Henry steadied Claire. "Are you all right?"

"Don't be silly," said Claire, her voice shaking. "It'll take more than some dusty old books to hurt this body." She gasped as September began stacking the fallen books in a pile. "Be careful with those. They're extremely valuable."

Picking up J.R.R. Tolkein's *The Hobbit* with illustrations of trees and snow-covered mountains, Claire ran her hand over the faded dust jacket. "This was your grandfather's dream acquisition, Farley. Tolkien designed and illustrated the dust jacket himself." She opened the cover. "See that tiny inkblot? The name 'Dodgeson' was misspelled in the first issue. After the publisher discovered his mistake, he personally corrected each book by hand. There are only few copies left containing his corrections."

"How did Grandfather end up with the book?" asked Farley.

"It's not hard to find a first edition of *The Hobbit* if you know where to look. Finding a first edition with the original dust jacket is much more difficult. There were copies for sale in the high auction houses in London and New York, but the cost was too dear. Our only hope was to come across it at an estate sale or at a used bookstore."

"He found this in a used bookstore?"

"No, I did."

Ten-year-old Claire had found *The Hobbit* in a box marked "discounted" in The Novel Hovel. It wore the dingy brown cover of another book, but underneath was the original dust jacket.

"I yelled, announcing my find," said Claire, her eyes shining. "I'll never forget the way Father scooped me off the ground and hugged me."

Unfortunately, the owner of The Novel Hovel had also heard Claire's vivacious hollering. By the time they brought the book to the cash register, Mr. Franco had adjusted the price upwards to somewhere in the area of a small fortune.

"But that's not fair," said Farley.

September shook her head. "You must have been crushed."

"I fell apart, right there in the store. It was all my fault. Father kept saying it didn't matter anyway, the fun was in the hunt. But I couldn't stop crying. Finally, he put the book in my hands. He told me not to let go of it; he'd be right back. He returned - with what we later found out was most of his life's savings - and paid Mr. Franco for the book."

Bumping along in the back of the streetcar, Claire took the crumpled notice out of her purse and read it again:

"Per our agreement, your interest rate of 11.9% is increased to 24%. In addition, there is a penalty fee of $985.75 for late payment."

There must be some mistake. She had made her payments on time – but they kept increasing the amount due, and then fining her for late payment and adding a penalty increase to the interest rate.

How was she supposed to pay this off, if they kept jacking everything up? A squirrel ran in front of the streetcar. He almost made it across the street and then zigzagged back. Claire closed her eyes.

"We want to talk to you."

Letting the door swing shut behind her, Claire looked from Farley to Veda Marie. She put her purse on the kitchen table and lowered herself into a chair.

"Something's going on with you," said Farley.

Claire started to shake her head.

"Don't bother contradicting us," Veda Marie piped in. "We've had it up to hear with your tomfoolery."

Claire put her elbows on the table and rubbed her temples. "I'm tired, that's all."

"That's because you haven't slept through the night for weeks. We hear you up at all hours, wandering around the house like a miserable ghost."

"At least I'm not hitting the refrigerator," said Claire, going for a little levity.

"That's another thing," said Farley. "You've lost weight."

"Not the good kind, either," added Veda Marie. "You've lost the kind that peels off overnight from a heavy load sitting on your shoulders. The kind that leaves you with nowhere to hide." She leaned in. "And you're not fooling anyone with these library meetings, missy. No offense Claire, but you haven't been a librarian for Lord knows how many years."

Claire huffed at that one.

"*Some people* happen to value my opinion," she said.

Veda Marie folded her arms. "Claire Sullivan, do you think this is the first day I met you?"

She closed her eyes. She was so tired. Almost beyond-caring tired.

"I owe a little more money than I thought."

"To whom?"

"Lowe & Son's."

"The company that did all those repairs for us?"

Claire nodded. "I don't know what happened; the bills got away from me. I just came from a meeting with Lowe & Son's. I was hoping we could restructure our payment plan, maybe extend it out a bit…but they weren't interested. But on my way out of the office, the receptionist pulled me aside and said I should give this company a call."

She slid a green business card across the table.

The Pilgrim Group
Low Interest Loans
For minority and female-owned businesses.

"I told her I've already been turned down by The Second Savings and Loan, but she said this company was less stringent. She said they were making a name for themselves helping small businesses."

"I don't like the sound of this," said Veda Marie. "We should talk to Ham."

"Ham's got enough on his plate." Claire picked up the card. "I'll call this lender first thing in the morning."

"What if they can't help us?" said Farley.

"We'll still be all right. As a cushion, I've decided to sell *The Hobbit*."

Claire woke from a full night's sleep feeling better than she had in a long time. Opening a large can of ground coffee, she took a whiff of the lovely rich aroma. She giggled. When was the last time she had stopped to smell the coffee? She giggled again as she pictured how silly she must look, grinning into a can of Maxwell House.

To the aroma of brewing coffee, she emptied the dishwasher: plates in the cabinet, pots and pans in the pantry, Veda Marie's ashtray on the fireplace. That was when she saw the beautiful wildflowers on the mantle. Next to the flowers was an envelope containing two hundred dollars in cash and a note:

To my wonderful Bridge Manor family,
I woke this morning and knew it was time for me to seek my next adventure. Oh, I will miss you! I love you all.
September Rose
PS. This is two extra months' rent.
PSS. Lucky the person who moves into Bridge Manor!

As she re-read the note, a sense of profound sadness washed over Claire. September had been such a bright, shining light in the house; she would be dearly missed.

The residents of Bridge Manor lingered at breakfast, trading stories of their beautiful September. It was late morning before Claire remembered her decision to sell *The Hobbit*. She flipped on the light in the library and opened the glass cabinet, then searched the shelves. *The Hobbit*, along with a number of other valuable books, was gone.

"Think about it, Claire," said Ryan. He leaned against the kitchen counter as she washed the dinner dishes. "What do we really know about September Rose? That's not even her real name."

"A thief does not leave money for two extra month's rent. Or write a loving goodbye note."

"Probably just to throw you off her scent."

"September's not built that way, Ryan," said Veda Marie, wiping down the table. "That girl is the very definition of love."

He let out an exasperated sigh. "I know how much you cared for her. We all did. But look at the facts: You told her about your valuable collection. Now she's gone. The books are gone. Face it; the girl wormed her way in here with her love beads and voodoo chants and carted off a fortune."

Chapter 30

"And finally," said Henry, wrapping up the staff meeting, "once Christmas is behind us we can start clearing out the back dining room and setting up for the Carter and Wilder New Year's party."

"Not Billie Kane again." Colette groaned. "That woman has no heart inside her chest."

"It's not Billie's party," said Henry. "It's a party for the *company* she works for."

Farley checked her watch as she pulled on her coat. "I have to go. Resa asked me to meet Eileen's bus. She had to stay after school for detention."

"Ahhh, detention. Takes you back, doesn't it?" Closing her notebook, Dion stretched. "What's she in for?"

"She punched a boy in the neck."

"Ouch."

"She's been getting into a lot of trouble lately. Ham hired Resa to make sure she's never home alone."

"We're finished here." Henry tossed his notes on the counter. "Want some company?"

"Sure." Farley slapped her hands together. "Hang on! I almost forgot. Christmas Eve falls on our day off this year. Veda Marie and Claire are planning an oyster roast, and they insist we're not allowed to lift a finger."

She pointed to Colette. "And I'm supposed to remind you that you're welcome to bring a guest. Which we all know is Veda Marie-speak for 'why in God's name are you still not attached?'"

Colette laughed. "Tell her it will be just me."

Eileen marched up the sidewalk, fists balled at her sides, head down, and curls flying from the hood of her black parka. With a start, Farley realized Eileen was becoming a young woman.

"Honey," she said, "what happened?"

Fury elevated Eileen's voice almost to a scream. "Sister Mary Ignatius made me get up in assembly and apologize to the dick-wad I hit *in front of the whole school*!"

Never underestimate the power of shame, thought Farley as she wrapped her arms around Eileen.

"Do you want Farley to teach Sister Monster Ignatius a lesson?" said Henry.

Eileen wiped a large snot-ball from her nose.

"Maybe next time."

Pulling the bottom of his tee shirt from under his jacket, baring his – Farley couldn't help but notice – impressively tight stomach, he placed his shirt under Eileen's nose.

"Blow."

"Gross, Henry. I'm old enough to wipe my own…"

"Blow."

She blew, twice.

"I'm impressed," said Farley. "There was a time you would have passed out cold if someone blew their nose on your shirt."

"That's not true."

"Oh, how quickly we forget shrimp-and-grits night."

Henry bumped Farley's shoulder with his. "It's different when it's someone you love."

Colorful baskets surrounded the tall Christmas tree; one basket for each person present. Everyone had been asked to contribute one dozen of any item of their choice. The result was a vibrant bounty: warm socks, gloves, a book, tiny ornaments made of shells, dried herbs, canned produce, and an envelope which read, in William's shaky handwriting:

Merry Christmas
From me to you.
A ticket in the cheap seats
to see
Those nice boys from Pittsburgh!
My treat.
With a myriad of love in my heart,
William Justus James.

Through her camera lens, Farley drank in the ambience of Christmas at Bridge Manor: the music and laughter, the gentle crunch of tissue paper, and the piney smell of the tree. In no time at all, she had gone through three rolls of film.

Paddy and Ryan were in charge of the bonfire. Chanting *'Men, Men, Men, Men, Men,'* they dug a pit in the center of the lawn, gathered firewood from the woods, placed large rocks in a circle around the pit and lit the fire. While the rest of the party set up for dinner, they monitored the flames and congratulated each other on such a splendid, manly fire.

Farley approached with a bucketful of cold beer. "Anyone thirsty?"

"Maybe just a splash to wash the dust from my throat," said Paddy. Pulling a beer out of the bucket, he tilted his head toward Ryan's yellow Mustang convertible. "That's another nice car you've got there, Father."

"I like to trade them in every few years." Ryan took a beer from Farley. "Cost me an arm and a leg, if you want to know the truth."

"How do you keep it so clean in this weather?"

"Altar boys," said Ryan, chuckling. "So, I hear your mill is still hanging in there. That's saying a lot these days."

Paddy shook his head. "Imported steel is so much cheaper than our American made. I'll tell you, Father, I don't know how much longer we can…"

"Hold that thought." Ryan turned and yelled across the lawn. "Joe! Do you have a date for New Year's?"

Joe leaned away from the smoky grill where he was roasting oysters. "I'm taking Sylvia to a party."

"How'd you like to take the Mustang?"

"Are you kidding?"

Ryan elbowed Paddy. "We're only young once, right?"

Laughter and chatter filled the air as they dined on oysters, hot beef stew, salad, and several giant loaves of bread. As the evening began to wind down, everyone moved to the bonfire. Benches and chairs had been set up around the fire, with blankets draped over the back of each chair.

"I want to sing a Christmas song," said William. "I know all the words…at least to the first part."

Fiddling with the hem of his cloak that he wore over his parka, he closed his eyes and proceeded to mutilate the first four lines of John Prine's *Christmas in Prison.*

Claire soaked in the laughter, shouting and singing as song after song was torn to shreds. She released a long, satisfied sigh. A sense of peace seemed to have settled upon Bridge Manor. If only for one night, they were all safe and healthy and happy. Nothing could touch them.

Paddy kicked the achy-ness out of his knees. He leaned down and kissed the top of Claire's head.

"Thank you for a wonderful Christmas, love."

"You're leaving?"

He cleared his throat. Wrapped in an old faded quilt with the fire's glow on her cheeks, his darling girl had never looked more beautiful.

"I thought I might pop into Mick's and exchange a few lies."

Dion applauded as William took another bow.

"Bravo!" she cried.

"Thank you." He struggled to hide his yawn by clenching his jaw, contorting his face into a comical strain.

"Come over here, you little nut." Dion held out a small envelope containing a gift certificate to Rosemary's Market. "This should keep you in ice cream for a while. It's a 'thank you' for helping me catch up in school. I couldn't have brought my grades up without your help."

"Yes, you could have," he said, this time letting a yawn rip. "You learn fast for a normal person."

Henry let his arm rest on the back of Farley's chair.

"I think it's time for *someone* to go to bed," he whispered.

Clearly he was talking about William. Still, Farley blushed like a schoolgirl. *Grow up,* she told herself.

(243)

"Come on, William." Claire folded her blanket across her arm. "I'll tuck you in."

Ryan stood. "I'm with you. I've got an early day tomorrow."

As they walked up the lawn, Resa zipped past them, wearing only a towel and a smile.

"Holy cannoli!" she yelled. "It's freezing!"

Ryan's jaw dropped.

"Calm down," said Claire. "We had an outdoor shower installed."

"What kind of a fool has an outdoor shower in a place like Pittsburgh?"

"This kind, I guess. The pipes are insulated. Everyone loves it, from Mr. Winston on down. Farley swears that nothing is better than bathing outdoors in the altogether." She elbowed her brother. "One of these days I might even get up the nerve to use it."

He winced. "Don't be disgusting."

Still seated by the fire, Mr. Winston put his gloved hand on Dion's arm. "How do you like your new home, my dear?"

Dion replied without missing a beat. "I feel more at home in Bridge Manor than I ever did in the house I grew up in."

Leaning back, he closed his eyes and let the fire warm his face. "Yes, I've found that Bridge Manor works wonders on the soul."

"Meet me in the library," said Henry. "There's a little something for you under the tree."

Farley's eyes twinkled. "I thought we were only supposed to give 'group gifts.'"

"I broke the rules."

"*You* broke the rules?" she said, her voice not betraying the pounding in her heart. "Now that you mention it, there might be a little something under the tree for you, too."

The library was lit only by the twinkling lights of the giant evergreen. From one of the trees high branches, Farley removed a white handkerchief tied with a thin gold bow and held it out to Henry. "You first."

He kept his eyes on her as he unwrapped his gift; a shiny silver Saint Lawrence medal.

"Saint Lawrence is the patron saint of cooks," said Farley. "He's a martyr. His torturers laid him across a grill to burn him alive. After a while he said, 'Turn me over, I'm done on this side.'"

Henry laughed, all white teeth and dimples. When he hugged her, she breathed in his spicy-clean-Henry-scent.

"Now you. Close your eyes." He reached under the tree, then placed something solid in her hands. "Open."

She stared down at the four shiny green leaves exploding from the rich dark soil.

"A lemon tree," she whispered.

"I pushed the seed into the soil last summer. I've been keeping it in the window of my apartment." He hesitated. "I wasn't sure…I hope you don't mind."

Pinching off a leaf, she crushed it between her fingers and breathed in its lemony aroma. She touched his face. His lips.

His kiss tasted like all the happiness in the world.

Farley woke to find William's face two inches from hers.

"I did it!" he cried, jumping back. "I woke with my forceful stare!"

"Leave me alone," she groaned. "I'm exhausted."

"How come you weren't here when I woke up?"

"I went to a sleepover."

"On *Christmas Eve?*"

"It was a Christmas Eve sleepover."

William pushed his glasses up. "How come Henry drove you home?"

"The sleepover was at his apartment."

Farley listened to William's shoes pound down the back stairs. *Henry.* She smiled, blushing as she pulled the covers up around her neck. They had made love as if they were starving. Henry was everything she had imagined and more; tender, loving, forceful, vulnerable. The way he whispered to her…touched her. The way he kept the lights on because he wanted to see all of her. She loved that he took his time, kissing and stroking and tasting. She loved him.

Farley shuffled into the kitchen, her hair forming a cliff on the side of her head. "Morning."

Claire covered the leftover turkey. "*Afternoon.*"

"Come over here," said Veda Marie, feeling Farley's forehead. "Are you all right? You haven't slept this late in years."

"Farley's exhausted," said William. "She had a sleepover at Henry's last night!"

Dion popped another beer and sipped the foam as she stared out over the windshield. The music from the radio was so loud, she didn't hear the knock on the window until it turned to banging. She resisted the urge to check herself in the rearview mirror and unrolled her window.

"Oh, it's you."

"Happy New Year to you, too," said Farley. "Let me in."

Dion unlocked the door and moved over to the passenger seat. Farley slid into the driver's seat.

"I guess Henry sent you to get his van back," said Dion.

"That's not it at all. We were worried about you."

"How did you know where to find me?"

Farley nodded toward Duncan's apartment. "Lucky guess. What are you doing?"

Dion took a long swig of her beer, then subdued a belch. "What does it look like I'm doing? I'm hanging around my ex-boyfriend's apartment on New Year's Eve." She opened her coat to reveal a red silk slip. "In my nightie. I was hoping to release my inner naughty on him. Pretty pathetic, huh?"

Farley wiped the condensation off the window. "Have you been here all night?"

"No. I went by my parent's house. Dad wasn't there; Ma said he moved to the night shift."

"You visited your mother in your slip?"

"I was decent at the time. Not that it mattered; she wouldn't let me in."

"I'm sorry."

Dion chuckled. "You should hear the stuff she said about Bridge Manor. Apparently she knows what goes on in our 'peccadillo nest.' All our wild parties and drug-crazed bonfire rituals and people – get this - having sex all over the place."

"The gig is up, then. No more fun times for us."

Dion drew a sloppy heart on the passenger window with her index finger. "Then I went to my Grandma's old house."

"You drove all the way to Washington County?"

"Her house isn't there anymore. Just a row of perfect little townhouses where my Grandma used to live. Remember that summer we stayed at her house and snuck out in the middle of the night?"

"God, yes. We must have walked for miles, all so I could see where *The Night of the Living Dead* was filmed. What a good sport you were."

"Of course. You were my best friend." She yawned. "You still are."

Farley started the car and pulled out into the road. For some reason her mind flashed back to Loretta, her fourth grade best friend, back when life went on forever and friendships were disposable.

"You're the only childhood friend I've ever managed to keep," she said. "You and Henry."

"You and Henry are perfect together," murmured Dion.

We sure are, thought Farley. Now I'm the one who's scared to death.

Chapter 31

"Bye, Mrs. Young," mumbled William, on his way out of the ice rink.

As usual the manager – a cranky woman with a brown cavity on her front tooth - said nothing.

"William, over here!" called Mr. Winston.

He waved his walking stick from across the parking lot.

William ran across the lot, his breath visible in the cold January air. "What are you doing here?"

"I felt like getting some fresh air."

"You walked all this way?"

"Don't act so surprised," said Mr. Winston. "There's still a little life in this body. Joe mentioned he was leaving practice early to meet with his advisor. I thought you might want some company."

"It's not dark outside," William mumbled as he walked alongside Mr. Winston. "I can walk all by myself."

"I hear you've been a big help to Joe at hockey practice."

William clicked his tongue. He loved his responsibilities: handing out water, picking up empty cups and towels off the floor, and blowing his whistle loud and clear to make sure everyone was off the ice when the Zamboni driver came on.

He got a thrill each time he put on his jersey with 'P-A-L' printed on the back. But most of all, William loved being one of the guys. And yesterday he ruined it. He accidentally offended not just *one* of the guys, but *the* guy: Peter Gaglio.

It all started when Sylvia stopped by the rink, her face all splotchy and red. When William suggested she might want to be tested for allergies she didn't even respond. She pretended to watch practice from the stands but he could tell she wasn't interested in the drills. And Joe acted funny, staring at his clipboard and hardly yelling at anybody.

After showers the guys tossed their blobs of sopping wet towels onto the floor. William was busy scooping up the blobs when Joe called him over.

"I need to talk to Sylvia," he said, untying his skates. "Wait for me in my office when you finish up in here."

"Okay. I figured out what's the matter with her."

Joe narrowed his eyes. "What did you hear?"

"Nothing. She's constricting her respiratory system. Her sweater is way too tight."

"Ha!" Peter Gaglio spread his legs and grabbed his crotch. "We know what's on your mind, piggy-pal-pal."

William had been elated. He didn't even care that Peter got the nickname wrong. Peter Gaglio never, ever, ever, *ever* talked to him! In fact, he usually acted like he was mad at William, even though William went out of his way to be nice.

"That's enough, Gaglio," said Joe. He put his blade guards on and stuffed his skates into his sports bag.

"It's all right, Peter," said William, nodding encouragement. "Masturbation is good for you."

The locker room exploded in peals of screaming laughter.

William had no idea what was so funny, but he laughed, too. He tried to think of what else he had read on the subject of masturbation. He held up a finger and shouted over the racket, "Although, a preoccupation with your penis can be an indication of penis envy!"

Peter Gaglio ignored the whistles, laughter and hand-slapping. He yanked on his pants, tossed the rest of his gear in his bag, and stormed out of the locker room.

William stood on the team bench and looked around for Joe and Sylvia. Other than a few well-placed safety lights, the rink was dark. Spotting them in the shadows near the side exit, he started across the ice. Aware that a slip on the ice could be incapacitating, he slid his feet in small increments and concentrated on keeping his balance.

As he neared the other side he lifted his head, prepared to remind Joe of the time. But something about the way Joe and Sylvia's dark silhouettes were so close to each other made him stop. Joe's shadow-hand wiped Sylvia's shadow-face. They hugged, two giant hand puppets moving to the rhythm of William's heartbeat. His penis strained so hard he worried his zipper would burst.

On the walk home, Joe explained why William's mention of masturbation and penis envy had embarrassed Peter.

"I didn't mean to make him feel bad," said William.

"I wouldn't give it another thought."

That evening, William approached Veda Marie about making a special treat for Peter.

"I did something I regret," he said. "I want to tell him I'm sorry."

Veda Marie smiled. "It takes a big man to apologize. What did you have in mind?"

William rubbed his hands together, his face flushed. "A peanut butter and marshmallow and barbequed potato chip sandwich."

"Chips *inside* the sandwich?"

"Yes." He bobbed up and down on the balls of his feet. "And some of your extra chewy nutty brownies!"

Veda Marie recruited Claire to help her make brownies.

"What kind of regrets could a boy like William have?" asked Claire, dipping her finger into the rich chocolate batter.

"Not a soul alive who can honestly say they don't have regrets."

As it turned out, Peter Gaglio did not return to the ice for five weeks. Having learned that his older brother Tony had finally made parole over at Eastern State Penitentiary, Peter had decided that the Gaglio brothers were due for some much-needed bonding. First he sprung his youngest brother, Rocco, from his foster home. Then - in preparation for a right and proper welcome home get-together - Peter and Rocco knocked off a liquor store, a photo booth, and a Kentucky Fried Chicken.

Reunited, the three brothers warmed themselves around a fire pit out behind the old glass factory, catching up as they washed down the chicken with Jim Beam. They laughed their asses off, reminiscing as brothers do. The time dad kicked the shit out of Rocco for being wasted on the lawn when the school bus pulled up. How about when mom leveled a gun at dad's nuts while he slept off a bender?

And who could forget the look on dad's face as he knocked tony's lights out for feeding a kitten to the dogs next door? And he had the wrong kid the whole time; it was Peter who did it! Too funny.

The Gaglio brothers embarked on a brutal, month-long celebration, during which Rocco lost his virginity, Tony lost a shitload of brain cells, and Peter lost one of his front teeth. Fuckin' a. The boys were back in town.

Veda Marie sprinkled potato chips on the marshmallow cream. She had to hand it to William; the concoction was a tasty one. She and Mr. Winston had gotten in the habit of splitting one for lunch.

"Joe, I don't mind making these sandwiches day after day. They don't go to waste. But is that Gaglio boy ever coming back?"

"He's supposed to be at practice today. Apparently he's had some family problems." He took a bite of sausage, exhaling through his open mouth to let the heat out. "I kind of hope he doesn't show. There's something really bad about Gaglio. He creeps me out."

On a bench in the locker room, William listened in on Joe and Peter's discussion about responsibility and trust and being a team player and what the hell happened to Peter's tooth. Peter gave Joe one word answers and grunted a lot.

By the time Peter emerged from the showers the locker room was empty. William waited until Peter's clothes were on before approaching him, then he stepped forward and put out his hand to shake like a man. Ignoring William and his outstretched hand, Peter sat on the bench to tie his shoes.

William clicked his tongue as he held up the paper bag.

"This is for you" he said. "I feel bad about what I said about you-know-what. I regret my words."

Peter stared at William, then at the bag. Clearing his throat, he spit a tight, thick lugie onto William's crotch. William opened his mouth to speak but nothing came out. He put his shaking hands on his hips and gnawed on the inside of his mouth. Brown mucus slid down his corduroys.

Standing, Peter raised a hairy index finger and poked William in the chest. Hard. Stunned, William dropped his paper bag and took a step back. Peter followed, standing uncomfortably close.

"You're a queer little fuck, aren't you?" said Peter, sliding his tongue in and out of the new hole in his mouth. He wriggled his fingers. "A queer piggy, prancing around in a faggot cape."

William stood, frozen. He wanted to run and hide, but his legs wouldn't move.

Peter poked him again and then spoke in a babyish voice. "Aww, what's the matter, fuck-face? Am I hurting the little piggy?"

"All right, William. I know how much you love that jersey," said Veda Marie. "But it's going to rot right off your body if we don't wash it. Hands up, high."

Reluctantly, William raised his hands over his head. Veda Marie pulled his coaching jersey off and stared in horror at the purple bruises and angry welts covering his chest. William hung his head, ashamed.

Dion's voice was calm. "We'll need to put some ice on these." She gently tilted William's chin. "Corn or peas, hon?"

"Peas," said William, trembling.

"Veda Marie, would you please bring us some bags of frozen peas?"

Farley knelt beside William and took his hand in hers. "Who did this to you, kiddo?"

Joe's fist connected dead-on with Peter's nose, spraying blood across the row of lockers. Peter grinned, blood and spittle dribbling down his beard. He spit twice, checking for more lost teeth.

"I take it the little piggy squealed."

"If he had, you'd be in jail right now," said Farley, gasping as she tried to catch her breath.

Her clothes were drenched in sweat and her left ankle was pouring blood from her misguided attempt to clear a wire fence. She had seen Joe tear off in the car and knew instinctively where he was going - and so she ran.

Joe kicked Peter's hockey bag.

"Get your stuff and get out," he said, his jaw tight. "And don't expect to play hockey in this city again."

Peter used the back of his hand to wipe a smear of bloody snot across his face. "You gotta be shittin' me."

Joe didn't reply.

"For what? Giving pussy-boy a few pokes?" He smirked and winked at Farley. A bubble of blood squirted through his tooth-hole. "Tell you the truth, I think he liked it."

Farley slammed her knee into his crotch. Peter went down. He lay on the locker room tiles, his beard mottled with blood, his face contorted with pain and rage.

"You shouldn't a done that, sweetheart," he gasped.

Peter fumed in the darkened showers, gathering up his strength. Fuck this, he thought. Who needs fucking hockey, anyway? He had better things to do with his time. No more grueling practices and tight-ass coaches. No more body-distorting muscle cramps and mind-warping head-aches. Still. He knew this was the end of the easy, 'come-fuck-me' girls waiting for him after the game. The end of the other guys looking up to him. No more crowds scream-ing *'There goes Gaglio! Gaglio!'*

He buried his head in his hands.

"Shower's over, Gaglio!" the security guard yelled. "You're outta here, now!"

William closed the door to his bedroom. He unbut-toned his happiness cloak and folded it just so. He pulled his other cloaks out of his drawer and placed them all in the back of his closet, in a box underneath his old *Operation* game.

Chapter 32

The icy winter gave way to the gentle thaw of spring, bringing a sense of sanguinity and a 'fresh start' feeling to the residents of Bridge Manor. After enrolling in a Photo Criticism workshop at the Art Institute of Pittsburgh, a local magazine picked up one of Farley's projects: a black-and-white series combining the new, sleek architecture of the city with the desolation of the empty mills and factories.

Now the official timer for Joe's Frosty Devils, William wore his shiny stopwatch proudly around his neck. The team recovered from Gaglio's dismissal and made it all the way to the semifinals. They lost in a heartbreaking last-second shot through the goalie's legs. Joe was already stepping up the team's training plans for the off-season.

Dion had decided to abstain from men for a while – how long 'a while' was not specified; she was taking more of a 'one day at a time' approach. She spent many long hours studying with William and was rewarded with all A's on her exams. Encouraged, she applied for and received a generous grant toward next year's tuition.

Henry's restaurant continued to prosper; the number of repeat customers increased monthly. Freeman's canned produce turned out to be Henry's pot of gold. The preserved tomatoes, peppers, and other vegetables had become hot items, not only in the restaurant, but in two local supermarkets, as well.

Things weren't quite as peachy for the Kane family. Ham made a life-changing decision. He informed his company and his wife – in that order – of his plans to leave the firm and start up a non-profit aimed at providing legal aid to people in the city's lower socioeconomic levels. His partners and co-workers wished him all the best and told him they were proud. Billie said she wished she had never married him and told him to go straight to hell.

Eileen was now used to waking up to her father and Billie fighting. As a kid it had been easier to ignore. She would put her pillow over her head and pull her blanket over the pillow, tucking the edges under to make a fort. If she stayed in her fort too long it made her dizzy, but it wasn't a bad feeling. She would hum over the yelling and pretend she was somewhere else. Sometimes she pretended up an older brother to watch out for her. He would be like William, except his name would be Jeremiah. Or Cody. They would live with their drop dead handsome widowed father who adored them and couldn't get enough of them. He even let them stay home from school now and then, just for kicks. Sometimes she threw in some popular friends who looked up to her and were secretly jealous of her. In her cool bedroom with beanbag chairs and a lava lamp and a set of bunk beds, she and her friends would stay up all night telling secrets and eating pepperoni pizza and making prank phone calls to all the stuck-up bitches in her school.

But that was when she was younger. She didn't pretend anymore.

Mrs. Piotrowski was grateful Father Ryan would not be able to see the paper doily she bobby pinned to her hair at the last minute. She had been unable to find her hat or scarf, or anything else suitable to cover her head. Not that it seemed to matter these days. She clicked her tongue.

Whatever happened to the old Catholic Church where mass was said in Latin, when a lady would never dream of entering the house of God without stockings on her legs and a lace mantilla covering her head?

The main chapel was empty except for an elderly custodian pushing his mop back and forth. The light above the confessional blinked; the tiny room was vacant. Mrs. Piotrowski stepped inside. The red bulb above her clicked on as she knelt on the padded kneeler. The screen in the partition slid open and she squinted, trying to make out the outline of his slender body. She made the sign of the cross with her white gloved hand. She no longer kissed her thumb at the end. Only the Latinos did that anymore.

"Bless me, Father, for I have sinned. It's been one week since my last confession."

"Go on, my child."

My child. She shivered. Those words alone kept her coming back week after week. Leaning forward until her lips ever-so-lightly brushed the screen, Mrs. Piotrowski whispered her sins of the past week; omitting the small detail of her inclination to fantasize about the good Father. To embarrass this virtuous man would be a far greater sin than the fact that she allowed her imagination to run a little riot now and then.

As she prayed her penance of two Hail Mary's and an Act of Contrition, she kept a careful eye on the custodian. He was humming. Eyes closed, his hips pulsated rhythmically toward the broom as if he were dancing. Jesus, Mary and Joseph. She would report him.

While Mrs. Piotrowski glowered at the poor custodian, Eileen slouched down the aisle and into the confessional.

"Bless me Father, for I have sinned. It has been," she paused, "five months since my last confession."

"Welcome back, my child."

"Thank you, Father. Good to be back."

Deciding to let the girl's overly familiar tone go, he tried to wait patiently for the girl to begin; a feat made painfully difficult by the two bottles of red he'd drunk last night. His temple throbbed and he had a mad craving for something greasy and salty.

"I took more things that don't belong to me."

"Why?"

"It makes me feel better. Not the *stealing* part, but the *having* part."

"What do you think it is that you're trying to feel better about? Is something making you unhappy?"

Eileen's eyes welled up, but she didn't respond. Billie – and the fact that she didn't get struck dead by a speeding truck or a bolt of lightning – made her unhappy.

Sin free again, Eileen hopped on her bicycle and tore across the square. She smiled, relishing the unsoiled feeling in her heart. Whoever came up with confession deserves a medal.

Farley thumped down the back stairs and into the kitchen. "Are you busy?"

"I'm supposed to be studying," said Dion, spreading her books out on the table. "So naturally, I made a big breakfast, emptied the dishwasher, re-arranged my make-up drawer and examined my pores. What's up?"

"I'm late for work. Can you give me a lift?"

"Sorry, Joe took the car. He drove Claire to a library club meeting."

Farley groaned inwardly. *Claire, what are you up to now?*

"She sure does have a lot of library meetings," said Dion. "Hey, maybe she's having an affair."

"Not our Claire. That would be *wrong*."

"What do you think they talk about in those meetings, anyway?"

"Don't know," said Farley. "Who is overdue, I guess."

"Thanks, hon." Claire shut the car door.

Joe leaned across the seat. "Are you sure you don't want me to wait for you?"

"It's a beautiful day; I'll take the streetcar to the square and walk home."

She waited until Joe's car was out of sight and then walked the four blocks to the loan office. She could have told him – along with everyone else in Bridge Manor – where she was going, but she didn't want to jinx herself until the deed was done.

The numbers on the panel illuminated as the elevator rose to the fourteenth floor. With each floor a weight seemed to lift off her shoulders. For the first time in too long, the sense of overwhelming panic – a panic that she had gotten used to – was gone. Her application for a loan had been accepted. This morning she would sign the papers.

The bell rang and the elevator doors slid open. Directly across the spacious hall were the heavy glass doors of The Pilgrim Group.

The receptionist pushed her intercom button. "Mrs. Sullivan is here, Mr. Johnson."

She stood and walked around her desk. "If you'll follow me, I'll take you to the conference room."

Claire's jaw dropped as she entered the room. Floor-to-ceiling windows revealed a gorgeous view of the U.S. Steel Tower. There must have been thirty chairs around the giant conference table. In the center of the long table was a polished silver pot of hot coffee, with matching silver sugar bowl and cream pitcher, a tray piled with muffins, bagels, and fruit, and a crystal pitcher of orange juice, which Claire had a feeling was fresh-squeezed.

The receptionist introduced her to Mr. Johnson and his assistant, Stephanie. Admiring Stephanie's impeccably-fitted black suit, Claire wished she had worn a better outfit.

Mr. Johnson, a large man with tiny bifocals, insisted they all have a bit of food and some hot coffee before getting down to brass tacks. Claire took a few self-conscious bites and exchanged small talk with Stephanie. Mr. Johnson opened his briefcase and removed the thick contract.

The meeting itself went quickly. Mr. Johnson flipped pages, occasionally pointing with his fancy pen, his gold cufflinks clanking on the polished conference table.

"Sign here."

At first Claire questioned each page before she signed, and listened carefully to each lengthy explanation. But after a few responses of 'it merely acknowledges that you are aware of what the contract states,' and 'it is all standard, Mrs. Sullivan, nothing to worry about,' she began to sign without question. She was grateful for Stephanie. Stephanie was kind; she knew how intimidating these contracts could be.

As if reading Claire's mind, Stephanie smiled at her. "Would you like Mr. Johnson to go through it again?"

Claire raised her chin. "No, that will not be necessary."

Chapter 33

Claire decided to tackle the seldom-used dining room as her summer project, and was actually looking forward to jumping in. The hardwood floor was already covered with two giant tarps, as September had been preparing to paint the room before she left. Claire knelt and ran her palm across the patched area along the base of the wall. *Smooth.* September had done a fine job. She jumped as the back door slammed.

"Claire?"

"Back here!"

She gasped as Paddy stepped into the room. His eyes were glassy, as if he had not slept in days. His skin was an odd shade of grey and his shoulders wore a deep slouch.

"What is it, Paddy?"

"We're closing the mill."

Standing, she wiped the dust off her dungarees and reached for his hand.

"Come on. Let's get out of here."

They took a back table at Mick's.

Claire held up her beer. "To Porter Steel."

"To Porter Steel."

Paddy took a long pull of his beer and set it down with a heavy sigh.

"The riverfront is littered with the shells of abandoned mills. Even so, I thought we would be the ones to survive." He gave Claire a weary smile. "Hard to believe an entire industry is gone."

Claire put her hand over his. "But it *is* gone, Paddy. We have to face it and move on."

"Move on to what, unemployment?"

"There are jobs out there."

"Jobs in technology and computers and things I know nothing about. Who will hire me? All I've ever known is the mill."

"Paddy's right; these are tough times," Veda Marie said, struggling to keep up with Claire. "If someone as good as September can steal, things must be bad."

Claire stepped up her pace as they moved along the waterfront. Over time, their walks had evolved into a daily half-hour pre-breakfast brisk run/walk – an invigorating way to start the day.

"You know as well as I do September didn't take those books," said Claire. "And even if she did - which she didn't - if she needed money that badly, she's welcome to it."

"You're right," said Veda Marie. "Our September Rose couldn't steal a kiss. Because then she'd have to worry about coming back as an ant, or a flea in her next life."

They walked in silence for a while. Up ahead an elderly couple sat on a bench, holding hands. The man smiled at the woman as a young groom might gaze into the eyes of his new bride.

"I'm not afraid to be old," said Veda Marie, after they passed the couple. "I'm afraid to be old *alone*. I'm afraid I'll envy everyone who has someone else to grow old with. I fear the envy. After envy, it's just a quick hop, skip, and a jump over to hate."

"Stop it. You could never hate."

"Still, I can't remember the last time someone looked at me that way."

Claire snorted. "Then you've got blinders on. Do you really believe Mr. Winston pulls his chair so close to yours because he likes the smell of secondhand smoke?"

"Listen to this," said Veda Marie, tapping her newspaper. "They're selling a 'bum jiggle machine' at the Armory yard sale."

Mr. Winston lifted his reading glasses. "I prefer not to know what a bum jiggle machine is."

Claire got up from the table to turn on the radio. Mornings were much livelier now that Mr. Winston was a regular attendee. At some point over the summer, their morning coffee/newspaper ritual had evolved into a competition to find the most interesting – and absurd– articles.

"I've got a winner," said Mr. Winston. "A woman in Oxford, Mississippi found Jesus in her Frito. She is offering her Jesus-Frito up for sale to the highest bidder."

Veda Marie made a face "That's crazy talk. Everyone knows Jesus Christ wouldn't be caught dead in processed food."

"And now," purred the velvety voice of the Golden Oldies DJ, "here's a timeless classic by the delightfully demure, forever pure Doris Day."

"Que Sera, Sera!
Whatever Will Be, Will Be!"

"I always felt sorry for Doris Day," said Mr. Winston. "No one can live up to the pressure of 'pure.'"

It occurred to Claire that Ryan would beg to differ. To him, Pauline was Doris Day pure.

"Hold everything, folks." Veda Marie rumpled her newspaper. "Mr. Winston, I'll see your Frito and raise you one." She read aloud from the article:

> Mrs. Edna Bowman has five children and
> eleven grandchildren, and she is a convict-
> ed criminal. For the past seven years, Mrs.
> Bowman has swindled department stores and
> supermarkets out of hundreds of thousands
> of dollars, all in the form of insurance settle-
> ments. Dropping a tomato, spilling some liq-
> uid, or scattering a few grapes, Mrs. Bowman
> would lay herself down on the floor and wait
> to be discovered. Eleven companies have so
> far been identified as victims of her fraudu-
> lent claims, exceeding $550,000 of settlement
> money for erroneous neck and back injury
> claims.

Veda Marie slammed the paper on the table. "Get a load of that one. The woman got five hundred and fifty thousand dollars *just for lying down*."

"Shame on her," said Claire.

"What if she really needed the money? I mean, who was hurt, really? I'm sure this was just a drop in the bucket for the insurance company."

"That may be true," said Mr. Winston. "But right is right, and wrong is wrong."

Outside a squirrel ran across the windowsill, then back the other way, its tiny feet sinking into the mud.

"Those damn squirrels can never make up their minds," said Veda Marie, the newspaper article forgotten.

Claire picked up the paper and read it again.

Five hundred and fifty thousand dollars just for lying down.

It Burns a Lovely Light

Chapter 34

Veda Marie changed the sheets on William's bed while Farley ran a dust mop across the hardwood floor. William was supposed to be dusting his furniture, but he had gotten distracted by a Mighty Mouse figurine.

"I can't believe it's almost fall," said Farley. "The seasons are flying by."

Veda Marie gave her a knowing look. "Time always flies for the happy, lovey."

Farley turned and mopped away from Veda Marie's high-flying eyebrows. She was happy; happier than she ever thought she'd be again, and it terrified her. One look at Henry - one *thought* about him - and her heart began to do jumping jacks. Never mind when he held her...kissed her...touched her.

"There's a John Wayne movie on TV tomorrow," said William.

"John Wayne." Veda Marie sighed, fluffing a pillow. "Now *there* is a man."

"Too bad his real name is 'Marion.'"

Veda Marie jokingly wagged her finger at him. "That is a vicious lie, and you know..." She stopped. "What is that over your eye?"

"What?" William felt his forehead.

"Come over here." She steered him under the light. "Lovey, you've got a bald spot in the middle of your eyebrow."

William ran to the bathroom mirror and stared, horrified.

"Trichotillomania," he whispered. "The repetitive self-removal of hair."

After Veda Marie filled in William's eyebrow with her Maybelline charcoal black eyebrow pencil Farley tucked him into bed. Alone in the dark, he rubbed his palm with the binding of his blanket and stared at nothing.

"The man of steel takes a mighty leap and soars through the air," he whispered. "Leaving behind mean old Peter Gaglio, who gets tinier by the second."

It had happened during an ice cream stop on William's way home from Freeman's. Tearing the wrapper off his Fudgesicle - careful not to touch the ice cream with his hands - the most peculiar sensation had come over him. Someone was watching him. Despite the August heat a chill ran down the back of his neck. He turned his head, just enough. There - across the square, leaning against a telephone pole in front of the dry cleaners - was Peter Gaglio, lighting a cigarette. Clicking his lighter closed, Peter looked directly at William and grinned his toothless grin.

William sat motionless, ignoring the melting chocolate running down his arm. Mercifully, it wasn't too long before a bus came along and carried Peter away. William's heart was pounding so hard it hurt. He told himself that it was just bad luck. After all, they lived in the same city – they were bound to run into each other now and then.

He'd seen Peter two more times since that day. Each time, Peter had grinned at William as if he had a horrible secret.

Reaching under his pillow, William pulled out Farley's old – rejected - bracelet.

"I am brave and daring," he whispered. "I am brave and daring."

He tried to push Peter's leering face from his mind as the angry voices of Joe and Paddy drifted up to the window. Nothing was good anymore.

"What do you care if I quit?"

"What do I *care*?" Paddy was livid. "How can you ask me that? Am I supposed to stand by and watch my son throw his future down the drain?"

The screen door slammed.

"What the hell is going on out here?" demanded Claire.

"Our son is dropping out of college, that's what."

"I'm not dropping out," said Joe, running his fingers through his hair. "I just didn't sign up for fall semester. I want to take a break and focus on my coaching."

"A break! He wants to take a break!" cried Paddy, looking as if he might burst. "You've hardly finished your sophomore year and you've been in college for, how many years now?"

William had to strain to her Claire's voice.

"Keep it down or take this down the hill."

"This is my chance," said Joe. "We made it to the finals last season. The potential is there to do even better next season. If we take home the trophy next season, I might be able to break into the pro league."

"You *might*," said Paddy. "You might win it big in the lottery, too. The only sure thing is an education."

"How would you know?"

"This won't take long," said Joe as they crossed the square. "I need to talk to Ryan about something."

"I know; I heard the whole thing," mumbled William.

"I'm sorry about that, pal. Don't worry; everything will be all right."

"Good. Because my stomach is acting like it needs Saltines and ginger ale."

William waited in Ryan's study, munching on crackers and flipping through a book about the hardship and torture the poor saints went though. He couldn't understand why anybody wanted to be a saint. Sainthood was pretty much a guarantee of severe pain somewhere down the line.

"It was an awful thing to say," said Joe. "Paddy's been working in the mill since he was thirteen. He took night classes for years to get his high school diploma."

Ryan carried his glass of Bordeaux to his recliner. He raised the footrest, spilling some wine on his pants. When he spoke, his words were slurred, dragged-out.

"*Shhtop* worrying."

"I want to focus on the Frosty Devils. We're good, Ryan. A championship win could bring me the recognition I need to break into the pro's."

"Then I say go for it."

"What about Paddy?"

Screwing up his face, Ryan waved a hand. "*Jussss* ignore him."

After the boys left, Ryan chuckled as he struggled to uncork a second bottle of wine. Typical Paddy, missing a perfect opportunity to be a hero in his son's eyes.

Be nice, Mutt.

"Easy for you to say," he murmured. "You're dead."

"Bonjour, Monsieur William," said Colette, double-tying her apron around her tiny waist.

"Bonjour," he mumbled.

He slouched into the chair next to Farley's desk.

She pushed her papers aside. "How's my little brother?"

"Not very good." He hesitated. "Probably because of Peter Gaglio."

Farley tried to keep her voice calm. "What about Peter Gaglio? Did he touch you?"

William shook his head, then leaned down and scratched his ankle to hide the tears that filled his eyes. Farley and Colette exchanged worried glances.

"Is that hairy boy bothering you?" asked Colette.

"He's bothering me in my mind," he said, his voice muffled by his knees. "I keep seeing him everywhere."

"Sit up." Farley pulled him by the arm. "Tell me what happened. Did he say something to you?"

William squeezed his eyes shut. He was getting that stomach feeling again. "He doesn't say anything. He's just there. I think I need a ginger ale."

Colette brought William a soda while Farley had him take a few deep breaths.

"I don't want you walking home alone anymore," she said. "If that creep comes anywhere near you...."

"...we'll rip every greasy hair out of his big hairy head," interrupted Colette.

William licked a tear from the side of his mouth. "Like superheroes?"

Farley smiled. William hadn't mentioned superheroes since the night he packed his cloaks away for good; saying they were for babies. She removed his glasses and wiped his face with a tissue.

"Are you are still planning to be an antibody for Halloween?" she said.

"It's called an immunoglobulin."

"I have a better idea. Why don't you go as a superhero? I mean, you *do* have the most authentic superhero cloaks around."

"It would be such a shame to waste a good costume," said Colette.

William tugged on his eyebrow. A cloak wouldn't be babyish on Halloween. *Everyone* dressed up on Halloween, even grown-ups.

Chapter 35

Henry and Farley spent most of their days and nights together. Their lives became so entwined, it was as if they could read each other's thoughts. A glance…a touch…a particular tone of voice was immediately understood. She could draw a map of his body in the dark. He knew what made her laugh, what made her cry, and what made her scream in agonizing ecstasy to please, please don't ever stop.

It seemed as if happiness had not only settled in, it was putting down roots. But somewhere deep down, Farley knew better. Because when horror once again reared its spineless head, she realized she had been waiting for it all along.

Rather than have costumed children trudging up and down the steep hills on Halloween, the citizens and merchants in and around Grady Square hosted The Big Boo; a Halloween party for trick-or-treaters of all ages. The annual event kicked off with the Goody Boo at precisely four o'clock in the afternoon. Traffic was blocked off in the square so that costumed children could safely move from merchant to merchant, collecting goody bags and treats. The Grady Boo Strut, a costume parade down to the waterfront and back, followed trick-or-treating.

Farley photographed the colorful celebration: a toothless old woman, grinning as she watched the parade from her window; the diapered behinds of three tiny ballerinas holding hands; the tender look on Henry's face as he knelt to place goodies in a child's plastic jack-o'-lantern. However, her favorite shot was of William studying his reflection in a store window. Just as she had raised the camera to her eye, a gust of wind sent his cloak soaring behind him, Superman style.

"Did you get that?" he cried. "It was just like I was flying!"

"I got it," said Farley, laughing.

William turned and studied his reflection again. "It was like I was a real superhero."

"You *are* a superhero." She held up her camera. "We have proof."

William threw his arms around her and squeezed. "This is the happiest day of my whole life."

Farley held her breath. She was unable to remember the last time her brother allowed – never mind instigated – an embrace.

Parade participants and spectators returned to the square to enjoy a barbeque buffet. Freeman's donated spicy chicken wings, cheeses, and beer. Dion and Colette arranged the trays on long tables decorated Big Boo-style. Farley and Henry stocked iced coolers with beer.

All but Henry were dressed in costume. Dion went as a college co-ed. She wore a Pitt letter sweater and an illegally-short pleated skirt. Farley was dressed as one of 'those nice boys from Pittsburgh' in an old football uniform of Joe's and a swipe of reflector makeup under each eye. Colette was the quintessential Cat Woman, sexy in her black leotard and tights, tail, and kitty ears.

Across the square, Billie elbowed Claire as Mr. Winston iced the keg. "I've been meaning to tell you how impressed I am with your Mr. Winston. Talk about articulate!"

"Why wouldn't he be?"

But Billie was already on the move - Shimmy, Shimmy, Ko-Ko-Bopping her way across the square in her swinging poodle skirt and tight sweater.

"Here comes trouble," said Farley, biting into a chicken wing.

Billie inserted herself between Farley and Henry. She gave Farley's stomach a poke. Although Farley had long ago outgrown her 'skeletal' look, hard work, walking the hills and healthy eating kept her trim.

"I don't know how you stay so thin, eating like you do," said Billie. "Don't you love a healthy eater, Henry?"

Henry locked eyes with Farley. "I certainly do."

Billie cocked her head. "And just where is your costume, Mr. Freeman?"

"You're looking at it. I came as an exhausted chef."

"How unimaginative," she pouted. "My heart was set on a more debonair look. Maybe a tuxedo…or a pair of ass-less chaps."

As the evening wore on, young parents carried their sleepy goblins home to bed, the music was turned up and the makeshift dance floor grew crowded.

"Too loud!" shouted William, his fingers stuck in his ears. "I think my ears are bleeding!"

Claire bent down so they could hear each other. "Do you want to go to Father Ryan's for a little while?"

William shook his head, appalled. "I can't, Aunt Claire. He's sick."

Each Halloween Ryan avoided the conflict of supporting local fun - versus supporting a pagan holiday - by conveniently 'coming down with something.'

"Besides," he said, "There's something wrong with Father Ryan. He keeps acting weirder and weirder all the time."

Claire frowned. She, too, was concerned with Ryan's increasingly morose behavior.

"I'll be on the bench, counting my Boo-goodies," said William, starting across the square.

"Maybe Eileen could join you."

"She's too busy dancing all night long," he mumbled to himself.

William watched the dancers from the safety of his bench. Mr. Winston and a delighted Eileen made their way across the floor. Eileen wore a black witch's gown and a smile that stretched across her whole face. Resa, Dion, and Colette and Veda Marie danced in a circle and took turns putting on a show in the center. Claire scolded Paddy as he tried to fake-dip her. William had to laugh as Henry - all lean body and graceful rhythm -guided Farley around the dance floor. Her knees jutted out at random and her body's rhythm seemed to be in direct conflict with the beat of the music.

Billie narrowly dodged Farley's flying elbow as she weaved through the dancers. Having zeroed in on a shy young accountant, she dragged him on to the dance floor and clung to him as if they were at a junior high sock hop. Mr. Bieberich, owner of Grady's Dry Cleaners, chuckled as he observed Billie's painful-to-watch overtures.

"My wife calls her 'Billie Kong. Not to her face, of course."

"Of course not," said Veda Marie, her cheeks bright red from her turn on the dance floor. "That would be rude."

Veda Marie worked her way back through the dance floor and grabbed a shocked Billie by the hand.

"Your husband needs you," she lied.

Turning, she collided head-on with an oversized bumblebee as he spun a fashionable sunflower.

"Look who it is!" cried the bee.

Veda Marie disappeared into an embrace of petals and wings.

"Billie, this is Tami and Timothy England," she said. "We go back for more years than I care to mention. I'm ashamed of how long it's been since we've seen each other."

"We met at Patty's birthday party," said Tami, beaming at Billie. "That Eileen of yours is adorable."

"She is a treasure," gushed Billie. Turning to Mr. England, she tilted her head flirtatiously. "But I have not had the pleasure of meeting the famous Mr. England."

"It has been a while, Billie." Timothy's antennae bobbed in all directions. "But I can't believe you don't remember me."

She batted her eyelashes and tried to control her glee. "I hate when this happens, don't you? I am so embarrassed; I don't recall our exact meeting."

"Patty's birthday party. I was the clown."

William sat upright and clutched his happiness cloak. His candy bag fell to the ground. Across the square in the gloom of Saint Xavier's shadow stood Peter Gaglio, giving William a great big jack-o-lantern, Peter-Peter-pumpkin-eater grin.

"Let's dance."

"I don't want to, Joe." Seeing the hurt in his eyes she softened her tone. "I'm going the ladies room."

Hurt, he watched as Sylvia disappeared into the crowd. He barely registered the harsh tug on his shirt.

"Joe," said William, a higher-than-usual-panic-pitch to his voice. "We need to go home now."

"Not now, Pal. Go ask Farley."

Billie teetered on the edge of the dance floor, eyes closed, hips grinding to the music. As the song ended, she opened her eyes and tried to focus. Ham was walking toward. No, two Hams. A double whammy-Hammy-jam-jam. Ha! She giggled. Both Hams wore her mother's fur with two dead foxes on the collar. Both of Ham's jaws were tight.

She wobbled. "That has to hurt, all that clenching."

He replied, but she couldn't make out what he was saying. *"...had enough...need to get Eileen...to go home."*

Billie stared at her husband in his pitiable getup. What was he supposed to be, anyway? Just as the music ended she let out a frightening cackle. The crowd grew quiet.

"You used to be somebody." She waved her arms, sloshing her drink. "A big partner in a big firm...country club...money flying in...now you want to chuck it all away for a bunch of *lowlifes*!"

"Claire," said Ham, never taking his eyes off his wife. "Please get Eileen out of here."

Billie steadied herself. "That's right; ask your not-so-secret infatuation to help you protect the little princess."

Ham took hold of her arm. "Come on, sweetheart. Let's go home."

"Come on, sweetheart," she mimicked, yanking her arm away. "What a pathetic loser you turned out to be. *A fucking loser!*"

Ham opened his mouth to say something and then decided against it. He stared at his wife.

"Goodbye, Billie."

As he turned away, she lobbed her half-empty cocktail glass at the back of his head. It was a direct hit.

"You need to get this looked at," said Dion. "You might have a concussion."

"I'll be all right." Ham flinched as Henry applied a makeshift ice pack to his head. "Where's Eileen?"

"Claire took her home," said Farley, having seen her hurrying Eileen across the square while Billie was still getting ramped up. She scanned the almost empty square. Claire must have grabbed William, too.

"At least let us give you a lift." Henry fished his keys out of his pocket. "Joe, do you mind bringing my van up? It's parked out back of the restaurant."

"No problem," said Joe. "Tell Sylvia I'll be right back."

Unlocking the door to Henry's van, Joe heard muffled laughter. He scanned the empty lot. Almost hidden by the shadows, a man leaned against the brick side wall of Freeman's. A woman pressed against him, pelvis to pelvis. Joe chuckled. As he turned the van around, his headlights flashed on the couple. Sylvia held up a hand to shield her eyes from the glare.

Neither spoke on the drive to Sylvia's apartment. Joe stopped in front of her building and let the engine idle. The two of them stared straight ahead.

"Who is he?" asked Joe.

"Someone I went out with a few times before I met you." She fumbled with the clasp of her purse. "I'm sorry, Joe. I don't blame you for hating me."

Joe put his head on the steering wheel. He waited until a large truck rumbled by before speaking. "I could never hate you."

"Fine. I hate myself enough for both of us, anyway."

He reached across the seat and found her hand.

"I can't do this anymore," she said, choking back a sob. "Every time I break up with you, you end up talking me into trying again. I don't want to try anymore. I can't even look at you without remembering…"

He continued holding her hand, almost hypnotized by the brief, brutal rain that washed over them as she cried.

"Trust me," said Ryan. He spoke with the deliberate annunciation of a drunk who thinks he's hiding it well. "She's not worth it. There are so many… *better* girls out there. Good *clean* ones. We need to find you a *clean* woman."

"Kissing someone else doesn't make her dirty," said Joe, leaning away from Ryan's red wine breath. "It just makes her someone else's girl."

"We both know what kind of girl she is."

"Don't talk about her like that." Joe's voice was flat as he tried to control his temper. "Sylvia is a nice girl."

"She's a nice alright," sneered Ryan. "She showed you such a *nice* time, you two had to take a *nice* drive downtown for a *nice* abortion."

Instinctively, Joe raised his fist.

Ryan defiantly lifted his chin. "Go ahead; hit me."

Chapter 36

Farley met him at the kitchen door. "Is William with you?"

"No," said Joe. "He's not here?"

Claire hung up the phone. "I've contacted everyone on the list except Ryan. His phone is busy."

"Thank God." Farley put her hands to her heart. "If his phone is busy at this hour, he's trying to call *us*. He must have William."

"I just came from Ryan's," said Joe. "He was alone."

Farley grabbed her sweatshirt. "He probably *just* found William, sleeping on the couch...or something. I'm going down there."

Poor Joe, thought Ryan. The kid was probably already castigating himself...dialing Ryan's number over and over to apologize. Well, let him sweat. The first thing Ryan had done after Joe left was take the telephone receiver off the hook.

He poured himself a whiskey. He knew he was drinking too much. Pickling himself seemed to be the only way to quiet the voices – make that *the* voice – in his head. He raised his glass. "I will only accept a face-to-face apology. As my God-given right." Looking up, he stretched out a wet grin. "Right, God?"

And there it was – a pounding on the door. Uncouth, but at least Joe had the good sense to come back.

"Ryan? Open up, it's Farley!"

What the hell was Joe thinking, sending her? Ryan grabbed the bottle and slipped out the back door. He'd wait in the rectory until she was gone.

Farley opened the door. "Ryan? William?"

She checked Ryan's small house from corner to corner. Putting the phone receiver back on the hook, she dialed Bridge Manor. Henry picked up on the first ring.

"Hello."

"Henry, he's not here. Ryan's car is out front, so he and William must be walking up…"

"Farley…"

"I'll bet they took the steps," she continued, her voice shrill, "which is why I missed them…"

"We woke up Eileen."

She nodded into the phone, her heart in her throat.

"She saw William leave with a small man with hair on his face. We think it was Peter Gaglio."

Farley choked back a sob. "No, please…"

"The police are on the way. We're gathering people to help search. Bring Ryan's car."

The car was locked. Frantic, Farley tried all the usual places: the kitchen counter, the top of his dresser, and the pockets of all the coats in the hall closet. She pulled opened his top desk drawer and reached inside, cutting her finger on the sharp corner of a book covered with thick plastic. She tried all the drawers. No keys, just more old books.

"Think," she whispered, breathing heavily.

Ryan was organized. He would hide a spare. She opened the front door and lifted the flowerpot. A shiny silver key glinted in the moonlight.

"Thank God!" she screamed.

Sobbing, she started the car. The tires screeched as she turned around in the square and drove up the hill.

Watching from the rectory window, Ryan polished off the last of his whiskey.

"Poor Farley," he said. "Always with the drama."

Claire stayed behind to stay near the phone and to wait for the police. Neighbors and friends gathered out in front of Bridge Manor to help with the search. Veda Marie and Resa ran from car to car distributing hastily drawn maps. Joe handed out hockey sticks and baseball bats.

"Stick to the streets on your map," yelled Henry. "We're concentrating on the South Side for now. Keep your bats and sticks close. Drive slow. Ask everyone you see. If you run into trouble, lean on the horn and don't stop until help shows..."

"GET IN THE FUCKING CAR!" screamed Farley.

Henry threw the car in reverse.

"It's going to be all right," he said. "We'll find him."

Farley nodded, her head wildly bobbing up and down.

"We'll find him," she repeated. She felt as if she might suffocate from fear.

The Gaglio boys took turns shoving and kicking William around the dark alley. They taunted and ridiculed him, laughing as he crab-crawled backwards, struggling and whimpering like a cornered kitten. As the beating changed from something to avoid to something to survive, William curled himself into a ball and tried to cover his head.

Tony and Rocco began to lose interest. This was so easy, it was almost embarrassing.

"Where's the sport?" said Tony, flipping his lighter open. He took a long drag on his Camel, unfiltered. "Come on, Rocco. Let's go."

Rocco called over his shoulder as they sauntered down the alley. "Let it go, Pete. We're outta here, man."

But Peter couldn't hear a thing over the escalating roar of the crowd in his head. *Holy Moly, would you look at him go! Gaglio scores again! Another hat trick by Gaglio! And the girls go wild...Peter! Peter! He's our man!*

As the cheers escalated to a final earsplitting symphony of applause and adulation, Peter Gaglio went to town on the little piggy, teaching him a thing or two about what happens to little fairies who prance around in capes.

Mercifully, the agony quickly became too much for William to bear and he stopped struggling. His mind grew calm and unafraid and he began to lose consciousness. The distant squeal of a car on the wet road was like a warm, comforting whisper of death.

Mom and Dad, please don't be watching over this.

William Justus James closed his eyes to the flickering headlights shining on the street that made everything look so pure.

"We've gone too far, Henry. They're within walking distance, I'm sure of it."

Henry slowed, preparing to make a U-turn. Farley was right; not even a monster like Peter Gaglio could get William into a car without one hell of a fight.

Someone would have heard something. As he turned, the car's headlights flashed on a small dark spot in the shadows between two abandoned buildings.

"Stop!" screamed Farley.

She opened the door and jumped before the car came to a stop. Tripping, she tumbled face first onto the pavement. Henry threw his door open and ran around the front of the car. Farley, stunned by the fall, was having trouble getting to her feet.

"Stay here!" He tore the flashlight from her hand and ran down the alley. Crouching next to the body, he gently lifted what was left of William's bloody cloak. Hot bile rose in the back of his throat.

"Oh, Christ," he choked.

Farley felt her way along the dark alley. "William?"

Henry heard the escalating hysteria in her voice. There was no time to wait for help; they had to get to a hospital. In the span of a few seconds he considered what would be worse: having Farley drive or having her hold her possibly dead brother.

"I need your help," he said, purposely shining the flashlight away from William.

The light landed on a pair of bloodied superhero underpants.

"Farley."

Henry met her eyes as she glanced in the rearview mirror. He spoke slowly, his voice firm.

"You have *got to slow down.*"

She nodded, her teeth chattering. "Slow down. I have to slow down."

William's warm blood seeped through Henry's jeans as the car sped across the Liberty Street Bridge.

Gripping each other's hands, Claire and Veda Marie tore through the hospital corridor. They stopped at the elevators, each trying to remember if they were to take a left or right.

Veda Marie grabbed a passing orderly. "Can you tell us where…"

"Veda Marie?" Henry appeared from a room down the hall.

Moaning, she covered her mouth. Henry's shirt and jeans were covered with blood.

Farley and Claire leaned against each other and tried to absorb what the surgeon was saying. *"…coma… ventilator…blunt injuries…head and torso… shattered femur … severely traumatized."*

Farley tried to swallow but her throat was too dry.

"But…he'll be all right," she whispered. "I mean, he's not going to…"

Dr. Hugh hesitated. "Your brother survived a brutal attack that should have killed a man more than twice his size. As long as William is alive, there is hope."

"Doctor, I don't care what it costs," said Claire. "Whatever he needs. Experts. Specialists. Please."

"We'll do everything we can, Mrs. Sullivan. Having said that, if you have a particular priest…."

"Coming!" yelled Ryan, hopping up and down as he struggled to pull on a pair of pants. His temple was throbbing and he saw spots. He opened the door to find Paddy, soaking wet.

"It's William, Father. You'd better come with me."

Neither man spoke on the way to the hospital. Ryan worked his way through the Rosary while Paddy wondered where the love of God was when this good boy was being beaten to a bloody pulp and left for dead.

Farley was an inch from William's face. "I'm going to wake you with my forceful stare."

She sat back as Veda Marie entered the room. Behind her, Mr. Winston carried a leather suitcase.

Veda Marie kissed the top of her head. "How's our boy this morning?"

"Better now. Last night his monitors were going off all over the place."

A nurse backed a portable tray into the room. They watched in silence as she changed the bags and checked the complicated-looking monitors surrounding William's bed. On her way out she spotted the suitcase in Mr. Winston's hand.

"Is that for the patient?"

"Yes, it's for *William*," said Veda Marie.

The nurse reached for the handle. "I'll take it."

Mr. Winston held tight; a brief tug-of-war ensued before she released the handle.

"I'm sorry, sir," she said, "but only *immediate* family is allowed in here. I'm sure you understand."

"I certainly do." He clutched the suitcase to his chest. "And on behalf of my family, I would like to thank you for taking care of our William." He tapped the suitcase with the palm of his hand. "We'll put his belongings away. Our boy needs his things folded just so."

Veda Marie gently kissed William's forehead.

"There's my sweet angel," she said, trying to sound cheerful.

But her heart cried out as she looked him over. Most of his head was bandaged. One arm was in a cast, and his left leg was suspended in traction. His entire body was a quilt of sterile bandages, sutures, angry bruises, and swelling.

Mr. Winston crouched next to Farley's chair and put an arm around her.

"Ham Kane needs to talk to you, dear," he said. "He's in the lounge at the end of the hall."

"Peter Gaglio and his two brothers were picked up in upstate New York," said Ham.

Farley wrapped her arms around herself. She nodded, encouraging him to go on.

"They assaulted the owner of a mom-and-pop store early this morning. The old man wouldn't give up the combination to the safe. They beat him, then hauled the safe out to his station wagon and took off. A few miles down the road the car ran out of gas. They were staggering across a field with the safe when the police apprehended them. Apparently family loyalty isn't a Gaglio trait; the brothers are already pointing the finger at each other about a boatload of crimes."

"Including William's."

"Yes."

The bile rose in Farley's throat. Three of them. Against William.

Farley walked Ham to the elevator. "What about the old man?"

"You mean the store owner?" He hesitated. "He's pretty banged up, but he'll be all right."

Farley nodded, grateful for the obvious lie.

"The doctors say William may never remember anything about that night," she said. "But if he does, I don't want him to have to face them in court."

"I'll see about recording his testimony, when he's up to it."

She gave him a weak smile. "Thank you for not saying 'if he gets better.'"

"I'll stay on top of the Gaglio situation." He hugged Farley. "You just take care of that brother of yours."

Take care of your brother.

Let's go, Jack. She'll be fine.

The hospital chapel was empty. Farley took a seat in the first pew and stared down the cross on the wall.

Chapter 37

November was one long permeating chill. William's family and friends walked a tightrope, balancing the horror of his attack against the hope that he would – that they all would – wake from this horrific nightmare.

William's doctors encouraged the family to talk in a normal tone of voice, speaking and reading to him as if he were awake.

Farley spent every possible moment at the hospital. Veda Marie watched her TV soaps in William's room, offering her opinions on what that vixen Erica was up to now. Claire's fingers inelegantly forced the needle and thread as she sat by his bed. Resa decorated his walls with drawings from Eileen and cards that poured in daily from total strangers. Mr. Winston and Paddy took turns reading to William. Dion did her homework on his bedside tray.

Joe taped football and hockey games and replayed them in William's room. On a whim, he contacted a friend of a friend who worked in the Steelers organization to request a card from the players. The following day a handful of players showed up at the hospital, bearing a banner signed by the whole team.

TO WILLIAM JAMES, OUR PAL
GET WELL SOON
FROM THOSE NICE BOYS FROM PITTSBURGH

The sky gave way to an unruly downpour as Paddy read William the final paragraph of Leon Uris's *Trinity*.

> 'When all of this was done, a
> republic eventually came to pass.
> But the sorrows and the troubles
> have never left that tragic, love-
> ly land. For you see, in Ireland
> there is no future, only the past
> happening over and over.'

Paddy turned off the overhead light. Flecks of dust swam through the streak of light coming from the hallway. Careful not to disturb the monitors, tubes and wires, he made his way to the window. He smiled as he imagined the rain thoroughly scrubbing the soot and grime-coated buildings and streets of the city. Like Ireland, his beloved Pittsburgh was overcoming its sorrows and troubles.

"You might not be known as the loveliest land," he whispered, "but nor will you ever be known as tragic."

Dion squeezed William's foot. "Hi, fella."

A muscle under his eye twitched, which she chose to believe was a response. She pulled a chair up to the bed and began unpacking her notebooks.

"Pharmacology is getting hard. I don't mean to be selfish, but you're going to have to wake up soon. I need my study buddy back. I had to ask my professor's assistant for help."

She spread balm on his lips. "Get this; his name is Horsehead. Can you believe it? I mean, I'm sure it's a lie name. Probably a childhood nickname the poor thing couldn't shake. I'm meeting him later today. I'll let you know if the noggin fits the name."

Horsehead stood on the tips of his topsiders, stretching to scrawl the assignment across the chalkboard. He erased a particularly illegible word with the mock patched elbow of his sweater, purchased during a recent unsuccessful attempt to be hip.

Dion theatrically cleared her throat.

"Hello," he said. "May I help you?"

"I'm Dion Piotrowski. I left you a message…"

"I just got off the phone with one of your housemates. I'd be happy to help. I'm available any time after six Monday, Wednesday and Friday. Do any of those nights work for you?"

"Monday at six would be great."

"Monday it is."

As she turned to leave, Horsehead waved a piece of paper. "Oh, I have a note for you from admissions. They still need a copy of your birth certificate and social security card." He smiled. "You know how sticky they are about paperwork."

Dion stared. The man had a striking smile. And big, shiny green eyes with dark lashes. She tilted her head. His cheeks had a pink glow to them, as if he'd been running.

"Will that be a problem?" he asked.

"No problem."

She turned and put her rear end into high gear, swishing from side to side out the classroom door. No problem at all.

Dion went around to the side door of her childhood home and let herself into the kitchen. She inhaled the stale odor of dishrags, mold, and garbage. Same old kitchen, she thought. Living proof that time really can stand still. The red Formica table and metal chairs. Food and junk on all the counters; jars of pickles, crackers, bread. Magazines still piled on the corner table, along with a hairbrush and an ashtray full of cigarette butts. Same old misery.

She found the folder containing her birth certificate and hospital records. On impulse, she grabbed a piece of paper and a pencil.

Dear Ma,
I'm sorry I had to take my personal records.
I needed them for school and you wouldn't talk to
me when I called. (Or answer my letters, or come
to the door.) I know about the mill closing down.
Please tell Dad I'm thinking of him.
Your daughter,
Dionna
P.S. I think of you, too.
P.S.S. The South Side Rialto is bringing back *Terms
of Endearment* for the Saturday matinee. I always
sit near the front.

"We're not expecting a crowd tonight," said Henry, "but you know how that works."

Colette handed him an overloaded basket. "Stop worrying; I can handle it. I hope I made enough sandwiches."

He weighed the basket. "I think you made enough to feed the entire hospital."

"The Shepherd's Pie goes to Bridge Manor. Drop it off first. Tell Veda Marie the heating instructions are taped to the top." She held the kitchen door for him. "And don't forget to give William a special..."

"...a special kiss from Auntie Colette," finished Henry, kissing her cheek. "You're the best."

Blushing, she waved. "Get out of here."

As his van pulled away, Colette touched the spot on her cheek where he had kissed her.

Farley rested her chin on the metal side bars of William's bed and watched his chest move up and down.

"Please wake up," she whispered. "We'll go home to Bridge Manor and I swear I'll never talk about leaving again. I just want our life back. Please, kiddo."

A nurse backed into the room pulling a cart full of electrical equipment.

"Hello, dear. How is our superhero this evening?"

Farley straightened and stretched her back. "I swear, it almost sounded like he was humming."

"He probably was."

"That figures," said Henry, his face hidden by an enormous basket of food. "William can never remember all the words."

Farley and Henry held hands in the dark, watching William sleep. One of the machines hooked up to William beeped.

Henry jumped up. "Oh, God! What's happening?"

"It's all right," said Farley. "It's his IV monitor."

She no longer noticed the hissing, clicking, and beeping of the machines. The sound that caught her attention was the 'bad sound;' a high warning bleep-bleep-bleep that went off when William's frail body was perilously close to losing its battle. It had gone off twice in the days after his admission. Thankfully nothing since.

Two nurses brought a fresh IV bag, re-checked William's monitors, and dimmed the lights on their way out.

Farley put her head on Henry's shoulder.

"William believes Mom and Dad are watching over us," she said. "But I can tell you right now, they're not. No parent, dead or alive, could stand by and watch over this."

"Farley ordered a fancy security system with monitors and special codes," said Veda Marie. "She's got Joe buying new locks for Bridge Manor. And she wants to re-do every stick of furniture in William's bedroom for when he gets home."

Mr. Winston nodded thoughtfully, re-lighting his cigar.

"She's paying for everything herself," continued Veda Marie. "She insisted Claire take the money out of her trust fund. Claire got all sideways about it but Farley won out. The poor girl is a mess."

He puffed a few times to get the cigar going; the sweet aroma of cherry began to fill the room.

"Making arrangements for William's return gives her hope," he said. "Right now, she needs all the hope she can get."

"I know it."

Twirling a strand of hair, Veda Marie studied Mr. Winston's profile. She was certain the overall blend of his pristine, manicured beard, full lips, solid cheekbones and high forehead suggested wisdom.

"Have you always been this astute," she teased, "or is wisdom a reward that comes with old age?"

Mr. Winston's shoulders bounced as he chuckled. "Oh, I've made my share of mistakes."

She waited, sensing something more.

"I haven't seen my brother Leonard since 1975," he said. "One of the most talented musicians you'll ever meet. We had a fight."

"About what?"

"That's the kicker; the fight was about nothing of any importance." He shook his head. "Two grown men pummeling away at each other, with the table barely cleared from Thanksgiving dinner."

"I hear you, Mr. Winston. Holidays can be the worst."

He picked up the back of her hand and kissed it. "Don't you think it's time you started calling me Satchel?"

"I'll think about it." She climbed off the bed and perused the room. "Where do you think my overalls might be?"

"I haven't got a clue." He leaned across the bed to watch as she bent over to pick up her pretty lace bra. "I was quite distracted, you see."

She stuck out her bare behind and gave it a wriggle. "Why thank you, *Satchel.*"

Heavy footsteps clamored down the hall.

"Hang on, Joe!" yelled Claire. "I'll look in Mr. Winston's room!"

She was two steps in before she froze.

After a futile attempt to cover her most private areas with her bra, Veda Marie sighed and put her hands on her hips.

"I...I," stammered Claire. "I thought you were grocery shopping."

"We shopped fast," said Veda Marie.

An equally naked Mr. Winston removed the cigar from his mouth "What was it that you were looking for, my dear?"

"Uh..." It took her a minute. "The red blanket. For William."

"It's right over there." Mr. Winston gestured to the blanket, folded over the back of his armchair. "Please secure the door on your way out."

Chapter 38

At a corner of Liberty and Seventh a Salvation Army, Santa rang his bell. Harried people pushed by, clutching their coats. Claire put her turn signal on as she stopped for the light, her conversation with Mr. Johnson running through her head.

"I'm afraid your loan cannot be renegotiated, Mrs. Sullivan. We'll need your payment in full by Friday. Otherwise, the deed to Bridge Manor is transferred to us."

The blood had rushed from Claire's face. "That's not in the contract."

"Of course it is." He shuffled through the bulky contract. "Here we are: page one hundred and sixty seven, paragraph four. 'Failure to make payment will result in immediate transfer of deed of property: 1107 Overlook Trail.'"

Claire gripped her purse.

"There must be some mistake," she said. "I can assure you I would never agree to something like that."

Mr. Johnson tapped the bottom of the page. "Those are your initials, are they not?"

Putting on her reading glasses, she leaned over the contract. "Yes, but…"

"Mrs. Sullivan, you signed a legal and binding contract." He closed the contract and folded his hands.

"As I said, if you can't make your payment by Friday, the deed to Bridge Manor belongs to The Pilgrim Group. I am sorry."

Claire tilted the car's rearview mirror and examined her face. There were new lines around her eyes and above her lip. Her bloodshot eyes looked bruised. The tears came faster now, running down her cheeks and into the folds of her neck. Pauline was right; the rearview mirror really was the only honest mirror.

"You should get a load of me now, Pauline," she breathed, pulling a crumpled napkin out of her purse. God, she was exhausted.

Three tiny brass bells rang as she opened the door to The Novel Hovel. Mr. Franco, clinging to the top rung of a ladder, strained to reach a book. Below him, a woman in jeans and a puffy green parka glanced at her watch.

Claire's feet felt like cement as she climbed the stairs to the second floor and wandered through the dark aisles. The scent of old books and lemon pine wood polish brought back long-forgotten memories…Father reaching down to pick her up, spinning her around and around. *We found it, our treasure! Have you ever been so happy in your life?*

She lowered herself to her knees, then lower; down to the dark wood floor. Lie down. Just lie down.

Five hundred and fifty thousand dollars just for lying down…right is right…wrong is wrong… breathing under water was easy…she found him near the bottom… wrapped herself around him… kissing…tender and soft… Oh, Paddy…he stroked her face…kissed her…my darling girl…right is right…all right…all right…

"Are you all right, Mrs. Sullivan?"

"Wuhh." Claire jerked awake, her eyes slow to focus. She was shivering. Her face, wet by a thin layer of drool, was pressed against the wooden floor.

"Try not to move, dear," said Mr. Franco. He was kneeling beside her, holding her hand. "You've taken a fall."

"Here, hon." The woman in the puffy green parka unzipped her coat and draped it over Claire. "This will warm you up."

Mr. Franco's twisted arthritic fingers struggled with the buttons of his cardigan. He placed his balled-up sweater under Claire's head, and leaned back, his voice weak.

"This is my fault," he said. "I must have put too much polish on the floors last night." He gestured toward the parka woman. "This nice young lady will stay with you while I call an ambulance."

Holding onto the bookcase, he tried to pull himself up.

"Goodness," he said, embarrassed. "I seem to be stuck."

Green parka woman helped the old man to his feet.

Overcome with shame, Claire covered her eyes with her hand. "It's not your fault, Mr. Franco. They'll be no need for an ambulance."

Ryan pulled the car up to the curb. Farley jumped out and ran into the old bookstore. Mr. Franco met her at the door and chatted nervously as he led her through the cramped store.

"I'm sorry about your brother, Miss James. I've been following young William in the papers."

He opened the door to his office. "And of course, Mrs. Sullivan's brother comes in to the store now and then. He fills me in."

Farley knelt beside her aunt. "Claire, what happened? Are you all right?"

"I've lost our home," she whispered. "I've lost Bridge Manor."

"Sorry it's so tight in here," said Ham, as the residents of Bridge Manor crowded in.

Claire looked around the room. His new office was about the size of her pantry. The wall behind his desk was floor-to-ceiling books, cardboard boxes and framed photographs and degrees. "I love it."

"What an amazing view," said Farley.

Mr. Winston draped an arm around her shoulders and pointed toward the Lower Hill. "There's my old stomping grounds. Leonard and I used to hang on the corner of Wylie and Fifth with our buddies, trying to out-cool each other." He chuckled. "The Wylie Hooligans; we were something else."

Ham pulled Claire aside as the group pulled up chairs around the small conference table. "In light of the others in attendance, I need to ask if there anything you would prefer we address in private."

"This concerns all of us, Ham. Feel free to say whatever you like." She stared directly into his eyes. "In regards to *this* issue."

"I understand."

"What we're looking at is home equity fraud, plain and simple," said Ham, folding his hands on the table. "Claire was offered a payment plan to make repairs on Bridge Manor. The interest rate was high, and it grew higher over time. But it wasn't the interest they were after. Their goal was to take full possession of Bridge Manor."

"Sounds like a second mortgage to me," said Mr. Winston.

"Home equity rip-offs have gone big time," continued Ham. "They are organized and demographically targeted. In some cases they are even nationally franchised."

"If they're such a big organization, why waste their time going after me?" asked Claire.

"On the contrary, you represent their ideal target. Your home is paid for. It's in your name." He hesitated. "And, you're a single, older woman."

"How dare you," said Veda Marie.

Claire patted her arm. "Go on, Ham."

He took a sip of water. "When you could no longer keep up with the interest on your payment plan, someone tipped you off about a lenient lender."

"That lovely woman couldn't possibly be a crook," said Claire.

"That lovely woman referred you to The Pilgrim Group. They presented themselves as respectable lenders, mired you in legal jargon and buried you in paperwork." Ham held up a copy of the thick contract. "Deep inside the fine print is a one-sentence kicker: Bridge Manor was the collateral on the loan. These people - with their fancy suits, pretty secretaries, and elegant conference rooms - are loan sharks, pure and simple."

Claire blushed, recalling how impressed she had been with the breakfast spread and the fresh squeezed orange juice.

"Then why can't we have them arrested?" said Farley.

"Standing alone, each company *appears* to be a legitimate entity." Ham picked up the contract. "Generally speaking, this is a binding contract; signed, witnessed, and submitted through the proper legal channels." He turned to Claire. "Witnesses can and will state that you said you understood what you were signing."

Farley saw Claire's hand tremble as she removed her reading glasses.

"There has to be something we can do."

"We need to find a connection between Lowe & Son Restoration and The Pilgrim Group. If we can show proof of kickbacks or a conspiracy of any kind between the two companies, their involvement becomes illegal. Unfortunately, the odds are not in our favor for finding anything before that deed transfers. If you lose that deed, you lose the only remaining advantage you have: possession of Bridge Manor."

Suddenly the disappointment that everyone had so gallantly kept at bay saturated the room. Each one of them had secretly hoped that Ham Kane, like one of William's superheroes, would swoop in and save the day.

"No." Farley shook her head. "We're not losing Bridge Manor. When William comes home, he'll need everything exactly the way it was."

Clare and Veda Marie exchanged a worried glance. There had been no improvement in William's condition in weeks.

Ham nodded. "Then you've got to pay off the loan before the deed transfers. I'd say you have a week, at best."

"All right, then." Farley pushed back her chair. "We'd better get going."

"I'll be at the hospital," said Joe, as they left Ham's office building.

"Give our boy a kiss." Veda Marie shivered in her parka. "And tell Dion - I swear this is true because he told me with his own lips - a man by the name of *Horsehead* called looking for her."

Joe raised his hand and started down the sidewalk.

"My son is ashamed of me," said Claire, watching him go. "He barely said a word all morning."

Farley had also noticed Joe's somber mood, and she had an unsettling feeling it had something to do with her.

"Joe, wait!" She ran the half block and stood in front of him. "What's going on?"

He stuffed his hands in his pockets.

"Come on, Joe. If you're mad at me, the least you can do is tell me why."

"Fine." He looked at the car, where Claire and the rest of the group waited. "How do you think she got into this mess?"

"Claire?" Farley shook her head. "The bills got ahead of her. All those repairs..."

"She would have been able to pay for those. She was fine, until..." He stopped.

Farley frowned. "Until what?"

"Do you even *know* how much one year of William's school costs? His private teachers or your photography? How about that fancy new security system we're being wired for?"

"I earn my own money," said Farley, stung. "And my social security checks usually cover my film and developing. Claire pays the big expenses like the security system or anything school-related with our trust fund."

"You trust fund. You're sure about that."

A feeling of dread was beginning to come over her. She shifted her feet; her hands instinctively planting themselves on her hips. "Cut the shit, Joe. What are you trying to say?"

"There is no fund; trust, college, or otherwise. The small social security check you get every month is it. *There is no other money.*"

Farley took a step back. "That's a lie. Why would you say something like that?"

"My mother paid for everything. Now she's so broke she's visiting loan sharks and attempting insurance fraud."

"Joseph Francis Sullivan!" shouted Claire, rushing up the sidewalk.

One look at her aunt's distraught face and Farley knew it was true. She pushed past Joe and ran.

"Shame on you, Joe." Claire's voice shook.

"Mum, we're losing our home."

"What did you do, go through my private papers? Ham would never betray my trust, and no one else knew."

"Ryan knew. You must have told him."

"I didn't *tell* Ryan anything. I *confessed* it."

Chapter 39

Farley curled up in the window seat of her bedroom to read the Air Force documents.

She lowered the papers. "What kind of a dispute was it?"

"An officer at the party made a pass at your mother," said Claire. "Your father shattered his nose across his face."

"So all these years, you've been forking over money you didn't have." Farley shook her head. "I've been taking *your* money and stashing it away for some crazy dream."

Claire's hands slid up to her hips. "You also saved every penny of your own hard-earned money. And I wouldn't call having a plan to take care of your brother some crazy dream."

Farley gave Claire a sad smile. "William never wanted to leave Bridge Manor. That was all me. What *I* wanted." She put her head in her hands. "Meanwhile, you were getting in deeper and deeper. I'm so sorry."

"For what? You thought the money was yours. I knew I had to tell you someday, but I kept putting it off. I was counting on winning those appeals. And," she hesitated, "I couldn't bring myself to tell you that your security was gone because of something your father did. He was your hero."

"He made a mistake," said Farley. "That would never change the way I feel about him."

"It changed the way you felt about your mother."

"Pauline didn't make a mistake; she made a *choice*."

Claire took a seat next to her niece. "She sure did. And I hated her for it, for much longer than I'd like to admit."

"You did?"

"She should have at least tried to get out of that car. Instead of leaving you and William all alone."

Farley smiled. "But we weren't alone Clare. Fortunately for us...we had you."

Claire procured blankets from the hall closet. Bundled up, they faced each other in the window seat.

Farley tucked her chin on her knees. "I used to be so jealous of the bond the two of you had. You and your magical twin instincts."

Claire chuckled. "I still remember the feeling I got the moment you were born. I was in my office at the library. All of a sudden, an overwhelming sense of elation came over me. Your mother was more than a thousand miles away, but I knew you were born before the phone ever rang."

"Did you have one of those instincts when she died?"

Claire wrinkled her forehead, searching for words. "I woke up feeling…empty. Lonely. It never occurred to me to apply those feelings to Pauline. We had each other; we could never be lonely." She tweaked Farley's blanket-covered foot. "That's how I know your mother loved you every day of her life. I *felt* it. So please, don't let her entire life be defined by one final, impulsive act."

Certain they would have approved, Farley sold her father's gold West Point ring, along with her mother's wedding ring, engagement ring, and diamond hair clip to a reputable jeweler in Squirrel Hill. She emptied her savings account and removed all but two hundred dollars from her checking account. Then she cancelled her order for William's new furniture and the fancy security system.

"They say a dog is the best security, anyway," she said, sliding a check across the table.

"This is a lot of money, lovey." Veda Marie's eyes were moist. "Are you sure about this?"

Farley looked around the old kitchen. The photo of her mother, Claire, and Veda Marie in their work clothes. William's chalk drawings, still on the 'to do' board. Last year's hockey schedule. The large gas stove, where she loved to watch Henry work his magic. The massive table, where dinner was served each night at seven sharp. Where they all gathered; a family.

She imagined Abigail at the window, gathering her strength to walk into the river. Grandfather, stomping around in his grief. Pauline - a child, herself - nurturing her abandoned baby brother. And Claire, the *other* twin. Claire, who took in two lost, grieving souls and gave them a home.

"I've never been so sure of anything in my life."

Everyone gave what they could. Henry cashed in savings bonds. Joe emptied his bank account. Dion gave what was clearly her next semester's tuition - although she swore it wasn't. Mr. Winston liquidated his IBM stock. Resa contributed two and a half large jars of quarters.

"I'll have more when my classes start up again," she said, shivering. The heat had been lowered to cut down on the heating bills.

Veda Marie's cigarette bounced in her lips as she added up the money.

"Let's get this show in the road," said Mr. Winston. "Claire will be back any minute."

"No, I'm picking her up at the hospital," said Joe. "I told her to call when she's ready."

Veda Marie circled the total and tapped it with her pencil.

Henry scrubbed his face with his hands. "We're still thirty-seven thousand short."

"We'll sell the car," said Joe.

"Actually, we made it." Veda Marie pulled a crumpled check from her pocket and smoothed it out on the table. The check was for forty thousand dollars.

Farley cleared her throat. "Veda Marie, what have you done?"

She stubbed out her cigarette. "Pull your minds out of the gutter, people. I merely called in an IOU from my gambling days."

"I thought your gambling days were over."

"They are. Have been for more than twenty years."

Henry gestured toward the check. "You're saying someone owed you forty-thousand dollars…for twenty years."

"Trust me, twenty years goes by in a flash. You blink and 'poof!' it's gone. I swear, one minute I'm…"

"Veda Marie!"

She chuckled. "All right. A friend and I got in over our heads one weekend in Vegas. Already in debt, my friend lost much more than he could afford to lose. And at one point I was down so low I barely had the bus fare back to Pittsburgh." She winked at Farley. "But I ended that weekend on a blistering hot streak. My dollars doubled, then doubled again and again. It got so I couldn't do anything wrong."

She lit up and exhaled, enjoying her walk back in time.

"We were a pair of fools; I was just the luckier fool. So, I offered to pay off his debts, on the condition that we both quit gambling - forever. My friend agreed, then sat down and wrote me an IOU on a cocktail napkin. He's offered to honor it many times over the years, but I preferred to wait until I needed the money. Deep down, I think I was afraid I might start playing the numbers again and end up on the street. Timothy's money was my security."

"Timothy?"

Reaching across the table, Farley picked up the check. It was signed by Timothy England.

The shrill ring of the telephone cut through the animated noise of relieved laughter and chatter.

"That'll be mum." Joe signaled to Farley as she picked up the phone. "Tell her I'm on my way."

Halfway out the door, he heard her cry out.

Paddy chewed his bran cereal as he read the back of the box.

A prize in every box!
You could be one of our lucky winners!
Prizes Galore!
Money! Money! Money!

"See, nothing to worry about," he mumbled. "I'll just eat cereal and the riches will come."

"Dad?"

Paddy stood when he saw Joe's tear-streaked face. God in heaven. He made the sign of the cross. *Father, Son, Holy Ghost.*

"Oh, son," he swallowed. "It's our William, isn't it?"

"He's awake, Dad."

His long legs propped on William's bed, Henry read from a book titled *Fun Medical Facts.* "Did you know it is not possible to tickle yourself?"

William turned his head toward the window.

"Yeah, even I knew that one." Henry ran his finger down the page. "Did you know that men are twice as likely to contract leprosy as women?"

Nothing.

"Here's a winner; I'll bet you didn't know that Arri-azia is the complete absence of breasts."

"Henry," whispered William, his voice hoarse. "I want to go home."

He closed the book.

"I know you do, pal. The doctors say it won't be long now. And when you do come home, we're going to have a Merry Christmas, Happy New Years, and Happy Birthday-to-you party, all in one. Claire and Veda Marie are already planning it. The list on the chalkboard goes all the way to the floor."

With each passing week, William had become more and more adamant about going home. He would heal better in his own house, he insisted. He emphasized the uncontainable germs potentially lurking in the hospital. Then there was his lack of a consistent sleep pattern; getting a good night's sleep in a hospital was out of the question. But the *real* reason he kept to himself. He didn't want to die in the hospital. He wanted to die at home.

That night Farley and William watched an old western on the small TV in his hospital room. When his eyes began to close, she quietly gathered her things and tiptoed toward the door.

His voice was barely a whisper. "They really are there, you know."

She turned, the hairs on the back of her neck rising. "What did you say?"

"Mom and Dad. They really are watching over us."

Blood pounded in her temples. "Did you see them?"

"I didn't have to. I felt them in my heart."

Chapter 40

Billie brought her Mercedes to a stop. A line of elementary school children crossed the road, flanked on all sides by their teachers. Lowering her sunglasses, Billie re-applied the mole on her cheek and adjusted the scarf around her neck. She was pleased with her new Liz Taylor look. She would have preferred the full riding-in-the-passenger-seat-of-a-red-Mercedes-with-a handsome-man-who-wore-brown-leather-driving-gloves sort of look, but one thing at a time.

The morning after Halloween she had checked herself into a treatment center upstate. Upon her release she found an apartment on the North Side and the most expensive shrink money could buy.

"Be strong," she whispered, wishing she had never agreed to meet Ham for lunch.

Guilt was new to Billie. Her shrink said feelings of guilt and shame were normal at this point in her therapy as she faced her demons head on. She assured Billie that even the worst shame could turn to pride if one learned from her mistakes - which was the only reason Billie had agreed to meet Ham for lunch.

"I know why you asked me here," she said, as he pulled her chair out for her.

"What are you talking about?" Ham blinked innocently. "I just want to see how you're doing."

"That, and address my many transgressions." She gave him a coy smile. "A *true* gentleman would confess to a few of his own, just to get the ball rolling."

The air filled with the delicious aroma of baking enchiladas as William opened his gifts and quietly exclaimed over each one. A hospital bed had been installed in the living room, along with a stereo, a television set, and remote control black-out curtains to block out the light.

"Last one," said Farley.

She placed a large white box with a red velvet ribbon on William's lap. The long black cloak he unwrapped was a combination man's jacket and superhero cape.

"Wow." His voice was still raspy from the ventilator. "It's stupendous."

"We thought it was time you had a grown-up cloak," said Claire.

"We, my eye," said Veda Marie. "Your aunt made that cloak all by herself."

"Really?"

Claire blushed and waved a hand. "Really. So don't look too close."

"A grown-up cloak." William smiled; his face free at last of the unbearable swelling and bruises. "I have been wanting this for all of the years of my life."

"Hello?" Ham opened the front door. "Claire?

Stepping into the foyer, Billie wrinkled her nose. "It smells like a Mexican armpit in here," she whispered.

"Christ, Billie." Ham shook his head, amazed that he could ever have had feelings for this woman. "Wait here," he said, switching on a lamp in the formal living area. "I'll only be a minute."

Billie scrutinized her surroundings. Wide staircase, tiled foyer, tall ceilings, shiny hardwood oak floors. She was impressed. She had written Bridge Manor off as a tear-down when she listed it years ago. She picked up a framed photograph of Claire and her noticeably prettier twin sister. Amazing how an extra centimeter here, an overactive gland there determined one's happiness. Talk about unfair, she thought, sinking into a flowery sofa.

"Eileen misses you, William," said Ham.

"I know, she called me on the phone. She said when she comes back from camp, you're going on a long trip. Just you and her. She's happy about that."

"I'm happy about it, too," said Ham. He turned to Claire. "Can I borrow you for a minute?"

"We found a solid connection between Lowe & Son Restoration and The Pilgrim Group."

"Oh, Ham!" gasped Claire.

"Someone came forward," he continued, "and admitted to providing names of potentially vulnerable home-owners to Lowe & Son in exchange for a significant fee. If matters escalated to the point that The Pilgrim Group became involved, she also received an additional bonus."

"She?"

"Billie." His mouth twitched. "Apparently she has been providing information to Lowe & Son for quite some time. She is willing to testify to that fact in a court of law."

Billie Kane stood straight as a poisoned arrow as they entered the room. Claire approached the woman who had caused her family so much pain. So many nights of agonizing worry. The threat of losing their home. The help-lessness. She pressed her lips together. No, she thought.

Don't go there; don't give her the satisfaction. Leave the room without saying a word. Take the high road. Claire Sullivan turned to go.

Oh, what the hell. She spun and smacked Billie Kane across the face.

Joe handed his father an *Iron City* and settled onto the sofa. The two men had fallen into a Friday night routine of a few beers at Paddy's.

"Mum says you got a job as a night watchman at Magee Women's Hospital."

"It's only part-time." Paddy opened his beer. "Still, I'm happy to be earning my own money again."

Joe crunched on a handful of chips and washed them down with half a beer before speaking. "I'm thinking about heading back to school. Community college, anyway. Classes start in less than a month."

"What about your coaching job?"

"I lost the taste for it. I'll miss the game, though. Once I get a feel for my classes, I'll join a club league. It will be nice to play for fun again." He smacked Paddy's arm. "So, what do you think?"

"You know what I think, son. There's nothing more important than an education."

"Glad to hear it." Joe pulled a folded piece of paper from his pocket and tossed it on the coffee table. "I picked up a registration form for you, too."

On their way to the registrar's office, Joe and Paddy hopped over potholes in the campus parking lot.

"These cars sure aren't as nice as the ones at the university," said Joe.

"Who cares about the cars," said Paddy. "What I want to know is, what's the name of our football team?"

Joe put his arm around his father's shoulders. "It's a community college. We don't have a football team."

Farley tossed a stack of photographs on William's bed. "The Post-Gazette is interested in using some of my photos for their Sunday magazine. They want shots that reflect the city's transformation. Look through these and tell me which ones you like - and be honest."

William started to say he was always honest; then bit his lip. He took his time perusing the stack.

"I like the ones of the empty mills and factories," he said. "The shadows make them seem scary and orderly all at that same time."

"They want to focus on the positive changes." She flipped through another stack. "Like all the new shops downtown, or the mayor's new film commission, or all the buildings going up..." Her voice drifted off. "Hey, you don't click anymore."

"What?"

"You haven't clicked your tongue since you came home from the hospital."

Shrugging off her comment, he held up a picture taken through a broken window of Paddy's mill during the downsizing. Although more than half of the massive building was empty, one could still see shiny bright sparks coming from the far end of the mill.

"This one is positive," he said. "Even though the mill is sad, the light makes everything feel better."

"You're right," she said, looking over his shoulder. "The light makes it all seem...hopeful."

"It reminds me of that poem you tried to change, about burning the lovely light. I remember because you got detention for arguing with the nuns. That was so cool."

She smiled at the memory. "It was cool, wasn't it? I don't know where I found the nerve."

"I know." The severity of William's voice struck her. "You found the nerve because you're brave and daring. You jumped off the high dive. You fought nuns. And you stayed at Bridge Manor with me, instead of wandering free and taking pictures of Bigouden and exotic crannies… and all that."

"That was just a silly dream, kiddo."

"Why did you stop dreaming it?"

"I grew up." Pushing aside the photos, she crawled in beside William and put her head on his pillow. "There's not a lot of room for wandering free in real life. Besides, I think what I was chasing was more of a feeling."

"What kind of feeling?"

"You know that innocent, hopeful feeling that anything is possible." She smiled. "The thrill of wondering where the path would lead me next."

"So after you finished being young, your dream went away?"

"Yup." She snapped her fingers. "Disappeared into thin air."

William frowned. "That would make me sad if I believed you."

"The Post-Gazette might use some of Farley's work," said Claire, joining Veda Marie on the picnic table.

"It's about time," said Veda Marie, lighting a cigarette. "And don't make that face at me, Claire Sullivan. I'm practically down to four a day."

"Did I say anything?" Claire leaned back on the table. "Did I say one word?"

"You didn't have to. That sour puss on your face says it all."

"I just don't understand why you didn't start your chemotherapy right away. This is your *health* we're talking about."

"Putting it off for a month or so isn't going to kill me."

Claire swallowed, blinking back tears. "That's not funny."

"I'm sorry, lovey." She hugged Claire and wiped her tears. "Remember, mum's the word until William gets some of his strength back. That boy of ours is sharper than most doctors - he'll know something is up when my treatments start."

"All right, but then you promise to be a good patient and do everything the doctors tell you to do."

Veda Marie raised her right hand. "I swear on my bum jiggle machine."

Chapter 41

Henry set the bag of groceries on the kitchen counter and stepped across the hall to check on William. It took a moment for his eyes to adjust to the dark room. William was lying in his hospital bed, facing the wall.

"Hey, pal."

"Hi."

"It's awfully gloomy in here. Want me to turn on some lights?"

"I just turned them off; I'm trying to take a nap."

"Sorry. Where is everyone?"

William rolled over to face Henry. "Resa went to talk to Father Ryan about why Eileen's turning into such a monster."

"She said that?"

"No. I heard Veda Marie telling Mr. Winston."

Henry smiled. "Where are they?"

William gave an exasperated sigh and recited in a monotone voice. "They're having quiet time in Mr. Winston's room. Farley is dropping off pictures at the newspaper office. Everybody is pretending to do their own thing - even though somebody shows up *every single hour* just to say 'hi.'" He glowered at Henry. "You must be my eleven-o-clock."

"Busted."

"What did Veda Marie tell you?"

"That you've had it up to here with everyone checking on you like you're a baby, and not the most educated person in this house."

"*And?*"

"And you had a good physical therapy session yesterday so it's no wonder you're a little run down."

William raised his eyebrows Veda Marie-style.

Henry shook the thermometer. "And… you're not happy Farley made you a doctor's appointment for tomorrow, because you're fine and *you should know.* Open."

He tucked the thermometer under William's tongue. "Don't be mad, pal. It's just because we love you."

"I love you too," mumbled William.

Henry placed the thermometer under the lamp.

"No fever. In fact, you're body temperature is lower than usual."

"See?" said William. "All I need is some sleep, and I can't sleep with everybody fussing and waking me up…"

"Point taken, pal. I'll put up a sign. How much time do you need?"

William wiped his eyes as he listened to Henry unpack groceries. He felt terrible about lying, but there wasn't any other way. He had recognized the symptoms when he woke up this morning; his body was going into Septic Shock. His heart rate had already begun to slow down. His body temperature was dropping, but his family was trained to be on the lookout for fever - not the other way around.

Without immediate treatment, his blood flow would quickly slow to the point that it couldn't feed his lungs, his liver, his heart…everything would shut down. And he welcomed it; he was grateful for this sudden solution.

William had known for some time that his frail body would not survive its brutal beating. Having sadly accepted the inevitable, his main concern was for his loving family. Now they would not have to watch him suffer. Given his compromised immune system, he expected his organs to shut-down within a matter of hours. As for the pain, he was already managing it with morphine pills he'd stockpiled…just in case.

And so he claimed 'tired.' And waited.

"How's he doing?" Farley dropped her portfolio on the table and gave Henry a kiss.

"Ornery. No fever, though. He said he just needs some sleep – which is difficult with us checking on him left and right. I promised we wouldn't bother him until three-o-clock."

Henry pointed to a note on the blackboard:

At the request of William James,
PLEASE BE QUIET
DO NOT WAKE HIM UNTIL 3:00 PM.
At which time he will return to his pleasant self.
Thank you very much.

"I'm still not cancelling his doctor's appointment," Farley murmured, as Henry pressed himself against her and kissed her neck. "I don't care how mad he gets."

"That's my girl."

"Where is everyone?" she whispered.

"Nap, quiet time, church and errands." He slid his hands down her body. "What do you say we go upstairs and have our own quiet time?"

Farley pulled away, her cheeks flushed. "First, I need to show you something."

Unzipping her portfolio, she sifted through photos of various sizes. Finally, she handed Henry a photograph of snow-capped mountains. In the forefront stood a group of evergreens weighed down with snow.

"Remind you of anything?"

He studied the photo, then shook his head. "You got me."

"The cover of *The Hobbit*. It came to me as the image appeared in the developing tray. And that's when I remembered where I last saw the book."

Henry roused Veda Marie to watch William while Farley called St. Xavier's. She confirmed Ryan would be hearing confession until noon. She and Henry would have just enough time to get in and out of Ryan's house without being seen.

"What the hell happened?" whispered Farley.

Henry stretched the collar of his shirt to cover his nose. "And what is that disgusting smell?"

Ryan's usually spotless cottage was a mess. Dirty dishes littered the countertops. Trash overflowed onto the kitchen floor and a sharp, sour odor permeated the entire house.

Henry gagged.

"You'd better wait outside," said Farley, heading straight to Ryan's study. "I'll just be a minute."

She slid open the top drawer to Ryan's desk.

I never got what all the fuss was about, buying old, mildew-ridden books.

She was careful as she reached inside, expecting to hit something sharp. All she pulled out was a half-eaten bag of miniature snickers and a handful of candy bar wrappers.

Cost me an arm and a leg, if you want to know the truth.

Except for more trash, the next drawer was empty.

Of course, Mrs. Sullivan's brother comes in the store now and then.

She found them in the deep bottom drawer. Six books, each covered with a thick plastic protector. Picking one up, she ran her finger across the small inkblot where the name 'Dodgeson' had been misspelled.

Farley clutched the box as Henry drove up Overlook Trail.

"Here Claire's out hawking her jewelry," she fumed, "*barely* stopping short of committing a crime to keep Bridge Manor, while her brother – a *priest*, mind you – is *stealing* from her! He probably stuffed a book down his robe every time he came to dinner. And on top of all that, he blamed September!"

"You're going to take these back right now," said Claire, re-packing the box.

"No, we're not," said Farley. "You can't let him get away with this, Claire."

"Ryan's not getting away with anything, hon. The poor man is becoming more and more wretched with each passing day."

Henry pulled a book from the box. "At least keep *The Hobbit*."

Claire screwed up her mouth. "I don't want it. Now hurry; put them back where you found them."

"Too late," said Farley, checking the clock. "Confession's over."

"You still have time. Resa and Eileen are meeting Ryan in his office after confession."

"To talk about Eileen's stealing," murmured Farley, holding the door for Henry. "Oh, the irony."

"I want to talk to Father alone, first," said Resa as they entered the reception room. "Do you mind waiting in here?"

Eileen shrugged. She couldn't give a rat's ass.

Since returning from her grandmother's, Eileen had begun to exhibit more and more disturbing behavior. The last straw was earlier that morning; Resa found her lighting the spray from a can of Veda Marie's hairspray - using an engraved lighter she'd lifted from Mr. Winston.

"Here's something to munch on while you wait." Resa tossed her an apple. "Be good."

"*You* be good," she mumbled, pulling a book of matches from her sock.

Ryan watched as Resa paced the length of his office, droning on and on and on. When her back was turned he removed a medicine bottle from his pocket and tossed two pills in his mouth. He had found the expired sedatives in Claire's pantry – prescribed years ago for William. He shook the bottle. Damn. Only a few left.

Poor baby. Then what will you do, darling?

The next time Resa's back was turned, he popped the remaining pills in his mouth. He swallowed them down with a gulp of whiskey he had discreetly hidden in his coffee mug.

Eileen let the match burn down and dared herself not to flinch from the pain. As her fingers began to blister, it occurred to her that Resa would notice the burns. She stuffed the matches back in her sock and wandered around the room examining framed portraits of old priests. Through the window she watched a man high on a scaffolding, power washing the bell in the big tower.

Dropping the apple core over the tower's edge, Eileen enjoyed the 'splat' as it hit the cobblestone below. She saw Henry and Farley walk up Father Ryan's driveway. Farley's lips flapped away; probably talking about something boring like what movie to watch or what to eat for dinner. Eileen lit two matches at the same time and dragged them along the sawdust covered wooden floor. A thin trail of smoke emerged and the sawdust caught fire – snapping, popping, and flickering like fireflies.

Crossing the lawn to his cottage, Ryan had an overwhelming sense that he was being watched. He glanced to his left, then right. He spun around. Nothing but a few shoppers in the square. He gave them what he hoped was a pastoral nod. Paranoia, he decided. Probably from the pills. Or the alcohol. Or the pills mixed with alcohol. He covered his mouth and giggled. His personal confession would be a doozy this week.

Confession. Ryan laughed out loud. Mrs. Piotrowski's confession had been a scream! The woman had actually tried to negotiate a smaller penance, then launched into a diatribe about how insufferable things were these days.

"Nothing surprises me anymore, Father," she had said, lips mashed against the confessional screen. "What with the half-naked, gyrating pelvises all over the television. Not to mention that Shirley MacLaine. I mean, *really*; playing a shameless floozy at her age."

"He's coming." Henry's voice was muffled by the layers of fabric softener sheets wound around his mouth and nose. "He's taking an awfully circuitous route. We'll have to go out the back."

Farley dropped the books in the bottom drawer and hurried through the living room.

She slowed halfway across. "Why are we sneaking around like a couple of criminals? We're not the ones in the wrong, here."

Henry separated the fabric softener sheets to make room for his lips. "Color me silly, but mightn't breaking and entering fall under the category of 'wrong?'"

"We're not breaking and entering. I'm his niece, stopping by for a long overdue heart to heart."

"Don't do this."

Scanning the room, she took in the rotting garbage and piles of dirty clothes. She reflected on her uncle's increasingly dark moods and bizarre behavior.

"When did this happen?" she said. "How could things have gotten so bad without any of us noticing?"

"Between William's recovery and the potential loss of Bridge Manor, I'd say we've had other things on our minds. Come on; let's get out of here."

"No, Henry. I want to talk to him."

"Claire specifically said she didn't want…"

"I won't say a word about the books. But Ryan is having some sort of breakdown right under our noses. I want him to know we're there for him."

"I don't think he's going to like finding us loitering in his living room."

"I'll be the loiterer. You'll be gone; it's better if I talk to him alone."

Ryan's shadow crossed the living room window.

"Go." She shooed him with her hands. "I won't be long."

Chapter 42

Ashen-faced, Ryan leaned against the foyer wall.

"You scared me to death," he said, mopping his face with his sleeve.

"I'm sorry," said Farley. "I thought I'd come by. I haven't been here since..."

"Is William all right?"

"I'm afraid he's getting depressed. We were warned that his recovery would be up and down, but still..."

"I'll visit him tomorrow." Ryan blinked, trying to focus his eyes. "Try not to worry; the kid's a fighter."

Bingo. Farley's voice took on the enthusiasm of a cheerleader. "You know who else is a fighter? You are."

Ryan frowned. I'm either going to pass out or throw up, he thought. I need to lie down. A relieved moan escaped as he stretched across the sofa, indifferent to the god-awful clutter and stench.

Sweeping a paper plate of dried chicken bones off the ottoman, Farley pulled it up to the sofa and sat. The sharp smell of whiskey threatened to overwhelm her, in spite of the room's competing funk.

"I remember when I was depressed," she continued, coughing a bit. "I didn't care about anything or anyone. I completely let myself go…"

Ryan covered his eyes with the crook of his arm and snickered. And she's off! Blah, blah, blah.

Farley stopped talking. "What did you say?"

She kicked an empty milk carton on her way out the door. What did she expect? The man needed professional help, for crying out loud. She could hardly help herself! She should be home with William, not playing shrink to Father Sybil. Stopping, she took a deep breath of fresh air. And another. There we go. In with the good, out with the...

"Fire!" she screamed.

Ryan cursed as he stumbled across the lawn. He could barely see, never mind climb a tower. Of all times for a fire.

Farley pulled the fire alarm, grabbed the extinguisher off the wall, and started up the long spiral of wooden stairs. As she ascended, her body slowed. *Don't look down. Keep moving.* Ignoring her wobbly legs and the suffocating thrash of her heart, she pushed on.

The door at the top was closed. She pressed her hands against the wood, testing for heat. Feeling no abnormal warmth, she opened the door. The fire seemed to be coming from the floorboards to her left. Wind gusting through the tower's large stone openings fed the flames.

It didn't take long to put the fire out, but Farley kept spraying until the extinguisher was empty. Finally she dropped the extinguisher on the saturated floorboards. As she tried to catch her breath, a flash of movement – partially obscured by the edge of the large bell - caught her eye. Stepping forward, she gasped. Ryan had climbed onto the stone ledge, his robes drifting and floating around him like a ghost. Distant sirens wailed as she took another careful step toward him.

"Ryan..." she said, using what she hoped was her sensitive tone. "What are you doing?"

Something about the way he giggled made her hair stand on end. He waved his arms to balance himself. "I'm looking down from on high. *On high*, get it?"

"Please come down. You're scaring me."

"I'm scaring *you*?" His face crumpled. "You're the one who's scaring me."

She shook her head. "I didn't mean to upset you. I saw your house…I only wanted to help."

He let out a frantic laugh. A sliver of drool dangled from his lips. "Some help you are! I'm not the one who died and ruined everything." He pressed both hands against his temple and squeezed. "People tell me their sins! I hold their souls in the palm of my hand. What more do you want from me, Pauline?"

Pauline.

Farley gasped as he shifted his weight. One more shuffle backward and he would be gone.

"You said you'd always be there for me," he snarled, gritting his teeth. He wobbled, then righted himself. "You lied. You didn't even *try* to get out of that car."

The door flew open and two firemen advanced, cautiously testing the charred floor with each step.

"Stay where you are!" screamed Farley, waving them back. As she turned back to Ryan, she unconsciously gave her hair a Pauline-style flip. "I made a mistake, Mutt. I wasn't thinking clearly. I'm sorry." Raising her voice, she pointed to the floor. "Now come down off that goddamn ledge before you kill yourself."

While Claire spoke to someone from the clergy, Henry and Farley watched as Ryan was loaded into an ambulance.

"I should never have left you alone with him," said Henry. "His house alone practically screamed 'breakdown.' I must have been blind."

Farley shook her head. "I'm the one with blinders on. Claire's meeting with loan sharks right under my nose." She gestured toward the ambulance as it pulled out of the square. "And each time I saw that poor man, his behavior was more bizarre than the last."

"All right; you win. You're blinder than I am."

She elbowed him. "You're just saying that to be nice."

Lest she find any more trouble to get into, Henry and Claire squished Farley between them in the van.

"What's going to happen to Ryan?" asked Farley.

Claire wiped her forehead. "After he's released from the hospital, he'll go to a place called The Sanctuary. It's a sort of rest home for priests. St. Xavier's is making the arrangements, and they've assured me he can stay as long as he likes."

Farley yawned, suddenly exhausted. "Is crazy hereditary?"

"Let's hope not, hon," said Claire. "That sounds like a question for William."

"It seems like an eternity since I saw him this morning."

Henry consulted his watch. "Believe it or not, it's just now three-o-clock. Veda Marie is probably waking him up as we speak."

"I'm sorry," said William, his breathing jagged.

"Shhh." Farley smoothed his hair off his forehead. His ashen skin was cool to the touch. "You're going to be fine, kiddo."

He swallowed. "Nothing hurts, I promise."

Dion pressed her index and middle fingers over his small wrist and stared at her watch. His blood pressure was faint and steadily dropping.

"How many pills did you take?" she asked.

"Just enough for the pain."

Claire and Veda Marie hastily packed William's small suitcase. From the kitchen, the measured tap-tap-tap of Mr. Winston pacing the floor with his walking stick, along with the murmur of Henry's somber voice reciting the address of Bridge Manor.

"...all the way to the top of Overlook Trail," he said, his voice cracking. "It's urgent. Please hurry."

William reached for Farley's hand. "I'll watch over you."

"Don't you dare," she said, angrily swiping her tears away. "Stop talking like that."

He closed his eyes, no longer able to keep them open.

"I love you," he murmured.

Farley put her face right up next to his.

"Open your eyes!" she demanded.

Suddenly, a gentle wave of oblivion seemed to wash over him. Even as he floated into unconsciousness, the sweetest remnants of his smile lingered.

Henry ran outside, as if he could somehow hurry the ambulance up the hill. Dion continued searching for William's vital signs. Clare and Veda Marie cried in each other's arms, while Mr. Winston wrapped a protective arm around Farley. But all she could do was stare at her brother.

For the first time since before his vicious beating, William's face was peaceful. Free of fear, and worry. Free from the unbearable pain he'd endured for so long. Free. She pressed her forehead against his, the way their father used to do.

"All right, kiddo," she whispered. "Go ahead. Fly."

And like a brave and daring superhero soaring through the atmosphere, William Justus James gave a final sigh and drifted...up...up...and away.

It seemed like the entire city turned out to say goodbye to you, my sweet William. The entire staff from Freeman's. The Frosty Devils. Even some of your 'nice boys from Pittsburgh.' Dr. Hugh, Nurse Becky, most of your physical therapy team. A man who looked a lot like Mr. Winston turned out to be his brother, Leonard. All the teachers and faculty from The Significant Me, and many of your old classmates. Marcus Shultz told me you kept him in snacks for years. I never knew that.

After the service Henry hosted a small dinner for our Bridge Manor family. We cried and eventually laughed as we shared magical William stories. When we finally went to bed, Henry held me close as we slept...almost as if he knew.

I crept out of bed without waking him. The barest hint of sun was coming up as I took the hillside steps. Tiptoeing up to my room, I pulled out my old backpack and camera case. That's when it hit me, kiddo. Suddenly and absolutely, I knew you were happy - and that you were watching over me.

I didn't see you, but I felt you in my heart.

Chapter 43

"Those buildings weren't even there when we first came to Bridge Manor." Farley pointed to the left. "And the old glass factory is a park now. Hard to believe, isn't it? It's like the whole city started over."

Henry got off the table and stood between her legs, his arms looped around her neck. He spoke slowly, giving her neck a gentle shake to emphasize his words.

"The city didn't start over. It adapted. And over time, things got better."

"I know." She clutched his arms. "Henry, for the first time in my life, I can honestly say this isn't about starting over. It's about starting the next phase of my life."

He pressed his forehead against hers. "But not here."

"I'll be back. I promised Claire and Veda Marie I'd come home at least once a year. And Dion threatened to hunt me down if I'm not there for her graduation."

"And then you'll leave again."

Instead of answering, she brushed the hair from his face.

"I hate the thought of you out there, alone," he said, squeezing her face in his hands. "Even if you are brave and daring."

She smiled; her tears making it hard for her to see. "I love you, Henry."

"I know it."

They were quiet for a long time, memorizing each other's faces. He kissed her. Without having to say a word, both knew this would be their goodbye.

"What is she doing now?" said Veda Marie, as Mr. Winston moved the curtain aside and squinted.

"Still sitting on the lawn," he said, heading to the kitchen door. "Staring into space, looking miserable."

Knees popping and creaking, Mr. Winston lowered himself onto the grass and wrapped his arms around her. Farley rested her head on his shoulder and together they sat; watching the night sweep in around them.

Legs folded on the cement entrance to the greenhouse, Colette watched Henry spread charcoal around the outer circle of the grill. He put an empty tuna can filled with water on the top grate, then put his hickory chips in a bowl of water. Then he rubbed the inside of the turkey with half of a salt and olive oil paste.

"The salt paste helps the moisture to stay in the turkey while it's smoking," he said. "You want your bird to be moist, but not salty."

"It's quarter after two in the morning," she said.

After trussing the turkey and slicking it down with more oil, he went to work on the basting mixture. To the rest of the salt paste he added parsley, minced onion, red wine vinegar and finely ground black pepper.

"Do you want to talk about it, Henry?"

He sprinkled the hickory chips over the coals, placed his bird on the greased grill. After checking to be sure the cover was on tight, he opened the vents. Then he stuffed his hands deep into his pockets

He continued staring at the smoking grill, even as she kissed the back of his neck.

"I'm here for you Henry," she whispered. "If you want me."

The night before she left, Farley slipped down to Freeman's. Safely obscured by the dark shadows of the greenhouse, she watched Henry through the kitchen window. Amid the chaos of constant bodies in motion, he moved smoothly from pan to pot to oven and back again. She wiped the condensation from the window and pressed her forehead against the glass.

"Farley?" Colette closed the greenhouse door, a basket of cut herbs in one hand. "What are you doing out here?"

"I don't know." She squinted as Henry disappeared and then re-appeared from a cloud of steam. "God, what a beautiful man."

"Have you changed your mind?"

She shook her head, her eyes never leaving Henry. "I leave in the morning."

Collette set down her basket and joined her at the window.

"That man adores you." She nudged Farley. "Too bad for me, eh?"

"For you?" Farley was stunned. "Oh, honey..."

"What can I say? I have a sickening habit of falling for unattainable men." Colette kissed her friend once on each cheek and tilted her head toward Henry. "Leave him be. He is already hurting enough, don't you think?"

Back at home, Claire thrust a small photo album into Farley's hands.

"Something to look at during your long flight," she said. "Don't forget to call collect the second you land, and every Sunday afternoon, and..."

"…any time in-between," interrupted Farley, tucking the album in her backpack. "You don't have to worry about me, Claire. After all, I come from a long line of strong women."

Smiling, Claire pressed the palm of her hand to Farley's cheek. "Yes, you do. Just promise you'll be careful."

"I will. And *you* promise to keep me posted on Veda Marie's chemo treatments."

Claire's jaw dropped. "How did you…"

"How else? Our sweet William. He wasn't listening; he just heard."

"I knew it!" Veda Marie appeared from the drawing room and dropped her basket of folded towels on the table. "I swear to God, no secret is safe in this house."

Laughing through her tears, Farley enfolded both women in her arms.

"I'll miss you every single day," she whispered.

Just then, Resa and Dion came through the mudroom door. Dion carried a triple-layer cake with the words 'Bon Voyage' written in icing.

"Hey," she said, setting down the cake. "Can we get in on that?"

Long after the rest of the house was in bed, Claire stood alone in the kitchen. She breathed in the lingering scent of lemons, coffee, freshly folded laundry, and firewood. The silence echoed with the refrains of laughter, sorrow, love, loss and joy. This beautiful, dignified old house had seen them through it all, she thought, opening the mudroom door.

There, under the chilly blue-white glow of a full moon and the fairylike flicker of the stars, Claire Sullivan stepped out of her clothes. Wearing only a smile, she grabbed a towel and mad-dashed-it down the lawn to the outdoor shower.

"Ladies and gentlemen," said the pilot. "We have reached a comfortable altitude. Please feel free to move about the plane."

Farley unbuckled her seat belt and stood.

"Excuse me," she murmured as her backpack grazed the leg of the woman sitting beside her.

Sitting back down, she dug through her backpack until she found the photo album. Inside the cover was an old black and white photograph of Bridge Manor, with an inscription along the bottom in Claire's messy handwriting:

The splendor of wandering free is knowing you have a place to come home to.

Farley flipped to a page in the middle. Pauline and Veda Marie in their standard pose: facing sideways, one foot pointed, stomach in. In the middle stood Claire, boldly facing the camera head-on. Farley ran her finger over the image.

On the last page was the family photo she had taken so many years ago on the hood of the old Buick. Us four. She smiled, struck by how young her parents were. Jack, the setting sun reflected in his aviator glasses. Pauline, her head on his shoulder, cheeks flushed and hair disheveled. Sweet William and his gleaming silver headgear. And her own face, so full of hope, squinting against the burn of the lovely light.

The End

It Burns a Lovely Light

Note from the Author

Thank you for reading *It Burns a Lovely Light.* I am truly honored.

The initial seed for this book was planted in the early 1990's when I spent three wonderful years in Pittsburgh, working in feature film production. Scenes were often shot in the cavernous, abandoned steel mills and factories in and around the city. I was fascinated by stories of the city's survival after the demise of its great steel industry – and overwhelmed by the kindness of the people of Pittsburgh.

After fifteen years as a writer and producer of radio and television advertising campaigns and documentaries, I finally put pen to paper.

It Burns a Lovely Light is a work of fiction. The characters in my book were pulled directly from my imagination and not intended to represent anyone in particular – with one exception. Jack James' experiences over the Gulf of Tonkin were taken (quite literally) from the recollections of my father, Brigadier General Robert I. McCann.

It Burns a Lovely Light

Acknowledgements

My deepest gratitude to those who inspired and encouraged me on this journey, reading (and re-reading) draft after draft and providing me with valuable advice:
My beautiful sisters, Kelly Maffeo, Maureen McCann, and Stephanie Elia. John Pennington, Alex Venners, Daisy Venners, Robert I. McCann, Patricia McCann, Becky Parrish, William Woodward, Lara Rota, Christina King, Elizabeth Lawrence, Ann Macleod, Lorraine Field, Rachel Cartwright, Patrick Jordan, Pietro Schechter, Charlie Trefzger, Bob Hudson, Roberta Franklin, and Alison Dunavent, from the Art Institute of Pittsburgh.

It Burns a Lovely Light